I0579233

RED ROSE

Red Rose

Copyright © 2020 by Rebel Hart

Photo by Regina Wamba

Cover by Robin Harper of Wicked By Design

www.RebelHart.net

All rights reserved.

No part of this book may be reproduced in any form or by any electronic or mechanical means, including information storage and retrieval systems, without written permission from the author, except for the use of brief quotations in a book review.

RED ROSE

RED THORNS CREW BOOK 2

REBEL HART

1

DANI

"Up here, on the right, should be--"

I sighed. "Max, I know what your house looks like."

He chuckled. "And here I thought you were too busy staring at my ass to know."

"Nope. That's your job."

"And don't you fucking forget it, Daddy's girl."

I rolled my eyes at the nickname as I gingerly maneuvered into his driveway. The lights were on at the back of the house. A good sign that John was there. But I still wasn't sure. For all I knew, no one was home and the light was on as a simple precaution.

Either way, I had to get Max inside.

"All right, you massive man. Come on. We have to get you out."

Max chuckled. "And here you keep flattering me. I half expect it to come with a kiss."

I shoved my door open. "Shut up and help me as much as you can."

"Wow. Such sass. Just makes you sexier, Bambi."

I walked around to his side of the car. "You know, those names are going to get old quickly."

"Then I guess I'll simply have to start calling you by your real name."

I slipped his arm around my shoulders. "Dani?"

His lips fell to my ear. "More like 'gorgeous.'"

How the hell that man could make me blush while he's practically growling in pain, I had no idea. But I wouldn't let his soft, warm words deter me. He needed help, and quickly. The bags underneath his eyes had already bruised over. The way he held his ribs had me more than concerned. And his stupid lip was still bleeding.

"All right. Take the steps slowly. With me. Ready?"

His grunts with each step didn't fill my gut with ease. Night hung heavily around us while the crickets chirped and the bats fluttered around. Probably trying to figure out what kind of chaos I had brought to their doorstep, no doubt. Max reached out and opened the door. Just opened it. Unlocked, in the middle of the night, bordering on the woodlands.

His brother has to be here.

"John?" I called out.

"I need to sit."

"John!?"

"Over there. I'm sorry, but I can't--"

I snickered. "Don't be silly. There's no reason to apologize. John!"

I heard something crash open. "Who the fuck is yelling in my house?"

"It's--it's me. Dan--!"

"Fuck," Max growled.

His foot stumbled over mine and we both went crashing into the wall. I felt Max's arm wrap around my waist, pulling me from the wall as he ground his teeth through the pain. I kept apologizing underneath my breath as I helped him get to the couch before I spilled him against the cushions. And when he let out a sigh, I heard another set of footsteps cantering down the hallway.

"Who the hell is in my--?"

"It's me, Dani. I have Max. He's really hurt."

I sat next to Max as the cantering footsteps accompanied by his cane rushed down the hallway. I leaned against the arm of the couch, spreading my legs for Max to snuggle against. I reached my arms out for him and pulled him toward me. His head settled just underneath my chin. I felt him trembling, tears in his eyes that he refused to shed. I wanted to help him. I needed to help him. Why the hell didn't he want--?

"Jesus. What the hell happened to you?"

I smoothed Max's hair away from his forehead as he drew in a deep breath. But when he went to speak, he started coughing and sputtering. Trying to catch his breath, he rolled over to the edge of the couch and vomited onto the floor.

"I'm concerned he's got a concussion," I said.

John looked at me before he grabbed a wooden chair from the corner of the room.

"All right. Let's take a look atcha."

I shook my head. "He needs a doctor. Isn't there someone we can call?"

John gripped Max's chin. "For emergencies, yeah."

I snickered. "And this isn't an emergency?"

Neither of the guys said anything. As Max continued to try and catch his breath, John studied his face. I reached down and pulled up Max's shirt, showing John the extensive bruising I hadn't even seen yet. It made me gasp. There were distinct imprints on his skin where the impact had taken place with spidered veins of black and blue and red branching out from all of those impact points.

"Can you roll over so I can see the other side?" John asked.

Max grunted. "Do I have to?"

I huffed. "Are you serious right now?"

John eyed me hotly. "Leave. You're not much help right now."

Max growled. "She stays."

Their eyes connected as I sat there, continuing to smooth Max's hair back. I felt him sweating. He was in too much pain.

"We have to get him some pain medication. He's going to pass out," I said.

John nodded. "Spit for me."

I paused. "What?"

Max leaned off the couch again and spat onto the hardwood floor.

"No blood. That's good," John murmured.

Max's jaw moved around. "Not broken. But I think I chipped a t--oh, fuck."

"What?" I asked quickly.

Max opened his jaw for his brother. John moved as if he knew what to do with the motion. Everything that took place between the two of them seemed consistent. Routine.

As if they'd done this before.

"Yep. Your canine's chipped. But your back left molar's missing. That's gonna be an issue."

I sat up. "Let me see."

But when Max grunted at my movement, I quickly sat back into place. And found John's stare on me again.

"You can support him or work on him. But you can't do both. Choose your place, and choose it now."

I nodded slowly. "Support. Always."

I felt Max's hand fall against my shin. His fingertips drew soft designs against the fabric of my pants. I started running my fingers through his hair again, pulling my eyes away from his brother, who was staring at me with a look I couldn't interpret.

"It's going to be okay, Max. Just relax," I whispered.

John scooted closer. "Do you have any idea who jumped you?"

I paused. "How did you know he was--?"

Max held up his hand. "No clue. But they got a damn good piece of me before they bailed."

He sighed. "That much is obvious. Another question. Was this Red Thorn related? Or random?"

Max snickered. "Is it ever random, in our lives?"

I furrowed my brow. "What does that mean? You think someone intentionally did this to you? Why? What possible reason could they have?"

Max wrapped his hand around my leg. "Support, gorgeous. Keep it that way."

I closed my eyes and clenched my jaw to keep myself from flying off the handle. I hated it when people told me my place. Especially when I wanted to help. My parents did that to me a lot. Shooed me away whenever things were getting too rough. Or too heated. Or too angry for me to supposedly witness. They treated me like I was weak. Like I was some porcelain China doll. Like I was some bumbling baby deer just birthed…

Bambi.

Did everyone around me see me as weak?

"You got anything to go on?" John asked.

Max coughed. "No. But Dani's right about one thing. This pain is getting to be a bit too much. You got something here I can take? Or are we really gonna have to ring up that damn doctor?"

My eyes flew open. "Yes. Doctor. Now."

John shook his head. "I've got something you can have for the pain. And since you don't need stitches, I can clean you up. The rest is just, well, rest. Sleep. Food, until your body heals itself. Except for this tooth shit. You'll have to find a dentist or something for that."

Max sighed. "Great."

John shrugged. "At least you didn't lose your front tooth."

Were these guys being serious right now?

"Dani, got a job for you. Gotta get out from behind Max."

John's voice pulled me from my trance. "But you said--"

He nodded. "Uh huh. And now I'm telling you different. I need you to go into the bathroom. Right there in the hallway. Underneath the bathroom sink is a big first aid kit. Grab it, go into the kitchen, grab the red bottle off the top of the fridge, and bring it all back to me. I need to get Max out of his clothes and look him over."

Max chuckled. "Don't worry, gorgeous. I'll let you have a look before he patches me up."

I snickered. "Last thing on my list right now, Max."

John started chuckling as I gingerly moved myself. As I slipped off the couch, John's chuckling grew to laughter. Which grew to guffawing. And as I made my way into the bathroom, I heard him practically fall out of his chair. Max's voice mumbled, but I didn't know what he said. All I knew was that once I gathered everything up and came back, John was wiping tears away from his eyes.

"Someone want to fill me in on what he's laughing about?" I asked.

Max rolled his eyes. "Another time."

John held up his hand. "Holy shit. Oh, man. That--I needed that on camera."

I paused. "Needed what?"

His finger pointed between Max and me. "You rejecting him. Holy shit. I've never--never, ever seen a girl just--HAH!"

I blinked. "Can we fix him up now so he doesn't die on your couch?"

Max grunted. "I'm not dying."

I dumped the stuff on the floor at John's feet. "We'll see come morning, I guess."

John immediately stopped laughing and glared at me. I didn't know what the hell was so funny, but it seemed like I was the only one taking this issue seriously. And I wouldn't have these idiots botch things because they were laughing while Max could hardly move!

"What next?" I asked.

John nodded his head. "Get out of my way."

Max sat up. "Or help me get my clothes off."

I nodded. "I can do that."

I gingerly helped him out of his shirt and tossed it to the side. The bruising made my eyes water as my hands slid to the belt of his pants. After stripping him down to nothing but his socks and his boxers, I stood back, watching as John scooted up closer to his brother. He reached for the red bottle and popped the top. My eyes widened as he held it up to his lips. He took two long gulps before passing it to Max. And when it took five, I started reaching for the bottle.

Before he moved back and took two more.

"What is this?" I asked.

I finally got the bottle away from Max and passed it back to John.

"It's whiskey," Max said with a growl, "and it's going to help dull the pain while John works."

John nodded. "It'll be a nice treat when I drug him up for the night, too."

I scoffed. "With what? A tranquilizer?"

John picked up the first aid kit. "No. With my lifetime supply of pain medication, courtesy of my chronic pain."

I paused. "Oh."

John nodded. "'Oh' is right. Now watch and learn, or get back on the couch."

I stood by the outer arm of the couch and watched as Max laid down against the cushions. With his feet resting against my thigh, I felt his toes curling into me every time John moved to work. First, the split lip. A small butterfly band-aid closed the wound, but not before he rubbed it down with alcohol. Something that made Max wince. And when his hands moved toward his nose, I quickly reached down for the red bottle.

"Hold on," I said.

I walked around to Max's face before I opened the bottle.

"Two more large gulps, okay? You can't risk any more than that," I said softly.

I lifted his head and counted the pulls. One, swallow. Two, swallow. And another small one, just in case. I settled his head back down and put the bottle off in the corner, hoping and praying Max didn't buck too much during this. Setting his nose was going to be rough. Even John knew that. And as I looked up at him, I watched him nod.

"On the count of three," John said.

Max took my hand and squeezed it. Hard.

"Ready," he grunted.

"All right. On my count. One--*SNAP!*"

And the roar of pain Max let out watered my eyes.

"Sh-sh-sh-sh, it's okay. I'm right here, handsome."

I pressed my lips to his ear and whispered as many sweet nothings as I could. John started from Max's nose and worked his way down his brother's body, patching up what he could and poking at what he couldn't. He got ice packs for the bruised ribs. He checked Max for any signs of a concussion. John checked every joint from his toes to his shoulders, just to make sure nothing else was out of place. And when we sat Max upright, my hand slid down the nape of his neck.

Fiddling with something that felt swollen.

"John?" I asked.

Max groaned. "Damn it, that hurt. The hell did you just run over, gorgeous?"

I peered down at Max's neck, confused by what I was seeing. There were circular indentations with designs that looked weirdly specific in nature. John got up and lumbered around to where he could see, trying to move Max as little as possible.

And when John's eyes landed on the bruising, he smacked his lips.

"Were the guys wearing rings, Max?"

He cleared his throat. "Yeah, they were. Bunch of fucking pussies. Might as well have had brass knuckles."

John nodded. "All right. I'm going to take pictures of this bruising pattern. They've hit you so hard back here that their rings left imprints."

It boggled my damn mind how these men thought a hospital wasn't necessary for any of this.

2

MAX

The world felt as if it was swirling around me. That's what pulled me from sleep. My eyes refused to open, and I felt some crusty shit trying to poke my eye out. I coughed, feeling my chest jump and my face explode with pain. And with every part of my body that became more aware of the morning sunlight pouring against my body, the more pain dawned on my conscious mind.

"The fuck."

I heard birds chirping as the crusty outer layer to my eye finally gave way. It sent involuntary tears slipping down my face. I lifted my fist to wipe it away. With every movement I made, I thought I was going to puke.

From the pain.

"Here, this should help."

John's voice seemed far off in the distance. I felt something sink into my upper arm, pinching and piercing, sending my 'fight' signals into overdrive. I clamped down onto a wrist and tried to pull whatever it was that was stabbing me out of my damn arm. I felt something bony press down against my major artery in my thigh, causing my head to spin.

"Fuck," I groaned.

John sighed. "And we're gone. You always did hate needles, you weird, tattooed little fucker."

My eyes had a hard time focusing. I got my head turned and gazed around the room. Shit. No wonder I felt like hell. I'd fallen asleep on the couch in the damn living room. I reached up for the curtains to the window beside me and I tugged them shut, trying to get that hot sun off my skin.

"Come on. Let me help you up. I need to see if you can at least sit up straight."

John's grip was tight. He helped me up off the couch and sat me up, leaning me against the arm of the piece of furniture. I felt like death warmed over. It had been a long time since I'd felt this kind of physical pain. And as I gazed around the room, my eyes fell onto a curious sight.

Dani, with her legs curled up against her chest, passed out in the recliner.

John's recliner.

"She wanted to sleep last night with you propped up against her. I told her that wasn't possible."

I nodded slowly. "So you gave her your recliner?"

He snickered. "No. She helped herself to it and refused to leave. It's being held hostage. I expect you to fix that."

I buried my smile. "Yep. Will do."

He chuckled. "I'm sure you will, loverboy."

I rolled my eyes as I braced myself against the couch. John hovered around me, holding his arms out just in case I fell or some shit. But I knew I wouldn't. The more I stood, the more stable on my feet I felt. Despite the fact that the pain was excruciating.

At least my heart doesn't hurt.

I shuffled myself into the kitchen. I needed a cup of coffee and some bacon. Some grease. Something to knock this cloud away from my mind. I leaned against the counter and used my shaking hands to pour myself a mug. I drew in the scent by the noseful, feeling my muscles already relaxing and the pain already slipping away.

"Pain meds look good on you. Just don't make them a lifetime thing."

John limped up beside me with his own mug clenched in his hand.

"I'm lucky she was there to peel me off the fucking pavement," I murmured.

My brother nodded. "Lucky indeed. She says there were four of them."

I shook my head. "No. Three."

"Not what she said."

"Well, she's not the one that got her ass handed to her by them."

"From her point of view, she says there were three who jumped you, then hopped into a black SUV. And that none of them got into the driver's seat."

My eyes found his. "Fuck."

He nodded. "'Fuck' is right. There were four men there. One manning the car."

I sighed. "It was a hit."

"Who the hell have you pissed off?"

I rubbed the back of my neck. "You mean other than Dad? I can't think of anyone we've pissed off lately."

John nodded. "I was hoping you could shed light on that, since I'm not much use in that department any longer. There's no crews you've come into contact with? No turf wars happening? No shit like that?"

I shook my head. "No. Nothing like that."

Then it dawned on me.

"You don't think…?"

John interrupted me. "Dad's a fucker, but he's not that stupid. If he wants something done, he'd want to come watch it for himself."

"He could've been that fourth person. The one in the car."

"You know that's not how he rolls. I mean, the garage incident tells us that."

I paused. "How the hell do you know about that?"

He chuckled. "The real question is how you thought you could keep it from me. Yes. I know Dad sicced his men on you in the garage. But if he was there, you would've known he was there. This isn't Dad. He's a sick man, but he's not mental."

"Says you."

I chugged back the rest of my coffee and poured myself another mug. I hated this feeling of not knowing. It felt like my head was being held underwater.

And when I felt like this, that put the entire crew at risk. My men, who depended on me, were now in danger.

And I didn't have the slightest clue as to who the fuck was doing all this.

"You need to warn the guys," John said.

I nodded. "I'll get to that, yeah. Once I've got something to fucking tell them."

"If someone is after you, you can't just--"

I held my hand up. "Your reign as president is over. I know what I'm doing. Let me do it."

He huffed. "Suit your fucking self. But if any of them get hurt or killed because you're too chickenshit to go to them with stuff like this before *you* figure it out? That's on you."

"What did you just call me?"

"Like you've got the energy to do anything about it. Pour yourself another mug while I cook us up some bacon. And eggs. I'm sure your girl's gonna be hungry when she wakes up."

"She's not my girl."

He snickered. "Could've fooled me."

He did have a point, though. As John rummaged around in the fridge for shit to cook for breakfast, my mind wandered. If these bastards had the bold balls to jump me like that in the middle of a damn college campus, then no one was safe. I was the president of the crew that owned these streets. I called the shots. I made the rules. And if they weren't afraid to jump me, they sure as hell wouldn't be afraid to jump anyone else.

Did they see Dani at all?

Worry pooled in my gut. If these assholes had seen Dani, she was a target. I shook my head. I should have resisted the urge. I should've buried the pull she had on me. Now, not only was Dani a target in my father's crosshairs, but she was possibly a target to some unnamed entity I had no information on yet.

"John?"

"Yeah?"

I set my mug down. "Tell the others to meet me at the pub. Whoever gets there first can shut it down."

He snickered. "I thought you were the president."

I shot him a look. "Just do it."

He nodded. "Glad you finally came to your senses. But you need to eat."

"No time."

"You need something in your stomach other than pain medication and booze from last night. You won't be able to function with a clear head otherwise. I'm telling you. Eat."

I blinked. "Something quick. I have to inform the crew as soon as possible."

"And it'll do you no good to do that with a swimming head. Trust me on this, Max. I've been living with pain meds and booze for years now. I know what works and what doesn't. Give yourself two scrambled eggs, bacon, and another mug of coffee. You'll feel better."

"We need to make sure everyone knows someone is gunning for us. They have to be able to protect--"

He pointed at me with a spatula. "Sit. You look like shit, and you need food."

"I don't have time, John. I need to handle my crew."

"And you will. After food. Go wake Dani. The more you bug me, the slower your food's going to come up."

Normally, I didn't take orders from anyone. Not even my damn brother. But he was right. My head kept sinking deeper under water and my vision was starting to blur again. Plus, my stomach was angry with me. Very, very angry.

"Fine. Maybe just a bit of food," I murmured.

John snickered. "Let Dani know I'm going to make her a small something, too."

"Yeah, yeah, yeah."

I lumbered down the hallway and slipped into the bathroom. I had to piss. But I also wanted to take a look at myself. Really do a damage inspection on my body. I stuffed myself back into my boxers and slowly turned around, preparing myself for what I was about to see.

Nothing could have prepared me, though.

"Holy fuck."

I had a makeshift stint over my nose. The area underneath both of my eyes was black and yellow and a bit purple. My eyes were puffy and red. The deep black bruises against my ribs explained why my footsteps hurt like hell. And when I craned my neck, I saw the soft round marks those gold-ass rings had left behind on the back of my neck.

I'm going to slaughter you all.

I straightened my back and dipped underneath the sink faucet. I chugged mouthfuls of water until my stomach settled down. Then I headed out to where Dani was. Her soft snores made me grin. Her beautiful body curled up against the leather arm of the recliner made my heart slam against my chest. She looked so peaceful. So calm. So settled.

I almost didn't have the heart to wake her.

"Hey there, gorgeous. Wake up for me."

I reached down and softly shook her, watching as her eyes fluttered open.

"Hmm? Max?"

I chuckled. "Morning, Daddy's girl. Time to get up."

She frowned up at me. "Don't call me that."

I paused. "Call you what?"

"Daddy's girl. Or Bambi. I have a name. Use it, please."

I nodded slowly. "Oh… kay. Morning, Dani."

She smiled up at me. "Morning, Max. It's nice to see you up on your feet."

"You need to get back to campus for class."

She stood up. "I'll be fine. Don't worry."

"You'll be late for class."

"Well, then it's a good thing I'm not going to school today."

I blinked. "And why not?"

John poked his head around the corner. "Breakfast is up."

Dani pointed. "See? Breakfast. Can't leave until I eat, can I?"

I nodded. "Then you'll after you're done eating."

"No, I won't."

She said the words so coolly. So plainly. And when John started chuckling to himself, I wanted to chip his tooth to match my own.

"Getting bolder, I see, Daddy's girl."

Her eyes flashed. "Don't you call me that anymore. I'm not some weak-willed little porcelain doll who bats her eyes only for her father. I'm more than that."

I paused. "Is that why you think I call you that?"

She snickered. "Is there any other reason?"

John poked his head back around. "Hate to break up this little lovefest, but breakfast is going to get cold if you guys don't come eat. Now."

I threw my hands up. "Why the fuck won't people just listen to me?"

Dani made her way into the kitchen. "Because you're talking nonsense right now. That's why."

John let out a roar of a laughter that made me clench my fists. Where the hell was my sweet, innocent little college girl?

You're killing her. She's almost in the ground. That's where she is. Because of you.

I started for the kitchen. "Dani, you need to get back to campus."

She sat down at the table. "Care to tell me why?"

I licked my lips. "Because what's happening is dangerous, and I don't want you anywhere near it."

"And what if I want to stay with you?"

"What if you fail your classes if you start missing them?"

She waved her hand in the air. "Missing one day won't hurt. I'm two weeks ahead in my homework and my reading, anyway. No tests. No quizzes. I'll be good."

"Dani, this isn't what you--"

"I'm staying with you, and that's final."

I looked over at John and he held up his hands.

"Don't look at me. I'm just serving up food."

Dani sipped her coffee. "Besides, someone's going to have to help you around today. You can barely stand up straight."

I glowered. "I don't need help standing."

John cleared his throat. "I mean, you are standing a bit crooked right now."

Dani held her arm out. "See? Even your own brother sees it."

I held back a sigh. "I have business to attend to today. Red Thorn business. Business you can't be part of."

John butted in. "Have you called a formal meeting? Or an informal one?"

"Will you shut the hell up?"

Dani set her cup down. "Please take me with you."

That innocent little twang of hers strummed at my gut. Tugged at my heartstrings. I looked over at her and saw her eyes growing wider. Begging me. Urging me to take her along.

"Dani, I can't."

"Please?"

I shook my head. "I'm serious. I can't risk you getting hurt."

John snickered. "I'm pretty sure the guys like her more than you at this point. They certainly won't let her get hurt."

"You're not helping, brother."

"I am helping. Just not you."

Dani nodded. "Thank you, John."

He grinned. "Any time, girl."

I shook my head. "What the hell is going on?"

Dani stood. "Please, Max. Take me with you. I'm worried about you. And if I go back to campus, the only thing I'm going to do is bombard you with text messages until I know you're okay again. I won't be able to focus on my studies, so I'll miss the lectures anyway. Me being on campus doesn't mean I'm going to be productive. Max, listen to me."

She took my hands and I already felt myself succumbing to her warmth.

"Take me with you. Let me help. I'm not as weak as you think I am."

And for the life of me, I couldn't figure out when the hell she ever thought I considered her weak.

3

DANI

I gazed around the pub, but the atmosphere was completely different. There weren't any playful waitresses squealing at having their butts smacked. There weren't men coming up to tables and asking for double dates with me and Max. There wasn't even food or drinks coming to any of the tables.

It seemed like a completely different place.

All of the men were standing around, huddled off on the other side of the room. And there I sat, in the booth Max and I had occupied for one of our first dates, alone. The only woman in this place. It felt awkward. Like I wasn't actually supposed to be here. But it seemed as if I was the only one that felt that my presence was off. None of the men clad in leather jackets and grungy jeans paid me any mind. Not like they had that night, anyway.

Then again, Max did look pretty beat up.

And they were all tossing questions his way.

"Who the fuck did this to you?"

"When did this happen?"

"Is this why you called the meeting?"

"They're going to die. Every last one of them."

The gruff voices made me shiver. Not with fear. I didn't feel fearful of my place in this establishment. Nor did I feel as if my safety was compromised. But the intensity and sincerity these guys used to speak of death. And revenge. And killing.

I'd never heard people so completely okay with those topics before.

"We wait until everyone's here," Max said.

The entire room fell silent.

One could almost hear a pin drop in the place. I heard my heart thundering in my ears. Max held a command over this place--over these guys--that I didn't understand. I mean, I knew they were all part of a crew. Their leather jackets were all the same. They had designs on the back in crimson red and gold. They all acted as if they had known one another for years. The best of friends, or even brothers.

I felt like I was missing something, though.

The door to the pub flew open and I craned my neck above the booth to see a massive man with a pot belly shuffling through the door. He let out a bombastic belch before scratching at the back of his head. The man looked like a cross between a pig and a moose. Towering over everyone else, but with a blank stare and an upturned nose on his face.

His expression changed the moment he saw Max.

"I've been waiting to get my hands bloodied recently."

"Grog. Nice to see you again."

Max walked up to him and the two clapped hands, welcoming one another into the night. Was the man's name really 'Grog'? Whether it was a nickname or not, it suited him. His eyes panned over to mine and he harrumphed through his nose. I could've sworn I saw a shadow of a grin playing upon his stubbled cheeks. His eyes returned to Max and I slid back down into the booth, wondering if everyone was finally here.

"All right. Time to round up."

Max's voice boomed through the pub and the men scattered. Chairs scraped across the floor and tables were moved out of the way. I saw each of the guys grab a chair and slide it up to the front, creating a circle as I was sure they'd done many times before. I watched Max sit down with a grunt. The men gathered around in their own chairs. There had to be twenty of them. Possibly even thirty. However, my eyes landed on the empty chair beside Max.

And I quickly scurried to take it before someone else did.

If my parents knew what I was doing...

I shook my head at the thought. What they didn't know wouldn't hurt them. And even though the rough-and-tumble men were studying me, I didn't feel the least bit threatened by them. If anything, I felt safer than I had in a while. If any threat of any kind came down onto us, I knew I was the first person they'd protect.

I don't know how I knew that. I just… did.

Grog clicked his tongue. "You gonna answer our questions now?"

Max stared at him. "Last night, I was the target of a hit."

The men started murmuring amongst one another before Max snapped his fingers, silencing them all with the smallest flick of his wrist.

Who are you?

"It wasn't a concealed hit, either. I was lucky that Bambi here was in close enough proximity to scrape me off the damn pavement."

One of the guys nodded at me. "That her name?"

I shook my head. "No."

Max put his hand on my knee. "It's her nickname, because you won't call her by her name. Only I do that. You all can call her Bambi."

I leaned toward Max. "Do they really have to call me that?"

He lowered his voice. "Just because you don't understand the nickname yet doesn't mean it doesn't suit you."

I had no idea what he could've possibly meant by that. But we weren't in a position to be able to discuss it. I let it slide as my hand draped over his on my knee.

"I was at her campus. Dropping her off. They jumped me, three of them. The fourth was in a black SUV that sped off into the night. They were wearing gold rings that dug into the back of my neck. John got pictures of the bruised insignias on my skin."

I saw some of the guys clenching their fists while others clenched their jaws.

"Whoever took this hit out made it clear to me that this is only the beginning. An appetizer, they called it."

Grog spoke up. "So you heard their voices."

Max nodded. "Yes."

My voice lowered to a whisper. "Why didn't you tell me any of this?"

He squeezed my knee, attempting to keep me silent, I guessed. It wouldn't work. He didn't get to control when I spoke with him and when I didn't.

"How bad is it?"

I looked over toward the voice and noticed the redhead sitting there. Oh, what was his name? Robert? Roland?

"What 'it' are you talking about, Rupert?" Max asked.

Rupert! That's it.

"The fuck you think I'm talking about? How bad are your damn injuries? What else happened?"

Max sighed. "You don't need a rundown of my wounds. All you need is--"

Benji cleared his throat. "Actually, a rundown might be nice. You know those kinds of injuries tells us how those guys moved. Pivoted. Where their strengths and weaknesses are. What they target on a person. That's valuable information."

I didn't even realize that slimy little jerk was here until he spoke up. And when he did, my eyes whipped over to him. He stared at me with a cool expression. One that was virtually unreadable. His eyes stayed locked with mine. As if he were somehow attempting to command me to get up and walk out. I held my head up high, though, trying not to show Benji how shaken I still was from our personal encounter.

"I wanted to call this meeting not to give you a rundown of what happened to me, play by play, but to warn you. As a crew. Whoever took this hit out on me not only has balls, but deep pockets. Those were expensive guys. Or stupid. I'm not sure yet. Either way, there's a chance this person could be targeting other members of this crew. I wanted to bring you guys together and inform you of that."

Rupert shot up from his chair. "You got any idea who this might be from? Because I'm gunning for a fight."

Some of the other guys stood up and nodded their heads with the man as Max sighed.

"I know you're all upset. Trust me, no one is more upset than I am. I have no theories as to who's behind this right now. We have many enemies, and just as many friends. Until I've got something to start narrowing the playing field, we all keep an eye over our shoulders and on our loved ones."

Grog nodded. "How do you start finding information on this?"

Rupert sat back down. "Yeah. How do we even go about figuring any of this out if no one saw anything of value?"

Max threaded our fingers together. "We have the insignias on their rings to go on. John thinks he can enhance the images enough to make them out. From there, we should be able to track down who sells the rings, and hopefully go from there. But right now, it's the only lead we've got."

Benji snickered. "It's a shit lead."

Max nodded. "Trust me, I know. Keep your eyes open and your ears to the ground. Keep your noses as clean as you can. And if you get yourself into a situation your gut doesn't like, get out. Immediately. We can't take any chances right now. Especially with loved ones. And if you hear any whispers, you come straight to me. Is that clear?"

The men nodded. "Yes, boss."

The unanimous echo. The snapping of his fingers. The way the guys hung on to his every word. My eyes slowly widened as Max nodded his head, dispersing the men to put the tables back in their rightful places. I slowly turned toward him. My eyes danced along the profile of his face.

"Are you their boss, Max?"

A grin ticked his cheek before his eyes flickered my way.

"And if I am?"

My lips parted in shock. He really was. He was their main man. The boss. The big cheese. Their president. I'd been doing a bit of research on crews like this. Their hierarchy. Their strategic thinking. Their traditions. The president wielded all the power. Well, except for the owner of the crew. Did Max own them, too? Or was John the owner?

I didn't see John at the meeting. Even though he was mentioned. And he was apparently helping.

Maybe this is a family thing and his brother owns the group.

As Max and I sat there, watching the men put the room back together, I wondered what this meant for me. I felt more powerful than ever, sitting next to him, being protected by his hand on my knee. Quickly becoming the object of his affections. Something wild stirred within me. Something that tugged a smile across my lips.

Something I'd never felt before.

And something I wanted to keep on feeling.

"Anything else, boss?"

Benji's voice rose above the clamor and everyone turned to face him. Benji and Max stared off for a long time. I looked back and forth between the two of them, and what I wouldn't have given to be a flicker on the inside of Max's mind.

"Nope. You're all dismissed."

And everyone did as Max commanded.

No wonder he's used to getting what he wants.

The men filed out the door, and some of them even waved to me. I still wasn't a fan of any of them calling me Bambi. Especially Benji. But I had to figure out what Max meant by his statement.

About me not knowing what the nickname meant.

I know what Benji means when he says it.

Max turned to face me. "Hope that wasn't too boring for you."

I snickered. "Are you kidding? It was thrilling. Thank you for bringing me along."

He laughed. "You really need to get out more, gorgeous."

"Then take me out anytime you'd like."

A growl fell softly from his lips before he pulled my chair closer to him with one hand, not stopping until our knees touched. His hand wrapped around the back of my head, pulling me quickly to him. And as our lips crashed together, I drew in a deep breath.

Before melting into his embrace.

I moved from my chair, straddling his lap as I sat close against him. I laced my arms around his neck, tilting my head off to the side just to taste a little more of him. I felt him grunt and tried my best not to lean my full weight against him. It was hard. His arms cloaked my back, pulling me closer despite the pain he was in.

"Max--mm--your nose is--oh--and your ribs--fuck."

He kissed down my neck. "Shut up and let me dote on you."

I sighed. "My pleasure."

His kisses felt delightful. His hands traveled the expanse of my body. As we sat there, alone in the pub, I felt more connected to him than ever before. His lips wrapped around my clothed, puckered nipples. His hands slid up and down my trembling thighs. I felt his raging erection pressing against me, begging to be set free from his jeans.

Then he pulled back.

I panted softly as my forehead fell against his. I felt his nose nuzzle mine softly as his hand cupped the nape of my neck. I gazed into his eyes. Those glorious, powerful, brooding eyes. They ignited with lust for me.

I saw them sparkling. Aching for me, the way I ached for him.

"Are we alone?" I whispered.

Max looked around quickly before grinning.

"All alone, gorgeous."

I smiled. "Good."

I captured his lips with my own again, refusing to let the moment pass us by. Max made me feel free, in control of my own life, spontaneous and beautiful. Important, and wanted. I didn't want that feeling to end. I wasn't ready to relinquish it and go back to campus.

So I rocked against him as my tongue slid over the roof of his mouth.

His hands went straight to my ass cheeks for round two.

4

——————

MAX

I didn't know what the hell this second kiss was all about. But I wasn't about to stop her. I didn't give a shit how much pain my body was in. Nothing would ever stop me from enjoying her, holding her as close as I could get her. The pub had been abandoned. There wasn't a soul in sight. No staff. None of my guys. And certainly no one from the public. The lights were dimmed and the streets were silent, except for the roaring of motorcycles as they drove off into the distance. As my hands slid down to Dani's ass cheeks, gripping them with sheer delight, her giggle set off a need in me I had to fulfill.

The last motorcycle engine faded into the distance.

Her fingers plunged into my hair as she clung to me. I slipped my hands into the pockets of her jeans and gave her ass a nice little squeeze. Her giggle sent my heart fluttering. Her hold on me sent my cock pulsing. And her gasps--those little sounds of hers--sent the tip of my dick leaking.

I growled. "I need you. Now."

I fisted her hair and crashed our lips back together. The pain in my body and in my head dulled the second our tongues collided. With every grind of her hips against my own, it faded into nothingness. Her hands slid my leather jacket off. My fingers unbuttoned and unzipped her jeans. We pawed at one another, trembling with need. Heated, and wanton, and ready for what came next.

"Take me. I need you, Max."

I kissed her neck. "Why don't you be a good girl and stand up for me?"

She giggled as I gripped her legs, standing us both up. She clung to me as I carried her over to the bar, settling her onto its edge. I pulled up a chair and sat, admiring her pussy as it stared me in the face. I was ready to feast on her until she begged me to stop. Until she pushed me away and drenched this bar with a mess we'd have to clean up before we left.

"Lift those hips for me, gorgeous."

I looped my fingers into the belt loops of her pants and she did as I asked. She planted her hands and lifted that perfect body of hers into the air. Helping me to slide her pants over that perfect ass of hers. I wanted to know what that tasted like as well. Maybe I'd make a damn fine meal out of her tonight.

I reached down and unbuttoned my own pants. Pulling my dick out so it could breathe without pain.

And hopefully, so I could pull her back into my lap and sink myself into her warmth.

I pulled her pants down to her boots and slipped my head between her legs. With her wet panties taunting me with their scent, I nuzzled softly against the cotton fabric. Cotton. Such a harsh and plain fabric. I kissed it softly before my fingers slid them to the side, revealing to me the pussy lips I wanted to suck on as a little treat.

"We need to take you underwear shopping next."

Then I felt something vibrating against my back.

"What's that?"

Dani's voice was breathless as her head peeked up.

"I don't care. Lay back down."

Then it vibrated again.

"That's my phone. Hold on. Sorry, I just--"

I rolled my eyes as I slipped from between her legs. I watched her stuff her hand into the pockets of her jeans at her ankles as she sat there on that bar, looking more tantalizing than ever. Her cheeks were flushed red, her hair wild and free, her legs bared. Waiting for my lips to nibble until I had the lengths of them marked.

"Darn it. It's Hannah."

I grinned. "It really is okay to cuss, you know."

She stuck her tongue out at me before she answered her phone, much to my dismay.

"Hey there. Where am I? I'm, uh, out."

I shook my head as I leaned back against the seat. Of course she'd be a terrible liar. I mean, even when she was telling the truth, she still sounded like she was lying.

"Yes, Hannah. I know. I just needed a day to--yes, I know I don't miss classes. I'm sorry you worried. Yeah, I see--Hannah!"

I chuckled as I stood to my feet, turned my back to her, and rearranged my cock before regretfully burying it back behind my pants. I knew what was coming. As much as I didn't want to admit it, I knew this would result in her having to head back to campus. And while I knew it would, I was hoping to snag a piece of dessert for myself before I had to take her back. Especially since Dani had instigated it this time.

I liked that she finally wanted me, and wasn't afraid of it.

"Yes, yes. I'm coming soon. There's no need to--Hannah, you can stop it now. Stop it!"

I turned around to find Dani's eyes wide and her nose flaring. She tucked her phone against her shoulder, up to her ear. She reached for her pants and I walked toward her, gripping her at her waist. I picked her up and set her down onto the floor, then helped her get her damn jeans back up her legs.

Swallowing disappointed growls with every inch they covered.

"Yeah. I promise, I'm coming. All right? Yes. And you can stop yelling. It's not going to get anything productive done. Now, stop blowing up my phone. I'm on my way."

My eyebrows rose. "Trouble in paradise?"

She slipped her phone into her pocket. "I'm sorry, Max. But I have to go."

I nodded. "It's all right."

"No, it's not all right. I wanted--"

I quirked an eyebrow as Dani let out a heavy sigh.

"Come on. I'll get you home and settled."

"I can catch a cab or something."

She eyed me hotly. "Get in the damn car. I'm taking you home."

I grinned. "If you insist. Though I'm tempted to say 'no' just to rile you up."

"And why's that?"

I wrapped my arm around her. "Because you have no idea how sexy you get when you're fed up. It's a nice change of pace."

She blushed. "You're insane, you know that?"

"Maybe you make me that way. Ever thought of that?"

She paused. "This is probably very true. But you know you like it."

I kissed her forehead. "With all I have, gorgeous."

The drive home was excruciating. My cock practically screamed at me to pull the damn thing over. It needed release. And so did I. With her. With this college girl who fit in so weirdly effortlessly with the rest of the guys. This college girl who didn't even come up to the middle of my chest. This college girl with words of fire that only came out when stoked to her boiling point.

This college girl that had completely captured my attention.

I didn't want her to leave for the night.

"All right, Max. We're here. Let me help you inside."

I unbuckled myself. "I've got it. John's here, too. So I'm not alone."

"I'm coming in to help you."

"No, you aren't."

Her eyes whipped to mine. "I want to see you inside. Please."

"And you need to get back to campus."

"Hannah can wait a few more minutes."

"But I can't."

She blinked. "What do you mean?"

I growled softly. "If you come inside with me, you aren't leaving. Not of your own accord. Not until I release you. Which won't be until well in the morning tomorrow. So if you want to make it back to campus tonight for your roommate, you better not come inside."

She swallowed hard. "Promise?"

I sighed as I turned to her. I reached out and gripped her chin, making sure she was paying attention. I saw those stars in her eyes. Girls that rode with me got them all the time. They thought being with me came with power and glamour and money and freedom. When really, the only thing that came with me was death, destruction, and darkness.

"You have to go back to campus. Okay?"

She nodded softly. "Okay."

"You have classes. You have grades. You have a life."

"You're part of my life now, though."

"A small part of it."

"That's growing into a much bigger part."

I shook my head. "Go back to campus, Dani."

"And what if I don't want to?"

How my heart sang with those words. "Don't make me get angry at you, Bambi. Don't do that."

"What does that nickname actually mean?"

"What?"

"Bambi. That nickname. Benji started it, and I know it's a bad thing when he says it. Does it not mean the same thing when you say it?"

My eyes danced between hers. "No. It doesn't mean the same thing."

"Then what does it mean when you say it?"

I cupped her cheek. "If you tell anyone I've seen this movie, you're in big trouble. Got it?"

She snickered. "Yeah. I got it."

"Promise to go back to campus if I tell you?"

She sighed. "Yeah. Okay. I promise."

"In the movie, you know, Bambi, that little deer, isn't really weak."

"No?"

I shook my head. "No. In the movie, Bambi goes through a lot of loss. The loss of his mother. The loss of his forest. The loss of some of his friends. But eventually, Bambi finds love. Bambi finds a relationship with his father. Bambi has a family. Becomes the head of the forest to protect those he loves."

She grinned. "Maybe you're more like Bambi than I am."

I chuckled. "And maybe you're strong, like Bambi. Stronger than you think."

"You think I'm strong? That's why you call me that?"

"I think you're stronger than even you realize. So, yes. That's what I mean by Bambi."

She smiled. "I like that."

I kissed the tip of her nose. "Good. Now. Let me know when you get back to campus. Okay?"

I slipped quickly out of her car before she could protest any longer. I closed the car door and turned around, watching as Dani sat there. Making her decision. Trying to figure out what her next move was.

Just keep your promise. Be good for me, Bambi.

Then I saw her car backing out of the parking lot.

"There we go," I murmured.

I stood there, watching her until she drove off into the night, the sound of the car quickly dying in the distance. I sighed as I turned around, ready to hobble my beaten ass up the front porch steps. My raging hard-on kept jamming against the zipper of my jeans. It was well past time for another round of pain medication. And as I opened the screen door, the front door was ripped open.

Revealing my brother holding two white pills and a glass of water.

"I thought you'd never get your ass inside."

I chuckled. "Me neither, to be honest."

Then I took the pills and chugged the water, trying to wash my lust for Dani away.

"Come on. I got lemonade and food for you, Max. You can fill me in on what happened at the meeting."

I sighed. "And after that, a long-ass nap."

My brother laughed. "Yes, yes. A long-ass, drug-induced nap."

5
———

DANI

I white-knuckled the steering wheel as I headed back to campus. I was irritated. Frustrated. And pissed off at that phone call from Hannah. I wanted to stay with Max. I wanted to make sure he'd be all right. I wanted to get one more night under his belt with someone watching over him before I made my way back for classes tomorrow. Especially since I only had afternoon classes.

But no. My roommate had to call and practically ram her emotions down my throat.

"Fucking Hannah," I murmured.

I mean, who the hell was she, anyway? She was my roommate that wanted to get me laid. That's who she was. So I'd gotten laid. By a great guy. Who actually liked me.

She doesn't know any of that, though.

Yeah, and she won't if she keeps ruining stuff like this.

"Ugh," I groaned.

I pulled into campus and snagged a parking spot not too far away from the dorm building. At least I wasn't hiking across campus this time around. I dreaded going into that building. I dreaded riding the elevator. I could practically hear Hannah seething at the end of the hallway. I heard her pacing, her little heels clicking at an insane speed.

And when I rounded the corner to stand in the doorway, she whipped around.

"What the actual hell, Dani?"

I thumbed over my shoulder. "You know I can walk right back out."

"Oh, no you don't."

"Hey!"

She grabbed my wrist and pulled me over to my bed. She whipped me around, cornering me in my own damn room like a rabid dog. I felt my face fall and my back stiffen. I stared at her as she closed--and locked--our dorm door. I felt like I was at home again, like she had become my parent. Locking me away from the world because she thought she knew what was best for me.

She had another think coming.

"What the hell are you doing, scaring me like that?" she asked.

"Last I checked, you weren't my mother," I said.

She snickered. "Drop the tough girl act. It doesn't suit you."

"Then stop interrogating me like a parent. You call me up and chew me out over something that isn't your business--"

"Making sure my roommate and my friend is okay *is* my business, Dani. You had me worried sick!"

I held my arms out. "Sorry. I didn't mean to."

"You skipped classes."

"I'm two weeks ahead in my work."

"You never skip classes."

I sighed. "Can we get to the point?"

She took a step toward me. "Fine. We can. You aren't acting like yourself, Dani. Do you know how uncharacteristic it is of you to spend a night out?"

"No. Why don't you inform me?"

She snickered. "Like *very* uncharacteristic."

I nodded. "Very."

"Yeah."

"Got it."

"You sure? Because you never do shit like this. I thought something terrible had happened to you!"

I sighed. As I leaned against my bed, I couldn't deny the sincerity in Hannah's eyes. The fear. The relief that I really was all right. She wasn't trying to control me. She was just scared. Worried for my safety. That was what friends did with one another. And I, for one, would've been the same way had the tables been turned.

So I swallowed my frustration.

"Look, I'm sorry, Hannah. Really I am. I never meant to worry you or anything. I was just having some fun because I knew I could spare the time to have it. I never get to do things like this. Ever. And I wanted to experience it for once. That's all."

Hannah sighed. "Well, don't do something like that

again. Tell me when you're not coming back for the night. I barely slept. I couldn't eat. I mean, what you do with your grades is your business. I don't care about that. But I care about you. And whether or not you're alive."

"The next time it happens, I'll let you know. I promise."

She nodded. "Great. Thank you. Now, where were you, anyway?"

I thought about lying. I didn't feel like I could tell Hannah any of this without her chewing me out. Or getting upset. Or berating me for some reason. What I was doing wasn't wrong. Max wasn't a bad guy.

At least, I don't think he is.

"Dani."

I blinked. "Hannah."

"Where were you last night? What were you doing?"

Don't lie to your best friend. "I was with Max."

She furrowed her brow. "Who's that?"

I pointed to my leather jacket. "Max. Leather jacket man. The guy with the bike?"

Her face fell. "What?"

"Yeah. I was out with him last night."

"And you stayed out with him?"

The shrill tone of her voice made me wince. "Yes. I did."

"What the fuck were you two doing? Where the hell did you sleep?"

I swallowed hard as she took another step closer to me

"You didn't," she said.

I shrugged. "You'll have to be more specific than that."

She grabbed my arm. "Did you sleep with him?"

"You mean, did I occupy the same bed as him last night? No. I didn't."

"Don't you use semantics with me. Are you sleeping with him, Dani?"

"Ouch. You're hurting me."

Hannah dropped her hand. "Sorry."

I rubbed my arm. "And anyway, wasn't the whole point of this year to get me to give up my virginity anyway?"

She gasped. "You slept with that man?"

"Hannah, would you just listen to yourself? I didn't sleep with him last night. Max was hurt in a fight last night. And I just couldn't leave him there. He was hurt!"

"What kind of fight? Where?"

"Right outside the dorm, Hannah. He was jumped. He wasn't conscious. I wasn't going to just leave him there."

"Did you call the cops? Get him in an ambulance? You still would've been home had you done that."

I shook my head. "He didn't want cops or an ambulance. I drove him back to his place in my car."

She threw her hands up in the air. "You what!? He's a criminal, Dani. Only men who have records or a chance at arrest don't go to hospitals after they're jumped. Don't you know any of this?"

I raised my head high. "He was hurt. I wanted to

spend the night to make sure he was okay. That's what I did. If you don't like it, that sounds like a personal problem."

Hannah put her hands on her hips. "You want to know what I think?"

"I already know what you think. You've had no issues shoving it down my throat since I got back."

"Dani, I don't know what the hell's gotten into you--"

"Control of my life. That's what's gotten into me."

She sighed. "Dani. This guy? He's trouble. I know that just from looking at him. You need to walk away now, while you still can."

"See? That's the issue with people. Always judging others on the outside. Max is always judged, and so was I. But he didn't judge me. And I didn't judge him. That's why it's nice to be around him. Maybe you should take a page out of his book."

"What? Pissing people off so I can get jumped and not go to the hospital?"

I pointed at her. "You take that back."

She smacked my hand away from her face. "Never."

I felt my nostrils flaring with anger. "I'm not walking away."

"You have to."

"No."

"Dani, just listen to me."

"I am listening, Hannah!"

My voice rose so high that it echoed off the corners of our room, causing Hannah to wince.

"You're just like my mother. I do hear you. Everyone can hear you. The only thing is that I'm not listening. Why? Because I don't want to. I hear you. I get it. But I'm not taking your advice. And that's what's pissing you off."

She snickered. "And why won't you listen? Why won't you just trust me on this?"

I shrugged. "Because I don't want to."

She nodded. "Well, great. Wonderful. That's just dandy."

"You don't have to like it."

"Of course I don't like it, Dani. I want my best friend back."

"What? The one that wore the baggy clothes you always picked on her about? The girl who was always a pushover who you tried to get out to bars and clubs until two in the morning? The girl you forced into heels because 'that's what girls do'? Huh? The girl you dragged to parties that made her uncomfortable? You want that girl back?"

"Dani, that's not what I--"

"You know what's amazing about this scenario?"

"Dani, just take a deep breath. Please?"

I snickered. "What's amazing is that, if I were doing any of this with you, you'd be just fine. In fact, you'd be delighted. But it's with Max. And you don't like that."

"Because he's dangerous, Dani."

"No, because it isn't you. Because since the first time I met you, you're no longer the driving force in my life."

"What?"

I nodded. "Yeah. And it makes you fume. You're no longer the one telling me how to better myself and 'find myself' and 'experience college for all it has to offer.' And because it's not you--but Max--that makes you upset."

"Are you even listening to yourself?"

"I am. For once in my life, I am. And if you don't like the decisions I'm making with it because I'm following the beat of my own drum now, then you can butt out."

She gasped. "You don't mean that."

I stormed past Hannah and wrenched out of her grip. I scooped up my purse and rushed out the door, sprinting for the stairwell. I jammed myself into the door as Hannah called out after me, trying to get me to stop and talk to her. Trying to get me to come back.

I wouldn't go back, though.

Not after something like that.

My entire body trembled. It felt like fire had consumed me and turned me into a shivering pile of ash. Where in the world did all of that come from? That anger. Those words. It almost didn't feel like me saying any of it.

But, damn, did it feel good to say.

I burst through the doors and poured out onto the sidewalk. I gazed up the facade of the building, spotting my dorm room. I slipped my purse over my shoulder and started walking. I didn't know where in the world I was going, but I didn't want to go back up there. While part of me wanted to tell Hannah everything, I wouldn't. Because right now, it would only get me yelled at.

I don't like this at all.

"Dani!"

Hannah's voice behind me caused me to start sprinting again. I booked it for my car, pulling my keys out of my pocket. I just needed to get away from her. Away from campus. Away from all the expectations and all of the things people wanted me to do just to seem normal to them.

"Dani! Wait up! Please!"

I fumbled with my keys as I approached my car. I pressed the unlock button and tossed my purse inside. I heard Hannah's heels clicking, gaining on me. And as I slid into the driver's seat, I locked my car.

Just before Hannah started tugging on the other door.

"Open this damn thing now!"

She slammed her fist against the glass as I cranked the engine up.

"Don't you dare. Don't you dare leave again. Dani!"

I sped out of the parking space and got myself turned around.

"Dani, just stop, okay? I'm sorry!"

They were always sorry. After the fact. People were always sorry once tensions died down. But I knew the apologies never meant anything. Not really. Because the moment I stepped out of bounds again, they'd yell at me again for it. Like a petulant child.

So I sped away from campus again.

"What about your classes?"

It was the last of Hannah's voice I heard. I tore out of the parking lot and skidded onto the road, hearing another car honking its horn as I almost crashed into it. I gripped the steering wheel with all my might and sped toward the intersection, hitting the yellow light just as I careened left. I didn't know where in the world I was going, but I needed to get away. I needed to get as far away from campus and grades and tests and expectations as much as I could.

And the more campus dimmed in my rearview mirror, the freer I felt. I drew in deep breaths as I drove around town, watching the clock tick past midnight.

I didn't know what I'd do about Hannah. Or classes. Or Max. Or anything else. One thing was for certain, though. One thing I knew for sure.

However much of Max I was allowed to have, I'd take.

6

———————

MAX

I sat on the back porch and let the afternoon sun batter against my body. It felt good, actually. Like sitting in a dry sauna. I'd taken three warm showers already just to try and unlock my muscles. They were tense. Aching. Bruised and battered.

But mostly, they missed Dani.

"Want a beer?"

John sat a glass bottle in front of me and I snickered. I picked it up and took a couple long pulls, feeling it wash down the last of the pain medication that had been lodged in my throat for the past few minutes. I licked my lips and set it down, watching the condensation already rolling down its curves.

Dani's are better.

"How you feeling?"

I sighed. "As fine as I can feel."

"How'd you sleep last night?"

I shrugged. "Like shit."

"So normal."

I snickered. "Yeah, normal."

John nodded. "Dani seems nice."

"She's a good girl."

"Doesn't seem so good to me. Skipping out on those classes."

I grinned. "She's got some spunk in her if you give her a chance. Just doesn't know how to…"

"Let it out?"

"That's one way to put it."

"Oppressive parents?"

I shrugged. "Don't really know."

"Bad childhood?"

"Again, don't know."

"Do you know anything about this girl?"

I know she's incredible. "She's smart. Wanted to be a doctor at one point before switching her major."

"A doctor. Nice. What made her switch?"

I paused. "I'm sure she's told me, but I don't remember."

"Pussy too good?"

I growled. "Don't you talk about her that way."

He held his hands up. "Just making a joke. Damn."

I took another long pull from my beer before I heard footsteps beside us. I whipped my head over and kept the groan to myself. John stood up. I had my hand already gravitating toward the gun on my hip. When Rupert emerged from around the corner of the house, I sighed.

"You almost got shot, you know," John said.

Rupert chuckled. "I would've dodged."

I snickered. "He is good at missing those flying pieces of metal."

Rupert smiled. "I take it you're feeling better?"

He clapped his hand against my shoulder and I grunted.

"Or maybe not. Sorry."

I sighed. "You're good. I'm at that part of the healing stage where everything hurts."

He pulled up a chair. "That's good. Means your body's actually trying."

John cleared his throat. "Want a beer, Rupert?"

He smiled. "Don't mind if I do. Thanks."

I held up my bottle. "And get me another."

Rupert cocked an eyebrow. "You on pain medication?"

John chuckled. "You think he cares?"

Rupert pointed. "I think that girl of his will care."

I drained the last of my bottle. "Well, she's not here, is she? So fuck it."

Rupert chuckled. "Spoken like a man who's truly taken."

I didn't hate the idea. But it did make me bristle a bit.

"What brings you here?" I asked.

Rupert leaned back. "Coming to check up on you. See how you're doing. Generally talk about how fucked-up things are right now."

I nodded. "They're pretty rough, yeah."

He shook his head. "I don't know. I just… got a bad feeling about all of this. Something's not right. And I feel like it's closer than we think. You know?"

John set the beers down. "Yeah. I know."

I reached out and slapped Rupert's stomach. "Maybe it's all those deep fried pickles you ate at the bar before the meeting."

Rupert narrowed his eyes. "Fuck off with that nonsense. And I mean it."

I nodded. "I know you do."

"Max, you're sure your old man couldn't have had a hand in this? Because you know I don't trust the bastard."

I cracked open my beer. "Who said anything about ruling him out?"

John slammed his bottle down. "I did. You know damn good and well Dad didn't have shit to do with this."

I thumbed over toward my brother. "He seems to think that if my father was behind it, he would've been there."

Rupert shrugged. "Well, you said there was a fourth person in the car."

John clicked his tongue. "Dad would've had a front row seat to the damn show, and we all know it."

Rupert took a pull from his beer. "I mean, how close was that car, or whatever? He could've had a front row seat from there for all we know."

"Dad didn't do this."

"You got any proof of that?"

I held my hand up. "The two of you can stop now."

Rupert held up his hands in mock surrender.

"Look, all I'm saying is, we don't rule anything out until we have proof otherwise. Deal?"

I nodded. "Sounds fair enough."

John shook his head. "I'm telling you, this isn't Dad. We know Dad. We know his MO. How he works. You know this isn't him."

And as much as I hated to admit it, he had a point.

"Max, our father's a monster. Right? Even I get that. But he has lines he wouldn't cross. A man like him still operates on morals. Even if they're skewed."

Rupert snickered. "Ashton has no morals."

John hissed. "He does when it comes to his sons."

I scoffed. "I beg to differ on that."

"The garage was a one-time thing. Quit pissing him off."

Rupert paused. "The garage?"

I eyed John hotly. "Are you fucking kidding me right now?"

Shock rolled over his face. "What? How the hell am I supposed to know you haven't told your best bud about shit like that?"

"Tell me what? The hell's going on?"

I sighed. "Dad sicced a couple of his bodyguards on me in our garage a couple of weeks back."

Rupert leaned forward. "And you didn't tell me? The fuck's wrong with that man? And you're sitting here thinking he didn't order some men to jump you? After he did it himself?"

"That's what I'm trying to say," I said as I stretched out my legs under the table. "If this was Dad, he would've been there. Physically. He would've given the order himself. Yes, Dad has a code. And that code is to not kill his sons, but witness their ass-kicking if they need one. This isn't Ashton."

John took the reins. "Besides, we need Max. He needs Max. Without my brother, operations takes a hit. Without him alive, there's no one to hand this club to. He doesn't have any other sons. Or children, for that matter. Dad wouldn't kill Max. And these men clearly alluded to more coming. Right?"

I nodded. "Right. They're out to kill me. That, in and of itself, rules Dad out."

Rupert didn't look convinced. "I still think it's reckless to trust a snake, regardless of whether he's blood or not. He's done you wrong before, Max. And apparently recently. A dozen times over in the past, too. Even you can't deny that. So who's to say he wouldn't cross this line for the right price? Anyone can be bought. Your old man included."

Damn it. Now Rupert had a point.

I ran a hand over my scruffy face and through my hair and leaned back, feeling my spine crack back into place. I closed my eyes, drinking in the sun. I stretched my body until it shuddered. Then I sat upright back in my seat.

"Feel better?" Rupert asked, chuckling.

I ran my hands down my face. "Let's just finish our beers and order lunch. I'm about to eat my own damn foot, I'm so hungry."

John sighed. "Why the fuck didn't you say anything? I could've already had something ordered. What do you want?"

"Pizza," Rupert and I said in unison.

John chuckled. "Fine by me. The usual?"

Rupert nodded. "Oh! But with those cinnamon whatevers this time around. Those fuckers were amazing."

I sighed. "And extra dipping sauce."

John scooped up his phone. "Great. Be right back."

Rupert cupped his hands over his mouth. "And bring more beer!"

I winced. "He's right there, you idiot."

John barked with laughter. "Beer. Got it. Hold on."

As John retreated back into the house, my mind began to wander. Could my own father really be behind all this? I mean, he was a master puppeteer. That man had pulled off some of the most difficult and mind-boggling things in the past to flood his pockets and line ours as well. And if that was true--if my father really was behind this--it would be hard to crack. Very hard. My father was an expert in covering his tracks and pinning shit on other people. He'd risen to the heights of the underworld he held now because of those two reasons. Getting out scot-free and being able to pin it on others when he couldn't.

"Has your father ever put on a hit on someone? That you know of?"

Rupert's voice jogged a memory that sent a chill down my spine.

"Once," I said.

"What happened?"

I sighed. "He succeeded."

"Well, what was it your father wanted? Why the hit?"

My memories pulled me back. "He was making a play for a plot of land. Thousands of acres for him to sell off as he pleased, whenever it was convenient. The owner wouldn't take his offer because they had a 'bad feeling' about him."

"Are you telling me your father had someone killed over land?"

"Not just any land, Rupert."

John walked back outside with more drinks. "The land he now lives on."

I looked up at John as he set the cooler of beers on top of the table.

"Are you fucking kidding me?" Rupert asked.

I shook my head. "No. I'm not. He had someone killed in order to take that land for himself. Half of the money he has right now came from selling that land off piece by piece to the highest bidder. Our father is smart. So if there *is* a chance that he's behind this, it's because he's making a play for something."

John opened the cooler. "And what the fuck does his son have that he can't just go out and buy? I mean, really. Come on. This is ridiculous."

I paused. "Thanks. I think."

Rupert reached for another beer. "Well, let's play hypotheticals, then. It's all we've got right now, so we might as well."

I shrugged. "I'm down."

John rolled his eyes. "This is stupid. I have those pictures, remember?"

I turned toward him. "You got them enhanced and tracked down?"

John paused. "Well, no. But--"

I turned back to Rupert. "Okay. Hypothetically speaking?"

Rupert grinned. "If your father's behind this, what would be your most prized possession? The one thing you think someone might want to take away from you?"

Dani. "Nothing that's of any concern to him."

Rupert sighed. "Just play the game. Come on. What's the most prized thing you own? The most expensive thing you've got?"

I shook my head. "The only thing I can think of that's changed recently is Dani. But she's not even that big a part of my life. Just some girl riding around with me."

John pointed. "And attending meetings now."

Rupert nodded. "That's a hell of a step."

I shrugged. "I can't blame her. Dani's the one that found me after I was jumped. She wanted to come along and make sure I'd be okay."

John grinned. "Sounds a bit more than 'just some girl.'"

Rupert chuckled. "Same thing I was thinking."

I felt my face turning red. "Fine. Say my father wants Dani. Why?"

I didn't like how close to home this conversation was turning. Especially after the incident with my father that essentially put Dani on his shitlist. But as we all looked around the table, no one could really give me an answer as to why my father would want Dani. Or even want her targeted just to remove her from my life.

Dad did mention you were distracted.

I shook my head. "Let's just sit tight until John can do what he does best with those images. Those insignias are all we've got right now. There's no use in drumming up anything else like this, especially when we're talking about some innocent girl."

Rupert furrowed his brow. "What aren't you telling us?"

I snickered. "You really want to know?"

John nodded. "It would be nice."

I licked my lips. "If Dad's behind this somehow, he wouldn't be after a person. He doesn't give a shit about people. He only cares about what he can own. What he can claim as his own. Like his property. Or his money. Or his sons."

John snickered. "Good point."

Rupert propped his feet on the table. "So where does that leave us, then?"

I sipped my beer. "I think we're coming at it from the wrong angle."

John cocked his head. "How do you figure?"

I chugged the rest of it down. "If I can figure out what the hell is being targeted in my life--other than myself--that will tell us whether or not this is Dad. He's got very few things he treasures. But if we can figure out what this person is after--other than my death, of course--that might help us backtrack and figure out who the hell is at the helm of all this."

Rupert nodded slowly. "Shift the focus. I can get behind that."

I pointed at my brother. "Which means we need those pictures and anything you've got on them A.S.A.P."

John cleared his throat. "I'll get on it big-time after lunch."

I set my drink down. "Good."

And before anyone could say anything else, I heard the doorbell ring from inside. Signaling pizza, more beer, and the eventual need to work.

After a nice nap, though.

My body needed a fucking rest.

7

DANI

My eyes began wandering away from my textbook and over to the wall. And as I stared off toward the middle of the library, my thoughts wandered back to Max. My afternoon classes had been brutal. It was all I could do to focus in my lectures and take decent notes. I was so mentally fried by the time my second class was over that I had to take a nap before coming to the library to study.

And I still wasn't getting much done.

What has this man done to me?

I was worried about Max. I'd sent him a couple of text messages when I got up this morning, but I hadn't heard back from him. No phone call. No text reply. Nothing.

It had me very worried.

"Come on. Be there," I murmured.

I pulled my phone out of my leather jacket pocket and swiped at the screen. I had plenty of messages from Hannah. Memes. Pictures. Random shit she'd heard throughout the day. Nothing from Max, though. I cleared it all out. Everything from Hannah. The one missed phone call from my mother. Just to make way for when Max got back to me. I didn't have the capacity to speak with my parents right now. They'd hear the worry in my voice and my mouth would start running off at the first sign of them inquiring about my life. And I sure as hell didn't have the need to speak with my roommate right now. Especially since she practically chased me out of the dorm room last night.

I hadn't come back until I knew she was good and asleep.

Which wasn't until about two in the morning.

I kept thinking about Max's injuries. How beaten he had been. The blood. The pain. The way he grunted every time he moved. The man needed a doctor's watchful eye. He needed a hospital, for crying out loud. I wasn't even sure he'd called the doctor he told me he would. For all I knew, his brother was playing doctor and feeding Max his own necessary pain medications.

I'd never seen anything like that before.

You've never seen a fight in your entire life, Dani.

I picked up my highlighter and uncapped it. I had to stay focused. I had to get my mind back on track. There were videos of the lectures I'd missed posted online, which meant I had to dig out my headphones. I'm sure there were various things I needed to jot down. Things I needed to highlight in the book. And I was prepared for that.

But as I rummaged around in my backpack, I couldn't find my headphones.

"Shit," I hissed.

"Sh!"

I whipped my head up and saw the librarian staring at me past her circular glasses. She had a mean glare on her face and her lips pursed into a tight pucker, staring daggers at me as if I'd just set off a bomb in the middle of the place. I nodded at her and silenced my movements, carefully moving my stuff in an attempt to find my headphones so I wouldn't have to go back to my dorm room just yet.

But they were nowhere to be found.

Seriously?

I closed my textbook in front of me and shoved it into the worn-out bag I'd had since my freshman year of high school. I stood up, sliding it over my shoulder to make the trek back to my dorm room.

And hopefully, encounter a more cheerful Hannah.

I couldn't remember a single thing I'd read in the library. I barely remembered my lectures. Worry pooled in my gut as I walked, my focus still elsewhere. I'd never struggled like this in school before. I'd never had an issue paying attention, or working ahead, or acing my classes. But even reading ahead hadn't prepared me for how much I'd really fallen behind by not being in classes yesterday. I couldn't recall a single fact.

I was much too distracted with something else.

"Evening, Bambi."

My head shot up and my eyes locked in front of

me. As I emerged from the doors of the library, the sight that held my gaze made me smile like a goofy little kid. There he was, leaning against his bike, his arms folded over his chest and his stare piercing straight into my soul.

"Got a few texts from you today. Sorry I never got back. Been busy."

I skipped down the steps toward him. "You look good."

He winked. "Always."

I giggled. "I mean, physically. You look like you're well. You know, better."

He nodded. "I feel a bit better, after some rest."

"How are your ribs? I'm sure riding your bike doesn't feel the greatest."

"Well, they feel well enough to do this."

He reached out for me and I squealed with delight as he whipped me around, pinning me against his bike. My butt had barely touched the leather of his seat before his knee pressed between my legs. His hand ran through my hair while the other softly slid down my torso and over my waist, finally settling on my hip.

I was trapped between the warm metal of his bike and the warm strength of his body.

"Glad to see you're getting your strength back, handsome."

He grinned. "Please tell me you're done studying for the night. I've been out here for a while."

"How did you know I was here?"

He shrugged. "I have my sources."

I narrowed my eyes playfully. "You saw Hannah at the dorm, didn't you?"

"I may or may not have ran into your very cranky roommate as she was coming out of the building."

"I'm surprised she told you where I was."

"You two okay?"

I shrugged. "Nothing I can't handle. She'll just have to be okay with the fact that she doesn't control my life."

He quirked an eyebrow. "You two have a falling out or something?"

I waved my hand in the air. "It's not important."

"It's always important between friends."

"Well, it's not important now."

"Dani."

I blinked. "What?"

"Friends are always important, no matter what."

"I know."

"They're a different kind of family when you can't go to your actual family."

"I get that, Max. I do."

"So whatever's going on, fix it."

I snickered. "I will, when she realizes she can't control me."

"What's she wanting you to do?"

I sighed. "Leave you while I still can."

He nodded slowly. "She's not wrong."

I was taken aback by his words. "What?"

"Let me guess. She thinks I'm dangerous, that I'm no good for you, and that I'll pull you off your path."

"Yeah. In not so few words, but yeah."

"Well, she's not wrong."

"So you agree with her."

He shook his head. "I never said that."

"So you're on my side?"

"I didn't say that either."

"Then what are you saying?"

He grinned. "That she's not wrong. What you choose to do with that is your business. But know she's not wrong."

"So you think you're no good for me."

He shrugged. "I'm no good for anyone. That's beside the point."

"How could you think that about yourself?"

"Easy. I just do."

I pushed at his chest a bit. "I don't ever want to hear you saying that again. Got it? You're a good man, Max. A great one."

He chuckled. "Oh, boy, do you have a lot to learn about me."

I paused. "What does that mean?"

He smiled wolfishly. "It means that truly great men don't do what I do. Means you still have a lot to learn."

"So you want me to stick around?"

"When the hell was that ever in question?"

I blushed. "Fair enough."

"Good. Because I've been waiting for you to stop talking."

"Wait, wh--? Mmmm."

His lips crashed against mine and everything fell to the wayside. Fire stoked in my gut and fireworks burst behind my eyes. I wrapped my arms around his neck, reveling in how he gripped my hips. He bent over me, leaning closer to his bike as he pinned me harder against its surface. I thought we might fall over, he dipped me back so deeply. I clung to his jacket, holding on as if my life depended on it. His tongue stroked the roof of my mouth. His hands slid up to my waist before he cloaked my back with his arms. I felt invaded by him. Warmed by his presence.

And I didn't want it to stop.

"Oh, your lips taste wonderful," he murmured.

My eyes fluttered open. "I think it's my lip gloss."

He licked his lips. "Mmmm, honey."

I smiled. "And vanilla."

"I think I'd like another taste."

I gripped his leather jacket once more and pulled him back to me. I rolled my body against his, not giving a damn who saw us. My legs spread for him, and I felt my nipples puckering against my bra as his hands wandered my body. I yearned for him. I ached to be filled with him. And as he sucked on my lower lip, I gasped at the feeling of his teeth.

"We need to finish what you tried to start yesterday."

I paused. "Huh?"

He kissed down my neck. "You know, when you left me hanging like that. Do you know what that does to a man?"

I moaned. "I didn't do it on purpose."

He chuckled. "Of course you didn't. But there are a few things I want to do to you on purpose. So where can we go"

It was hard for me to think. Feeling his teeth raking softly against my skin made me shiver and my mind fall blank. I slipped my arms out of my backpack and heard it drop to the pavement, spilling the contents onto the ground. I didn't care though. Not when Max was around. He gripped my ass cheeks and hoisted me up, sitting me on the leather seat of his bike. Then he stood between my legs. Forcing them open as his hands ran up and down my thighs.

"Where can we go, gorgeous?"

My eyes fluttered open. "Uh, Hannah's in my dorm room."

He nodded. "All right. Are there any other quiet places around this school of yours?"

"I--I don't--I'm not--uh."

He gripped my chin. "Come on, college girl. There must be some place we can go. Use that brain of yours."

I stumbled through the tipsy recesses of my mind, my body drunk off the feeling of Max. I closed my eyes, mentally walking my way through campus. And as Max's hands softly drifted along my body, I thought of an option.

"We could go to the pool."

My eyes opened and I found Max staring down at me, a grin slowly spreading across his face.

"I'm not into putting on shows," he said.

I shook my head. "It'll be empty at this point."

"You're sure about that?"

I nodded. "More than ever. Last year, nighttime

was my favorite time to swim because people were never around. And there are saunas."

He growled. "Really now?"

"Mhm. Two wet saunas for the students, and I can tell you for a fact they hardly get used."

His nose nuzzled against mine. "Then there's only one thing to do."

"What's that?"

His eyes found mine. "Show me where we're headed, gorgeous."

8

MAX

"Come on, Dani. You were the one who picked out this place."

I watched her toes grip the edge of the pool. "I didn't know you wouldn't let me go back to get my bathing suit."

"Like you said, your roommate's there. Did you really want to endure her questioning?"

"I would've, if it meant not skinny dipping."

I held my arms out. "I'm not skinny dipping."

"You're only in your boxers."

"And that means I'm not naked now, doesn't it?"

Dani kept looking around. As if this would be the one time a throng of students walked in to randomly take a swim at nine o'clock at night. There wasn't a soul around. After Benji ruined this place for her, I'd already had it in my mind to replace that memory with a much better one.

"I don't like it when people keep me waiting, Bambi."

She stuck her tongue out at me. "Too bad. You'll just have to wait until I'm comfortable."

I chuckled. "Women's underwear is designed just like swimsuits. Their purpose is the only thing that differs."

She paused. "That's… not a bad point."

"See? I have a good point every once in a while."

She grinned. "You have plenty of good points when you're not neglecting your health."

I saw her eyes drop to my ribs and I splashed her.

"Uh, uh, uh. You told me you wouldn't stare."

She sighed. "It's hard not to. Are you sure you're feeling okay for something like this?"

A shiver worked its way up my spine. "Better than ever, gorgeous. Now jump in or I'm coming up there to get you."

She pointed at me. "You better not."

I shrugged. "Then get your ass in here. Otherwise, I'm coming for you. And I'm throwing you into this pool with all of your clothes on."

"That would ruin my coat!"

"Then take it off and get in here."

She was the cutest thing in the world when she was flustered. It was too easy to press her buttons as well. Dani was easy to rile up. Part of that idea made me sad. It made me wonder what her parents were really like. Because being easy to rile up usually came with a lack of self-confidence and a lack of understanding of the world.

In some ways, her parents had done her a disservice.

"Five," I said.

"Hold on! I'm almost out of--"

"Four."

"Max, cut it out. I'm getting out of my pants now."

"Three."

"Damn it, stop!"

I snickered. "Two…"

"Fine! Fine! Look!"

She held her arms out as she stood there in just her panties and her bra. And when my eyes slid over her body, my cock stood at attention, tenting my boxers underneath the water. Her tan skin called to me. The soft slope of her waist had my fingertips tingling. She had power in her thighs. Her shoulders were broad and strong. The soft outer lines of her abs and the way her toned arms flexed as she held them out made me lick my lips.

Then she brought her hands together and bent forward.

I caught a glimpse of her back as she dove in. The lean muscles underneath her skin, going unseen up until this point. How had I not noticed her figure and her strength before?

She is a swimmer, you idiot.

Guess she wasn't the only person who didn't know much about the other.

I watched her glide through the water, her body straight and her eyes locked on me. Her dark hair ruffled underneath the water in small waves as her arms finally came down against her sides. She kicked her legs. She hadn't yet come up for breath. And as she made her way for me, she looked like a damn goddess.

She finally popped up. "There. Happy now?"

My eyes ran along her face, taking in the way her hair floated in the pool. Every movement she made was perfection, and I'd never noticed it up until now. I took snapshots in my brain of the moment. I didn't want anything to ever rob me of this memory.

"Max? You okay?"

I swallowed hard. "I'm always okay, gorgeous."

"You just looked--ooh!"

I reached out for her and pulled her into my arms. I spun her around, splashing water everywhere as she started giggling. Her hands slipped around my neck, holding me close as her legs wrapped around me. Her ankles locked, pulling me even closer to her. And as my cock pressed against the cloth of her panties, she smiled.

"Guess someone's happy to see me."

I growled. "I'm always happy to see you."

I fisted her hair and brought our lips together. I couldn't take it any longer. I needed her. I wanted her. And I had to have her. She'd been on my mind all day. All last night. And after seeing the texts she'd sent me today, I knew she wanted to see me as much as I wanted to see her. My tongue slipped along hers as my hands massaged the small of her back. She rocked against me, teasing my dick with her warmth as water started sloshing against our bodies.

"Max."

"Mmm?"

I kissed down her neck as her head fell back.

"Max, there are--oh--cameras."

I nipped at her skin. "Let them watch."

"I could--I could get--oh."

"Mmm, in trouble?"

I cupped her clothed breast and massaged it softly. I felt her nipple hardening against my palm, even through her bra. It made me chuckle. I loved the way her body responded to me. The way she shivered and undulated against me, her hands sliding along my skin. She sighed as her fingertips passed over the muscles on my abs.

"You know what doesn't have--Max."

I paused. "I'm listening."

"You know what doesn't have cameras?"

I nuzzled my nose against her pulse point. "What doesn't?"

"The saunas."

I slowly lifted my gaze to meet hers and I saw her pupils blow wide. She licked her lips, her eyes dancing along my face. And when she bucked against me, I popped. I fisted her ass cheeks and held her close. I marched my way through the water as she giggled and hugged me close. Her head tucked into the crook of my neck as I made my way up the steps, holding her as water dripped from our bodies.

"Tell me where to go."

She kissed my shoulder. "Through the door in the back that says 'ladies.' No one's here. We can use their sauna."

"Perfect."

I kicked our clothes over to the door, shoved my shoulder into it and used my feet to scoop them onto the tile floor. They were soaking wet at this point, but I didn't give a shit. The only thing I cared about was getting into that sauna and locking the fucking door.

Until I'd had my fill of this incredible woman.

"Left. To the left. The white door."

I continued kicking our clothes until they were in the corner. I swung the door open, meeting a large cloud of hot mist that forced me to inhale deeply.

"Oh, yeah. That's the stuff."

I grinned. "I'll have you louder than that by the time I'm done with you."

The mist encompassed us as I stepped into the sauna. I set her down on the highest bench, watching as beads of water and sweat already permeated her skin. The door closed behind us and I turned around, ready to lock the damn thing and ravish her body. I didn't want to take my eyes off her for another second. I didn't want to waste another minute without bringing her pleasure.

"All right, anything else?" I asked as I turned back around.

And when I did, I was met with a completely naked Dani.

"Holy fuck."

She grinned. "Just need you, big guy."

She spread her legs slowly and my cock pulsed. The smell of her pussy carried itself on top of the mist, wafting underneath my nose as beads of sweat dripped between her pert breasts. I pulled my boxers off and lunged for her as she giggled with delight. And as I knelt on the lower bench, I slipped her legs over my shoulders.

"Max, oh. I--oh, fuck."

I lapped slowly up her slit and relished her taste. I took my time, sucking and licking. Nibbling and exploring. Her bare heels dug softly into my back. I growled every time I felt her toes dancing against my skin. Her hands flew to my hair, clinging to me as she pulled me closer.

I kept my ministrations light to the touch. Barely there. Just enough to have her--

"Max, please. Please, please, oh. That feels--just a bit--Max, ugh."

Begging.

I lapped my tongue deeply against her slit. I felt her jump before she ground her hips against my face. I flicked her clit, feeling her legs contract as I chuckled against her pussy lips.

"Max, you damn tease."

I pulled back. "You have no idea just yet. But you will. In time."

She whimpered as I teased her, slowly tracing the outline of her clit with my tongue. She fisted my hair so tightly I thought she might pull it from my scalp. And I couldn't get enough. She was like putty in the palm of my hands. My cock leaked, with thick threads of arousal dripping against the bench of the sauna. Sweat poured down my back. I felt it dripping from her skin and intermingling with my own. I wanted to tease her until she cried for mercy.

But I didn't have that kind of patience.

"Fuck," I growled.

She gasped. "That's it. Max. That's it. That's it. Right there. Right there."

She rolled against my face as my fingers slid between her legs. I pressed my tongue against her clit, feeling her grind against me as my fingers danced against her entrance. I felt her walls throbbing as I breached her. I slid one finger in, listening to her moan. Her tight walls clamped down against me as she bucked harder.

"More. I need more. Please. Oh, please, Max."

I sucked her clit into my mouth as I slid a second finger in, feeling her juices dripping down my wrist. Fucking hell, she was so wet for me. Everything about our bodies was wet, and I adored it.

"Max!"

I crooked my fingers and sucked on her clit. I pumped slowly, feeling her meet me halfway with every thrust. Her heels propped themselves against my shoulders. Her legs fell off to the sides, exposing the whole of her body to me. My eyes flickered up, watching her skin flush and her tits pucker. Her face contorted in pleasure as I fucked her with my fingers and sucked her clit to painful peaks.

"Oh, my God pleeeease."

Her hands fell away from my head and she sat up. I moved with her, refusing to let her go as she changed her position. Her eyes peeked down at me, her tits bouncing with every movement she made. I slid my fingers away from her body and wrapped my arms around her thighs, pulling her back toward me, then watching her slide back down.

Watching her finally give in to me.

"Shit. Shit. Shit. You feel so good. So good. I can't--I can't--a little harder. Left. Left left le--yes!"

I growled against her pussy. "Come for me."

"I'm trying."

"Take what you want."

"I want you."

"And I want you to stop holding back. Come for me, Dani."

"Max!"

Her back arched and her gut jumped as I opened my mouth to receive her offering. I felt her juices trickle against my tongue and I swallowed every bit of her down. I slid my thumb between her folds, softly caressing her aching clit. She jumped and whimpered, gasping for breath as she choked out my name. I slid my tongue inside her, feeling her walls pulsate. Her heat rushed over me as my thumb slowed its ministrations.

"Oh, Max," she said with a sigh.

"Take a few deep breaths, gorgeous. Because once I get myself situated, you'll be at my mercy. Completely."

9

DANI

His words shot electricity through every part of my body. Even though I was spent, I felt myself rising to the occasion again. I should've been scared. Possibly intimidated. But as I sat up and drank in his strong physique, I realized something.

I wasn't.

I wanted him. All of him. He stood there, stroking his length, his back falling against the wall as his hand moved faster. Pumped harder. I bit down on to my lower lip as I picked myself up, sitting at the edge of the bench with my legs still spread.

"Now. I want you, please, Max."

He shook his head. "Hold on. Just a--fuck."

"Max, let me--"

"Shit, Dani."

I sighed. "Max, please."

"Almost there…"

His muscles twitched, his balls bouncing. And when

his cock shot spurts of cum from its tip, I gasped with every pump. He leaned heavily against the wall, dripping with condensation. Smelling of sweat and musk and me, a heady combination that wafted up my nostrils.

It was torture, watching him pleasure himself like that.

"Now I'm ready."

My eyes widened. "What?"

The second he charged me, I yelped. He scooped me into his arms and I fell against him. He sat himself down on the lower bench, his back resting against the upper portion. And as I straddled him, I felt his cock growing thicker than ever.

"Holy shit," I whispered.

He grinned. "I suppose that's one way to put it."

He commanded my hips and pressed them down the length of his cock. I moaned with pleasure, my head falling back as he fisted my skin. I sighed as he stroked my walls. I felt our hips bottom out together before his hand cupped the back of my head. He drew my eyes to his, our foreheads resting against each other. And after capturing my lips, he rolled his hips.

"Holy shit," I whispered.

"Just needed a quick one out of the way," he growled.

He rolled deeper, causing my toes to curl.

"Max, yeah."

He grunted. "So tight for me."

I wrapped my arms around his neck. He guided my hips, teaching me how to pleasure him. And the fireworks exploding inside my veins pushed me onward. A renewed sense of vigor filled my veins. I rocked against him, feeling his dick throbbing against my walls as his hands guided me faster. He picked me up, only to stake my body on his cock again. Over and over, making my breasts bounce as his face fell into my cleavage.

"Damn it, you're fucking gorgeous," he groaned.

I ground against him, taking as much of him as I could. My nails raked down his chest. I massaged my tits as my head fell back once more. It was all too much. Feeling him filling me, his hands massaging me, his lips marking me with every suck and nibble against my bare skin.

And with the steam swirling around us, I didn't stand a chance.

"I'm so close."

He grunted. "There it is."

"So close. Max. I can't--I can't--"

"Come for me, Dani. Do it."

I whimpered. "Oh, shit."

My body pulled taut and his arms blanketed my back. I quivered against him, my walls clamping down around his girth. I shivered as he stood up. I felt him sink to his knees, planting my back against the floor of the sauna. The heat seared through my skin, making me quake as my muscles contracted. And as I caught my breath, Max tossed my legs over his shoulders, bending me in half.

"Holy fuck!" I exclaimed.

He grinned down at me. "My favorite position."

"Oh, Max. I can't take any more. I can't. My body, it's--"

"You'll give me one more, and you'll love it."

"Fuck!"

He pulled back and slammed into me, causing my body to jump. It hurt so good. The pleasure was almost painful. I arched my back as he sucked on my nipples. My knees bent forward toward my chest as his hot breath caressed my skin. I raked my nails up his arms. The feeling of his wet balls smacking against my ass cheeks made my eyes roll back.

But, nothing compared to the feeling of being trapped beneath him.

"Max!" I wailed.

"Say my name."

"Max, Max. Oh, holy fuck, Max. Please."

"What was that?"

"Please, let me come. Please, let come. Please. Please. I can't--"

"Oh, yes you can, Dani. Come for me."

"Oh--shi--Ma--"

I couldn't even get the words out. As my body spiraled into an endless pit of darkness, I felt his cock stroking the whole of me. Sliding against places that made me shiver. Rutting against me as his pelvis ground against my swollen clit. I wrapped my arms around his neck. I pulled him back down to me, my body quaking beneath him as his cock twitched, thickened, and grew against my walls. Signaling his own end.

While his tightly-wound curls tickled my clit.

"Like that. Like that. Like that. Don't stop. Don't stop. Max. Holy fuck. What have you done to me?"

Orgasms poured over me, one after the other, robbing me of my voice and my breath. His teeth sank into my shoulder, sucking and marking. Lapping at me, as if he'd lost full control of his movements. I felt him spilling into me with every pump of his cock.

And when my body finally collapsed, he came tumbling with me, pinning me beneath his strength and the comforting tiles of the sauna floor.

My arms fell to the sides. My legs softly slipped from his shoulders. He kissed my neck, my shoulders, my cheeks, until our lips softly came together in a wanton kiss. I lay there beneath him, spread-eagle on the floor, quivering until he finally managed to move. I jumped as his cock fell from between my legs. The gush of fluids signaling our debauchery flowed behind it, wetting the floor beneath me.

"My God, Dani," he grunted.

I giggled. "My sentiments exactly."

He snickered as he pulled himself up to the first-level bench. After drawing in a deep breath, he reached down for me. He helped me into his lap and I curled up, my body still shaking after our adventure. His arms were strong. The crook of his neck smelled divine. He wrapped his arms around me and held me close, nuzzling his cheek against my forehead.

I didn't want the moment to end.

I wasn't sure how long we sat there. Eventually, Max moved. He picked me up and helped settle me onto my feet. Then the two of us finally breached the door of the sauna. We shivered as we gathered our clothes. We had a devil of a time getting them on, too. I giggled while he grunted. I cursed softly to myself, making him chuckle. I had to jump to get back into my skinny jeans, and I felt Max's eyes on me the entire time.

"Hell of a show," he said.

I rolled my eyes. "Such a horndog."

"Only for you, gorgeous."

How was it possible for him to make me feel so special like that?

"I'll walk you back to your dorm."

I waved my hand at him. "You don't have to do that if you don't want to."

He grabbed my wrist. "I said I'll walk you back to your dorm. I want to make sure you get there safely."

I nodded. "Okay. Thank you."

"Not a problem. Come on."

We started out of the saunas, the cool air conditioning greeting us. But it had nothing on the autumn breeze hanging softly in the air. As we walked back to my dorm, hand in hand, I felt myself drying off. The wind kicked up in the darkness, swirling dead leaves around as we ventured onward. I leaned my head against his arm, trying to cherish the moment as much as I could. Eventually, we got to the front door of my dorm.

And it was time to part ways.

"I had a really good time tonight, Max."

I looked up at him and saw him grinning.

"Me, too, Bambi."

I snickered. "I'm still getting used to that."

He ran his knuckles along my cheek. "Take your time. It's not going anywhere anytime soon."

"Oh. Thanks."

He chuckled. "You like it, don't even try to play like you don't."

I blushed. "Maybe a little bit."

"See? There's my Dani."

His Dani. "Are you feeling okay enough to drive home?"

"I feel better than I have in days, thanks to you."

"Good. I'm glad."

"Now, if I could just get one more…"

I smiled as his face gravitated toward mine, his breath pulsing against my lips. I closed my eyes, preparing myself for his warmth. I wanted as much of this kiss as I could get before we had to leave one another's presence.

Just before we connected, the dorm door swung open, ruining the moment.

"Finally ready to come inside?"

Hannah's voice grated on my ears and I sighed.

"Sorry," I murmured.

Max kissed my forehead. "Another time."

Hannah scoffed. "You can let her go now."

I shot her a look before Max backed away from me. I could've strangled that girl, if my body had the energy to do much of anything.

I hid my smile. "I'd better go. Got classes in the morning."

Hannah put her hand on her hip. "Among other things."

Max nodded. "Have a good sleep. I'll see you tomorrow?"

Hannah went to interject, but I put my hand up to silence her.

"Sounds like a plan. Just let me know when, handsome."

He nodded at Hannah. "You sleep well, too."

She scowled at him, but didn't say a word. Thank the Lord. Because I was two seconds away from figuring out what it felt like to smack someone in the face.

Max winked at me before he walked away and I stood there. Watching him go. And when he finally disappeared off toward the horizon that held the library, I sighed. I pushed past Hannah and made my way for the elevator. I didn't want to speak with her, I didn't want to look at her, and I sure as hell didn't want to talk to her.

"Hey, aren't you going to wait for me?"

Her arm jutted in between the closing elevator doors before she slid in.

"Damn. All right. I'm ready," she said.

I shrugged before I pressed the button for the top floor again.

"So you want to talk?"

I didn't acknowledge the question as the elevator kept pulling us up to the top of the building.

"Fine. I'll talk, then. Your relationship with him is unhealthy, at best. He shouldn't be pulling you away from your studies. And he damn sure shouldn't be seeking you out while you're on campus. That's creepy. And weird. And I don't like it."

The doors of the elevator opened and I strode out.

"Dani, are you even listening to me? I'm telling you this for your own good!"

I didn't stop moving until I was inside our dorm and standing at the window. Waiting and watching for Max to drive by. I was worried. The last time he dropped me off at my dorm room, he'd almost been killed. I chewed on my nails as I kept my eyes outside, half-listening to Hannah rattle her head off.

"I mean, look at you. You're already watching for him at the window. There's a life outside there, Dani. A life that wants to meet you. Friends that want to meet you on campus. Grades that need to be gotten. And you can't have any of that if you're too busy straddling the back of some dude's bike. He's going to get you in trouble."

Relief flooded my veins as I heard a bike off in the distance. The engine roared louder. And louder. Until finally I saw its headlights. There was Max, rounding the corner, his helmet turned toward my dorm building. I saw him lift his hand and I smiled as I lifted my own. I watched him drive off, no worse for wear, and I felt as if I could finally get a peaceful night's sleep.

"Have you heard a word I've said?"

I rolled my eyes. "Yes, Hannah. Unfortunately."

She snickered. "Unfortunately?"

I turned toward her. "Yes. That's what I said. You

don't even know the man, Hannah. You're all bent out of shape over literally nothing right now."

Her eyes widened. "Really? Because I think I'm the right amount of bent out of shape. He's bad news. You can practically smell it on him. You just have your blinders on because you think he's hot."

"Uh, when have you ever known me to be reckless? I don't take risks. I make calculated decisions."

"Well, you're not being calculated about this. And if you're not careful, he'll take you down with him, and you'll have nothing."

I watched as she reached for her shower caddy and dug around for a towel. She looked over at me before she snickered and stormed back through the door. I stood there, alone, in the middle of our dorm room, wishing I was anywhere else.

Preferably with Max.

I felt angry and frustrated. But, more than that, I felt policed. I felt as if I was right back at home, having my every move and my every word questioned. I didn't come to college for this. I came to college not just to get an education, but to get away from that bullshit. I loved my parents. I loved my childhood. But I was ready to be a bit freer with my life. Not always having to succumb to all these expectations and be someone I wasn't inside.

That's how I felt with Max.

I felt a little more like myself.

I turned back toward the window and gazed outside, wondering where Max was. What he was up to. Whether or not he missed me. Because I sure missed him. A lot. Being with him made me feel strong. It didn't make me feel like this weak-willed little people pleaser I had become. I was stronger at his side. More capable. I felt like I had a voice, and I felt like he listened to that voice.

I enjoyed who I was around Max. And no one would take that away from me. Not my parents, not my roommate, and certainly not my studies.

I finally felt as if I was coming into my own. Learning all about who I was and who I wanted to be.

Thanks to Max.

10

MAX

I shifted myself on the stool as I reached for my rag and wiped some wax onto it. I hated buffing. It was the bane of my existence. So much damn work just to get a few scratches and shit out of my bike. But there was no one else around here that took half as much care with my bike as I did. I'd gladly pay someone to do the damn job. But it was always half-assed.

So I sucked it up and did it myself.

"Fucking college campus," I murmured.

Every time I went to that damn place, I found a new scratch. A new piece of paint chipped off the side. A new dent I had to pop out. College kids were selfish. Brutal. They didn't appreciate the shit that had been given to them through their tuition. That was another thing I liked about Dani. She wasn't selfish. She took care of her things. Myself included.

Huh. Look at you, being someone else's property.

I chuckled at the thought.

"The fuck happened here?"

Benji's voice pulled me from my thoughts and I slowly looked over at him. His eyes danced around the garage as he shoved his hands into his pockets, his gaze landing on a hole in the wall. A hole I still hadn't patched from the goons my father had brought over a while back.

At least, it felt like a while back.

"You good?" he asked.

I clicked my tongue. "I'm great."

He pointed to the hole. "What happened there?"

I shrugged. "Something probably fell through it."

"Did you fall through it? Because that's a pretty big hole."

I sighed. "You got a reason for being here, Benj?"

"Dude, I can't believe your face is still fucked up like that. Have you seen a doctor?"

"I asked you a question."

"And I asked you one, too. I take it your ribs are better since you're hunched over that bike."

I whipped my eyes over to his. "You know what happened. You were at the meeting. What I want to know is why that meeting was the first time I'd seen you in almost a damn week."

He paused. "What?"

I stood from my stool. "You've been M.I.A. for almost six days. You haven't checked in with any of the guys. You haven't made your rounds. You sure as hell haven't been seen around campus lately. Where the hell have you been?"

He shrugged. "I've had shit to do, man. Studying.

Library time. College bitches to fuck. You know how that is. Right?"

He winked at me and I wanted to pull his throat out through his asshole.

"No. I don't know how it is."

He snickered. "Oh, come on, Max. Don't tell me she's made you soft. That nerd? She's got less going for her than a stripper on a Tuesday afternoon shift, and you--"

Before I could think, I charged him. No one spoke about Dani that way. Especially not a pea-sized vermin like my cousin. I fisted his shirt and barreled him against the wall. His back slammed with such a fury that his eyes widened. I lifted him off his feet, snarling as his hands wrapped around my wrists.

"Holy shit, Max. What the--put me down. Dude! It was just a fucking joke!"

I growled. "Say another fucking word, Benj. I dare you."

He glared at me. "Or you'll what?"

I pulled him away from the wall and dragged his face up to mine.

"Or I'll drown you with your own fucking teeth."

He scoffed. "Dude, relax. Seriously. You're wound way too tight. I'm just pulling your damn leg. Fucking hell, man. You're a really easy target, you know that?"

I paused. "What?"

He shoved my hands away. "I was just messing with you. You really think I'd talk about your girl like that seriously? Shit, I have more sense than that."

"Obviously not."

"Well, you've never fucking come at me for shit like that before. The hell's gotten into you?"

I took a step back. "What did you come here for?"

He sighed. "I'm worried about you, man. I've never known you to get so hot over the stupidest shit. Especially some chick. And this on the heels of, well, this?"

He ran his hand up and down in the air, signaling to my body. My crooked form. The bruises still shining on my face. My lip that still wasn't quite healed up.

I reached my hand behind my neck and rubbed at the bruises. They weren't welted any longer, but they still hurt to the touch.

"You sure you're doing okay, Max?"

I gnawed on the inside of my cheek. "What happened to you that night?"

He blinked. "What?"

"The night you called and told me you needed to meet me. To talk with me. What the hell happened to you?"

"I got a bit… distracted."

My face fell. "Let me guess. College bitches?"

He grinned. "Possibly."

"And then you complain to me because you don't understand why you haven't been initiated yet?"

He paused. "What?"

"Seriously, Benj. You crawl up my ass and make yourself a little home every time you want to harp on the fact that it's prospect season and I won't let you become one. And then you pull stunts like this and wonder why I don't induct you? You're irresponsible at best, unreliable at worst. And if you want to be part of this MC, you have to step up and be consistent."

"Wow, you're really being serious right now."

"Of course I'm being serious! Because you know what would've happened that night? The night I was jumped? Had it been any other guy holding me up from leaving, he would've stayed true to his word. He would've gotten his ass down there because he knew not to waste my fucking time, and he would've seen what was going on."

He blinked. "So, this is you being pissed because I wasn't there to help you fight off whoever it was that jumped you?"

"No, this is about you simply not doing what you said you would. And the consequences that stem from that. Had it been Rupert, or John, or anyone else, they would've come down, seen what was happening, and jumped in immediately. Because we're family. All of us are brothers."

"Well, I'm your cousin."

"I'm not talking about that kind of family, shithead. I'm talking about the kind that stands with one another. That stands by each other, through thick and thin. You want to know what I think?"

His nose rose higher in the air. "What do you think?"

"I think you saw what was happening and became chickenshit."

He balked. "I--what--the fuck did you just say?"

I took a step toward him. "You heard me. I think you came downstairs, saw what was happening, and got scared. Poor little Benji, not wanting to get his hands dirty."

"I get my hands dirty all the fucking time! Like that bullshit job we never got paid for."

His hands came down against my chest and he shoved me away. Or at least, he tried. I stood there like the rock solid human being I was. And the second he realized what had happened, he took a step back.

"Max, I'm sorry."

I narrowed my eyes. "You're what now?"

He held up his hands. "I'm just pissed off that you'd think, even for a second, that actual blood-family would leave you hanging out to dry like that."

I shrugged. "My father does it all the time."

"Well, I'm not your fucking father."

"No. At least my father has a pair of balls."

"Are you kidding me right now with this shit? I come over here to see how you're doing and you attack me like this?"

I held up my hand. "Save it. I don't have the energy for it. I'll only say this. You don't get to fuck around and go back on your word and only show up when it's convenient for you, and then get what you want. It's all or nothing. All of the damn time. You don't get to slack off because we're related and then get inducted. That isn't how shit works around here."

He shook his head. "Get the stick out of your ass, Max. You think I want to be part of that hellhole now? I've got better things going for me. Like school, for one. Hell, I don't even want to be part of your little rinky dink operation anymore anyway."

Good. "Glad to hear it."

He started backing up toward the driveway. "Oh, and another thing. What I've got brewing? It's better than the Red Thorns. Better than what you, or anyone else, could've provided for me. You can't even get us paid for fucking jobs we work. How pathetic is that?"

I quirked an eyebrow. "Oh? Did a better opportunity fall into your weasely little lap?"

I felt my anger mounting, but I was proud of how I kept my cool on the outside. I stared Benji down as he kept backing toward the road. His words were music to my ears. My cousin was young and stupid. He had too much going for him in terms of book smarts to be part of some shit like this anyway. This kind of life was for men who had nowhere else to turn. Nothing to give the world, except for their darkness. But as he continued backing toward the driveway, I noticed something.

I didn't see his bike around.

"And what if I did find a better opportunity? Huh? That make you worried?"

My eyes darted around the curb. "Not at all."

"You sure? You're not worried that your little Red Thorns might be in trouble without me?"

I snickered. "Gotta show up in order to contribute something, cuz."

He frowned at me. "How about you worry about your little small-time crew, and I'll worry about me. How does that sound?"

"Get the hell out of here while I'm still allowing you to go."

"Allowing me? With the condition your body is in, I'm sure you couldn't--shit!"

I charged him again, pushing through the pain as I ran after him. He spun around like the little pussy he was and raced for the road. Took a right and just kept on running. And running. And running. Until his body faded into the darkness. I panted for air as I stood there, waiting for the sound of a bike. Or the sound of an engine. Anything to signal to me that Benji was actually leaving.

I didn't hear anything, though.

Just the chirping of crickets as darkness fell upon my home.

I stalked back over to my stool, but something wasn't sitting right with all of this. Something in the back of my head kept nagging at me. Asking an impossible question that almost seemed too weird in its own right.

Does Benji know more about this than he's letting on?

I mean, it didn't make any sense. The boy was a nuisance. A fly I kept having to swat away because of his persistence. He couldn't organize his own damn school schedule, much less something like a hit.

No, Benji would've never done something like that.

That doesn't mean he has no information, though.

As I went back to buffing my bike, the question kept swirling around. I couldn't shake the idea that, somehow, Benji was wrapped up in all this. I mean, he got very defensive when I accused him of seeing what happened and being too chickenshit to intervene. I'd never seen him get irritated over anything the way he got over that. Benji knew better than to try and take me on.

So why did he get so bent out of shape over that assumption?

More questions, and still no answers.

Fucking story of my life.

11

DANI

I ran my fingers through my hair as I caught glimpses of Hannah in the mirror. I was excited about my date with Max tonight. But my roommate was still ignoring me. She wouldn't look at me if she didn't have to. She didn't acknowledge me, except to say 'excuse me' or 'need this?' It was awful. I hated it. But I wouldn't cave in. I wouldn't let her guilt me into admitting that I had somehow done something wrong.

Because I hadn't.

"Where are you going tonight?" I asked.

I tried pinning my hair back as I watched Hannah flip a page of her textbook.

"Getting into anything fun?"

She licked her lips and flipped another page. Much too fast to actually be reading. I rolled my eyes. I couldn't stand people who were passive aggressive. And I wouldn't live my second semester like this, either. I'd put in for a change in accommodations if things kept on like this.

"Can I borrow your purple lipstick? It'll go well with my blouse."

I just knew that'd get her to pipe up. She hated it when I called her favorite lipstick purple. "It's aubergine," she'd correct me before handing it over.

But all she did was flip another page of her book.

Fine. Suit yourself.

I slid my hands down my purple blouse. Another purchase by my mother snuck into my things. And while I usually complained about such nonsense, I wasn't tonight. I had on a pair of my tight black jeans with my chucks instead of heels. Especially since heels weren't very comfortable on the back of Max's bike. So to take things up a notch, I'd decided on this blouse. It cut a bit deep against my chest and had a flowing texture to it. One that drew the eye down my body.

And pairing it with my leather jacket made me feel strong.

"So is it all right if I…?"

I pointed toward Hannah's makeup bag, but she didn't say anything. So I walked over and rummaged around until I found the lipstick. Then I swiped a couple of coats against my lips. I felt her eyes on me as I did so, glaring at me. I rolled the lipstick down and tossed it back to her bag. I missed the opening and it clattered to the floor.

I caught her eye in the mirror. "Whoops. Sorry."

Her nostrils flared and I saw her hands white-knuckling her textbook. If she really wanted to work that hard not to talk to me, then it spoke to the pettiness of her character. And it wasn't something I'd give in to. I'd make her talk to me. There were two of us living in this dorm room and I didn't want to feel weird or isolated or smoked out every time she was around.

"Well, I'm off. You need anything before I go?" I asked.

I spun around and faced her, not shocked that she didn't respond.

"All right, then. Have a good time tonight. Don't wait up."

I gathered my things and walked out the door, not bothering to close it. Hannah had already hurt my feelings by flagrantly making plans in front of me after classes and not inviting me to go out. Not that I would've been able to. Max and I had already discussed our date plans this morning. But it would've been nice to have been invited.

At the very least, it would've been nice not to listen to Hannah as she made those plans. Right in front of my face. While standing in the middle of the dorm room. Giggling her face off.

Passive aggressive jerk.

But none of that mattered. I was only seconds away from seeing Max. From throwing my arms around him and racing off into the darkness of the night. I needed this, too. I needed him. To see him. To kiss him. To touch him. To feel him.

I hadn't seen him since our evening in the sauna.

And I was already having withdrawals.

While part of me felt guilty about the strain on my

friendship with Hannah, the other part of me didn't care. I liked Max. A lot. He was quickly becoming part of my world. And if Hannah didn't want to accept that, then there was nothing I could do about it. She didn't have a say in who I did or did not see. She didn't get to ice me out in an attempt to veto someone out of my world. This is what she'd wanted, anyway! For me to find someone. Make friends. Date someone. Lose my damn virginity.

Why was she suddenly pissed off?

Just focus on your date. Nothing else matters.

I smiled. Nothing else mattered at all. The only thing that mattered was the time I got to spend with Max. I pushed my way out of the dorm and started walking across the lawn. I slipped between two buildings before crossing the road, headed for that flickering lamplight. Why the city hadn't fixed it, I didn't know. But as I stood there, waiting for Max to arrive, I drew in a deep breath.

My eyes rose to the dorm and I saw a shadowy figure standing at the window. Hannah. I felt her eyes on me as she stood there with her arms tucked around her stomach. As if she were holding something in with all her might.

Guilt pooled in my gut before the sound of a bike tore through my thoughts.

The curtain fell in front of Hannah as Max turned the corner. I pulled my eyes away from the building and smiled as he rode up. I slipped my purse up my shoulder and held it close to me, watching. Waiting. Vibrating with anticipation as he pulled up. His bike sputtered as his feet touched down onto the pavement. He slid his helmet off and let his eyes slip down my body. The way he licked his lips shot fire through my veins. When he reached around to grab my helmet, I finally spoke.

"Missed you."

He handed my helmet to me. "Missed you, too. Ready to go?"

"I've been ready all day, handsome."

He chuckled. "Good. Hop on, Bambi. We got a night to enjoy."

I slipped the helmet over my head, priding myself in the fact that I was getting better at it. I stuck my purse in his storage compartment, then tossed my leg over the back of his bike. The more I rode with him, the more comfortable I felt. And when Max revved his engine, I saw a handful of students look our way.

Watching us as he revved his engine one last time.

I like how they stare at us.

I threaded my arms around Max's waist and leaned against him. I shifted down the seat, feeling the warmth of my inner thighs grace his back. I laid my helmeted head between his shoulder blades and drew in a deep breath. With one last pump of the gas, he took off from the curb.

Parting the seas of the night that swallowed us whole almost immediately.

I tightened my grip and held on to him. I fisted his jacket with my hands as I smiled beneath my helmet, moving with the bike. I clenched my thighs as tightly as I could, hanging on for dear life. I relished the feeling of freedom these rides always gave me. We rode in silence, my body drinking in the feel of his as I pressed even deeper against him.

His back rumbled with his growl.

I giggled at the sharp turns and squealed with the high speeds. It didn't take me long at all to figure out that Max took the long way to our final destinations. Not that I minded. On the contrary, I adored it. I liked the fact that he wanted to take me riding. That he wanted me there, clinging to him. Behind him. Seated against him, with him at the helm. Guiding us wherever he thought appropriate. With Max, I could let go. I didn't have to focus on tests, or midterms, or study dates, or family plans. I didn't have to focus on the drama with Hannah, or her expectations of me, or those stupid dorm parties I had stopped attending.

With Max, there was no pressure. The word 'no' didn't come with the silent treatment or some sort of retribution. It didn't come with failing grades or disappointed parents. All it came with was a head-nod and a suggestion of something different.

He respected my boundaries.

And I really liked that.

I felt the bike slowing down and I finally looked up. My grip around his waist loosened as he pulled into a parking lot. I heard music thumping from the walls of the building in front of us. There was a small line out the door and men dressed in black taking IDs and marking on the tops of people's hands. My eyes searched the building for a sign. Something that told me where we were.

Arbor Days.

Huh.

"Ready?" Max asked.

I had been in such a daze that I didn't realize we had parked. I felt my helmet being slid off my head and I tried to fix the shocked expression on my face. Arbor Days was one of the trendiest clubs around here. Just on the outskirts of town, it was a fabulous restaurant I couldn't ever afford during the day. And at night, it turned into a lounge and rooftop dance club with live music, great food and drinks, and college kids of all sorts trying to barge their way in and get a taste of things.

"It's so good to see you."

Max's breathless words made my heart stop. It finally pulled me from my trance and I gazed up at him. He tucked a strand of hair behind my ear before he cupped my cheek. His touch felt warm. It sizzled my skin and made the hair on the nape of my neck pucker. His grin sent my gut humming and I felt a flush working its way down my body. I had no idea why in the world this man made me feel the way he did, but I never wanted it to end.

I smiled. "I missed you too, Max."

He groaned. "Say it again."

I giggled. "I've missed you, Max."

His lips approached my own, nipping, but not kissing. I gasped as I felt his breath pulsing against my skin. When I leaned in to kiss him, he fisted my hair softly. He held me where he wanted me as his eyes found mine. And I sat there, waiting for his command.

"Say it one more time, gorgeous."

I blushed. "I really missed you. Please, let's not go that long before we talk again. Okay?"

He grinned. "Good girl."

I squealed as his arm wrapped around my waist. He picked me up, his lips still hovering over mine as he steadied me on my feet. I went in to kiss him again, but he pulled away. Not being able to kiss him made me whimper. And with that sound came a cocky little wink that promised so much more to come. His hand patted my ass and I pressed myself against him, seeking comfort within his warmth.

More and more, he had started to feel like home.

And I wondered if I felt the same way to him.

We walked up to the front door, our arms threaded around one another. But we didn't have to wait like everyone else. Max patted the bouncer on the shoulder, and after they each exchanged a smile, he let us in. Both of us. Without so much as checking our IDs. I heard people grumbling behind us. Judging us. Getting ready to gossip about us.

And I found it all so thrilling.

Max led me up the stairs. Up *multiple* flights of stairs, until we emerged onto the rooftop. The live music thumped and jello shots were already making the rounds on silver platters. People were grinding against one another on the dance floor. Swaying and bobbing to a rhythm all their own. I couldn't help but stare. Everyone looked so happy. And as Max pulled me to a rounded table tucked away in a corner, a scantily-clad woman walked up to the table.

"What can I getcha?" she asked cheerfully.

Max looked down at me. "Rum and Coke?"

I shrugged. "Sure, yes. A rum and Coke for me."

The woman's eyes fell to Max. "And for you?"

"Just a beer. Whatever your best is on tap that isn't dark. Then water after that."

The woman pouted. "Just one?"

He nodded. "Just one. Got precious cargo with me tonight."

For a split second, I wondered what that cargo was. Until he pulled me close. Then I realized what he was talking about. *I* was the precious cargo.

I love this man.

"All right, a rum and Coke and only one beer that isn't dark coming up. Any food for you two?"

Max's voice sounded far off. "Not for now. But maybe later, if she gets hungry."

Holy shit. I'd fallen in love with Max.

The revelation caught me off-guard. I wondered what that meant for us. For me. Did he feel the same way? Was he thinking it right now?

"Dani, can you hear me?"

I slowly looked up at him. "Huh?"

He furrowed his brow. "Did you hear me?"

I blinked. "What?"

"I'll take that as a no. I asked you how things were going with you and Hannah. I take it they're not much better?"

I love you. "Uh, they could be worse, I guess."

"Do you want to talk about it? I know she's your good friend."

I nodded slowly. "She is. I don't want to lose her."

"I'm sure you won't."

"She's just--not really talking to me right now."

"That what got you so distracted?"

No. "Yes."

He eyed me carefully. "You sure?"

"Yeah. I'm sure. It's just… sticky. I know she's very worried about my safety with you. I just don't get why she can't trust me on this. She doesn't even know you."

"In her defense, you don't really know me."

"And you don't really know me."

He grinned. "Of course I know you. You're Dani. College girl, close with her family, people pleaser. You do everything to the best of your ability and you have your life planned out. You never want to disappoint people, even if it means burning the candle from all ends until there isn't anything left of you."

I blinked. "Well, I know who you are, then. You're Max. President of a club, close with his chosen family, and definitely not a people pleaser."

He winked. "Just a people pleaser."

My gut jumped. "You only do the things you want to do to the best of your ability, and you make no plans. You go with the flow, you throw caution to the wind, and you don't give a shit about repercussions."

"Oh? What else do you think you know?"

"I know you don't care about disappointing people unless you care about them, too. You don't overtax yourself because so many depend on you. But that in and of itself makes you worry more than you should. You're strong. You're resilient. You're tough."

"Anything else?"

I smiled. "And you're more loveable than you make yourself out to be."

He snickered. "Hardly."

I shrugged. "I have spoken."

"Oh, you have, have you?"

"Yep. I have."

"Well, just know that your friend isn't wrong to worry about me. And your assessment of me is only partially accurate."

I sighed. "I know you'd never hurt me, Max."

"Not intentionally, no."

I paused. "What does that mean?"

And as my eyes held his, something sinister boiled behind them. Something I'd never seen before. Something that made me freeze against him before his arm fell from around me. Was this it? Was this the part where my world shattered and left me for dead?

Not intentionally hurting you is a good thing.

But that didn't mean I wouldn't get hurt, anyway.

And I was owed an explanation as to what that meant.

MAX

I didn't like the way she stopped moving against me. She didn't pull away, but she wasn't soft against me any longer. She was on guard. And she needed to be. Because this conversation was long overdue. I needed to let her know what she was getting into with me. She deserved the right to know exactly what I was involved with. Well, not exactly. But she needed to understand that my lifestyle was rough. That people did depend on me, but not just for money. Or jobs.

They depended on me to survive.

"I'm waiting, Max."

The waitress came by with our drinks, and not a moment too soon. I reached for my beer and took a long pull of it, hoping to relax a little bit. I wasn't afraid. I was never afraid of shit like this. Especially with some girl. But, Dani wasn't just 'some girl.' She was different. She made me feel different. And if I could get out of this without losing her, that's the outcome I wanted.

If it was even possible.

"Dani, what I do… it's not for the faint of heart."

She turned fully toward me. "All right. So tell me what you do."

I took another sip. "The life I lead is dangerous. I have enemies that take cracks at me all the time. That target me and my brother. They come after us on a regular basis."

"Like when you were jumped outside the dorm?"

I nodded. "Yes. Like then."

"You think someone's out to get you?"

"I know someone is. It's the nature of my business. What I do. The life I've chosen for myself. It's wild, and unpredictable, and dangerous. And even though I'd do whatever it took to keep you safe, I also can't guarantee I'll always be able to do that."

She blinked. "Well, I can take care of myself. I'm not completely incapable of something like that."

"I never said you were. But I'm not talking about existential crises here, Dani. I'm talking about moments where former clients have wanted me dead. Wanted men in my crew dead. I'm talking about times where things go haywire with a job and we piss off the wrong person. And suddenly, I'm patrolling neighborhoods and going dark for weeks at a time to make sure the guys in my crew--and their families--are safe."

"See? There. You keep them safe. You can keep me safe."

I nodded. "I know. What I'm saying is that you

could get hurt with me, Dani. Really, truly hurt. Not emotionally hurt. Not spiritually hurt. But physically, unfixably, hurt."

The look on her face was unreadable. As she reached for her drink, I watched those soft lips of hers wrap around the small red straw. She took long sips. I watched her neck bounce softly with her swallows. I wanted to know what she was thinking. How she was feeling. But all I had to go on was the muted profile of her face.

The reality of the situation was that she couldn't take care of herself. Not like she needed to for the life I led. I knew how easily Benji could make Dani back down. How easily anyone could make her a target and take her out at a moment's notice. And those people were small fish. My father--with all his bullshit--was still only a medium-sized fish in a massive ocean of people who had the capability to run us all over. Take us all out before the sun could rise on yet another day.

I lived with that threat, day in and day out.

And I wasn't sure Dani could.

I'm not sure if I want to let her.

"Look, Dani, all I'm saying is that life can change at the drop of a hat. One minute, things are going smoothly. And the next, you're face down in a puddle of your own blood. I would understand if you decided it was too much for you."

She stopped drinking. "What are you saying?"

"I'm giving you an out."

She put her drink down. "An out?"

"Yes. An out. A chance to walk away."

Her gaze found my stare. "As in, a chance to end this. You and me. What we're doing here."

I nodded. "Yes. One chance. You have this moment to walk away without any repercussions at all. But if you stay in this with me, then you're fucking in it. Because I don't let go when I want something. I never have, and I never will. And I've never wanted something the way I want you, gorgeous. Ever."

I watched her cheeks turn pink. I watched them heat as a soft smile crossed her face. Damn it, she was the cutest little thing I'd ever come across. And I'd be fucked if she left. She looked radiant in the moonlight. Her purple blouse matched her lips and her sparkling eyes stared up at me. As if I were the end-all-be-all of her life. She'd never looked so beautiful to me. So adorable. So cute.

I wanted to kiss her until she couldn't breathe. But I settled for slipping my hand against her knee. I resisted the urge to drag her against me and permanently etch that blush across the whole of her body. Right here, in this fucking booth. I had to resist. I couldn't sway her decision. She had to make this on her own. I couldn't make this choice for her.

"I've never wanted anything the way I want you either," she whispered.

I shrugged. "Might not be worth it."

"That's for me to find out, isn't it?"

I searched her eyes. "Danger is inevitable with me. Lots of it."

She threw her head back. "Hah! Hah! Hah! I laugh in the face of danger."

I furrowed my brow. "What?"

"*Lion King*?"

"Huh?"

She blinked. "The Disney movie?"

"Uh…"

Her jaw fell open. "Haven't you ever seen *The Lion King*?"

I shook my head. "No clue what you're talking about."

She scoffed. "How the hell have you *never* seen *The Lion King*? It's a classic, Max. What the hell did you watch as a child? Paint dry?"

"Wasn't much of a television kid. I liked mud."

"But what about snow days? Or sick days? Or rainy days? *Lion King* was my go-to movie on sick days."

"Rainy days are the best for mud pies. Snow's fun to play in. I never got sick."

"You never got sick as a kid."

"Not severely, no."

She snickered. "Well, then we're watching that movie together for our next date. You, me, Disney, popcorn, and a blanket. Oh! And soda. Can't forget the soda. With two straws. We're going to go old school for this next one."

I paused. "Does that mean you're not walking away from this?"

I hated how vulnerable that question made me feel. I hated the way my voice sounded. The desperation that laced it. I watched Dani bite down onto her lower lip. Her eyes danced around the barely-there bruises still on my face. Her hand fell against my chest and slid down my side. And when she got to my ribcage, her fingers splayed out. Almost as if she were trying to heal the rest of me that was sore.

"I'm in this, Max. I want this. I want you. No matter what comes our way. Okay?"

And the fireworks that went off inside my gut had nothing on the way my cock pulsed. The way my grin slid across my face. I wrapped my arm around Dani and pulled her close, crashing our lips together. Sealing our union for everyone to behold. Her hands danced against my body. She fisted my shirt, drawing me closer as our tongues danced together. The music thumped and our drinks were forgotten as she climbed into my lap and straddled me, grinding against me to the beat of the music filling the rooftop.

"No matter what, okay?" she whispered.

I sucked on her lower lip. "No matter what, gorgeous."

13

———

DANI

The door crashed open as we stumbled into the back room. The three rum and Cokes I had allowed myself went straight to my head. And my hands were connected to Max's body. His lips ravaged mine. His tongue raked against the roof of my mouth. I slid my hands down his torso. Around his back. I gripped his ass and pulled him close to me as my back fell against a wall.

A dark wall, in a dark room. Away from the thumping music and the glitter on the dance floor.

"More," he growled.

I moaned down the back of his throat as our tongues collided.

"I need more of you, Dani."

I gasped. "You have me. All of me. Take what you want."

His hands fisted my ass cheeks and he hoisted me against the wall. His lips found my neck, nibbling and sucking. My hands were gripping and tugging. I wanted him naked. I wanted his skin against mine. I needed to feel him. Be filled with him.

You're in so much trouble.

I was all in with this man. And holy hell was he a lot of man. My parents would be mortified if they ever found out. But I didn't care. I didn't give a shit about what anyone thought. I loved Max. I'd fallen for him. And he made me happier than anything else in my life.

Damn it all.

His hands slid up my shirt. I wrapped my legs around his waist as he pinned me between his body and the cold surface behind me. I gripped his hair and pulled his head up, gazing into his war-torn eyes. His nostrils flared. He practically gnashed his teeth at me. And when I pressed my lips against his once more, I felt his heart beating against my chest.

Keeping time with mine.

You're the one for me, Max.

"Mine," he grunted.

Always yours.

"I need to feel you," he whispered.

I took his hand and placed it against my breast. My forehead fell against his own as our eyes connected. He gripped my breast, tweaking the nipples until they puckered against my bra. I felt heat pooling between my legs. That dastardly grin he always had pulled across his face, making me blush. I felt his cock against my jeans. He ground against me, stroking me and teasing me.

Your parents would be very horrified right now.

"You make me feel alive, Max."

His head pulled back just a tad and my eyes focused on him.

"I know that sounds weird, and I know it ruins the moment. But, that's how you make me feel. Like I haven't really been living until I met you."

His eyes searched mine. "Don't say things you don't mean."

I shook my head. "Not a habit I ever entertained."

He stepped away from me and my legs unwound from him. His hand gripped my waist as he settled me onto my feet. Had I said something wrong? Had I made him upset? I craned my neck back to keep his face in view. The soft yellow bruises still underneath his skin sobered me up. I ran my hands softly down his torso, slowing down as my fingers rumbled over his ribs. I searched his face for any sign of pain. Any sign of hurt or discomfort.

"You're so easy to read, gorgeous."

I blinked. "Why did you back away?"

"Why do you think?"

I paused. "I'm concerned I've said something wrong."

He tucked a strand of hair behind my ear. "Not at all. If anything, you said something right."

"I'm not following."

He grinned. "Why don't we get the hell out of here and I'll prove it to you?"

My heart skipped a beat. "Your wish is my command."

"Good girl."

His hand slipped into mine and he pulled me farther away from the wall. The darkness slowly gave way to the lights and the sounds of the rooftop club. My heart thundered in my ears. He winked at me before he pushed through the door and led me across the floor. People continued throwing glitter into the air. Jello shots came out by the dozens. I had to push two trays away just to get through the chaos. And all the while, I felt Max's hand holding tight to mine. Gripping tighter. Refusing to lose me in the crowd.

I was ready to get this man alone.

My man.

I picked up the pace until I could thread my arm around his waist and walk alongside him. I loved the way he held me. The way his arm claimed me in public. Everyone knew who I belonged to. Who I was with. And everyone knew that Max was mine. That he belonged to me, too. I never wanted that to change. I never wanted anything about this to change. No matter what Hannah thought, or my parents, or anyone else I might come across.

I knew I'd always choose Max.

"Shit."

He stopped abruptly and held out his arm, stopping me in my tracks.

"Max?"

"Shh."

"What?"

He looked down at me. "Shh."

His eyes darted back up and the frown on his face made my heart stop. And not in a good way. He quickly spun me around and slipped behind me, his hands against my shoulders. He guided me back through the crowd. Away from the exit door as we made our way through the dancing throngs of horny people once more.

"Max, where are we going? Your bike is back that--ah!"

I almost ran into someone carrying a tray of drinks. I whipped around, intending to demand an answer from Max. But the fury in his eyes prompted me to keep my mouth shut. He twisted me back around and kept leading me. I felt the tension in his hands growing. He gripped my shoulders so tightly I thought he'd leave marks behind. And all the while, he guided me back to the back room.

Until we were shrouded in darkness again.

"Max, what's going on?"

He turned around and closed the door before I heard him rummaging around in his jeans.

"Max? Say something, damn it."

A light came on. "I said hush."

I lowered my voice. "Tell me what's going on. What are we doing?"

He started panning the light around, completely ignoring my voice. What the hell was going on? What in the world just happened?

"Max, please. Tell me."

He spun around quickly. "Do as I ask, or this is done."

I blinked. "Excuse me?"

"When you were sitting out in that booth, you made a commitment to me. Did you mean it?"

I stared at him. "Of course I meant it. But that doesn't mean--"

"When it's safe, I'll explain. Until then? Trust me to protect you."

My blood turned cold. "I'm in danger?"

"We both are. Follow me. There's a stairwell over here."

He wrapped his hand around my wrist and tugged me along behind him. I mean, it was all I could do to keep up. Even I heard the panic in his voice. And I'd never heard that before. Ever. Not once had he ever wavered. But the more he tried to keep me quiet, the more wavers I heard.

It made me nervous.

He opened the door to the stairwell and we rushed down it. I stumbled into him a few times. And every time, he turned around to catch me. Worry rushed through my body. It felt like I could hear everything within a five-block radius. Every single part of my body was on alert, waiting to be seen. Waiting to be yanked around.

Waiting to be jumped.

I followed Max while he followed his little light. And when we found a door with an 'exit' sign, we dashed in that direction. He eased the door open silently and I peeked outside. There was an alleyway outside.

"Come on. Stay close, gorgeous."

He certainly didn't have to tell me twice.

The alleyway was dark, with signs to direct trucks into a loading zone. I rubbernecked around, trying to take it all in, making sure no one was approaching us from any other angle. Max dropped my hand and jogged to the entrance of the alley, peeking out onto the sidewalk, his eyes dancing against something I couldn't see. I stood there, waiting for him. Waiting for our next move. But, as I watched him, I saw his shoulders tense.

Before he burst into a sprint back my way.

"Run with me, and keep up as much as you can," he said.

Not like I had a choice in the matter.

Nonetheless, I kept the pace Max set. The running helped me to dispel some of the nervous energy pooling in my gut. It didn't stop my entire body from shaking, though. I cursed my inner wimp. I needed to be able to handle shit like this if I was going to be with him. Our destination seemed to be the other side of the alleyway, away from the parking lot. Away from his bike. Away from the noise and the chaos and the crowd standing outside the restaurant-slash-club.

But before we got there, he pinned me against the wall in the darkness. He held his breath. He cloaked me with his body as the world fell momentarily silent around us with his hands on either side of my face as we leaned against the brick wall.

Listening for something I couldn't hear.

"Max?" I whispered.

His head kept darting around, looking up and down the alley. As if he were waiting for something. Or someone.

"Max?" I whispered harshly.

"Someone was waiting for me. I think they spotted me."

My hands rose to his chest. "Who?"

"I don't know."

"Then how do you know they were waiting for you?"

"They were by my bike."

I nodded quickly. "Okay, that's bad. Um, what were they doing? Were they carrying any--?"

He groaned. "Just give me a second."

"Do you know what they want?"

He growled. "Dani?"

"Yes?"

"Shut up and give me a second to think."

My stomach churned with nerves. Tears of fear rushed my eyes. I closed them, trying to hold them back because I didn't want Max to see me this weak. I didn't want him to think I couldn't handle this life. Or being out with him. But when my body began to tremble, I knew my anxiety had betrayed me.

Of course you'd walk into trouble the night Max warns you it'll come for them.

It was like the world was actively trying to separate us.

"Shit."

My eyes flew open. "What?"

He gripped my arm. "Come with me. Now."

I stumbled away from the wall. "Wait a second. What's happening. What--?"

"They're coming. We have to run. Now."

And again, he certainly didn't have to tell me twice.

14

MAX

I dragged Dani behind me until we made it to the back of the alleyway. I ripped her around the corner and spun her until she faced me, placing her back against the wall. Then I jammed my hand back into my pocket and pulled out my phone.

"Dani, I need you to do something for me. It's important."

I kept my voice as low as I could while she looked up at me with wide eyes.

"What is it?" she asked.

I slapped my phone in her hand. "Call a man in my contacts named Rupert. You remember him, right? Red hair?"

"Yeah. Yeah, I--I do."

"Good. Call him. Tell him where we are. Tell him I need him now. As soon as he can get here."

"What's going to happen? What's happening, Max?"

The tremble in her voice broke my heart. The tears she kept trying to blink back shook me to my core. The way her hand quaked as he wrapped her fingers around my phone made me wonder if I was a fool. If I really had done right by her in letting her make her own decision about this.

Then again, she was a grown woman. No longer the cute little girl I'd seen across the street moving into her little dorm room.

And baptism by fire was one way to initiate someone into my lifestyle.

"Dani, just do as I'm asking. Duck behind that dumpster and don't you move, no matter what you hear. Got it?"

She swallowed hard. "Max?"

I growled. "Just call him. And stay down. Do as I'm asking you to do, gorgeous."

I helped her to slide behind the dumpster before I started back down the alleyway. When I had peeked around the corner originally, I saw the two men come out of the club and go over to my bike, their eyes caressing my metal beauty as if they had a right to. But one of the guys moved quickly, practically snapping his neck as he peered over his shoulder.

And I'm pretty sure he spotted me as I dashed back for Dani.

I knew they weren't the friendly sort, either. They were both dressed in black. All black, like those guys who jumped me just outside her dorm building. I wondered if they knew the men that attacked me. Or maybe they were two of the four guys there that night.

One of them did tell you that was nothing but an appetizer.

In the pit of my gut, I knew this was connected. I didn't know how to prove it. But my gut never steered me wrong. It always kept me safe. It always kept my men safe. It always kept my brother safe.

Now I hoped it would keep Dani safe.

I stood in the middle of the alleyway, thankful that they hadn't turned the corner yet. Maybe if they saw just me standing here, they'd get their focus off Dani. Because I was almost certain they'd seen her in the wake of me trying to get away from them. I squared off my shoulders as two shadows rounded the corner. My hands balled up into fists as I stood there, my feet shoulder-width apart. I was ready for a fight. I was ready for a possible takedown. I was ready to re-open some injuries.

What I wasn't ready for was Dani getting hurt.

God, I hope she's calling Rupert.

The massive men kept walking until they were only twenty or so feet away from me. Then they stopped. They both looked me up and down before grins spread across their faces. After they were done drinking in their fill of me, one spoke up.

"Looks like the right guy to me."

The second man nodded. "I'd say so."

I licked my lips. "What do you want?"

I braced myself for a battle as the first man took a step toward me.

"There's someone who wants to speak with you."

I narrowed my eyes. "I'm sure they do."

The second one nodded. "You can make this easy, or you can make this hard. We're prepared for either."

I snickered. "Tell me who wants to speak with me and that'll determine how we do this."

The first man smiled. "And spoil the fun? Nah. We don't ever get this much fun in our profession."

The second man rolled up his sleeves. "So you can either come with us, or we'll take you ourselves."

"Your choice, tough guy."

I drew in a deep breath as both of the men stood there. I wasn't sure if Dani had done as I'd asked. So I didn't know if there was any point in pausing. Or buying myself time until Rupert got here. However, I did know a few things about this situation. Things that weren't happening.

I wasn't going with two fucking strangers to meet their mysterious boss.

Nor was I leaving Dani behind to be found by someone else.

"You know what, boys? I think I'll take my chances," I said.

The first man snickered. "Are you serious?"

The second man chuckled. "You owe me forty bucks."

I nodded. "Glad I could make someone a little bit of money."

The first man charged me, his feet moving quicker than I anticipated. The gleaming of his serrated knife in his hand caused me to step to the side. The second man ambushed me, clocking me square in my ribs with his fucking fist. And as I let out a groan, I prayed to any god listening that Dani did as I asked.

Stay where you are, gorgeous. Let me handle this.

I saw the knife coming straight for my face. I grabbed the man's wrist and pulled him to me before knocking the two men's heads together. I slipped out from against the wall they tried to use to corner me and picked up a metal pipe I'd stumbled over. With my back hunched and my nostrils flaring, I held my own in the middle of the alley. Ready to fight for the small amount of space I could give Dani as a safety threshold.

"What? That's all you got?" I asked.

And as the first man charged me again, I held the metal pipe over my head.

15

DANI

I scooted further between the dumpster and the wall as I held the phone to my ear. I heard the engine of a bike roaring on the other end of the phone. But I didn't know how much time had passed. I couldn't hear anything that was going on. I didn't know if Max had run. Or dipped back into the club. Or lured the guys in another direction.

"Rupert. Where are you?" I hissed.

"I'm less than five minutes out! If that!"

I winced at his yelling. "We don't have five minutes. I can't hear anything that's going on."

"Stay where you are. Do as Max asked. I'm serious. I'm not far away now."

"Hurry up!"

My heart thundered in my chest. The shadows cloaked me as I continued to grow more curious. I needed to know what was going on with Max. I needed to at least know that he was still standing.

"I'm going to try and see if--"

"Bambi, no. Just do as Max is asking you. He's trying to keep you out of trouble."

I rolled my eyes. "It's just a peek. Calm down."

"ETA two minutes!"

I slowly crept away from the dumpster and peered around the corner. With his phone held to my ear and Rupert rattling off some nonsense, I watched as one of the guys charged Max. My jaw fell open as the fight began, unraveling within the confines of the alley as I knelt there. Being useless.

"Rupert, they're ganging up on him."

"Stay where you are. I'm fucking serious. I'm about to--"

I watched as Max reached for something. I watched him hold it over his head. And as one of those guys charged him, he ducked as Max swung. Another guy came out of seemingly nowhere and slammed straight into his gut. I saw the man's knee connect before Max crumbled to his knees. And the sound of something metallic clanged off in the distance.

"Rupert. He's down. What do I do? Tell me what the fuck to do!"

"What the hell do you mean, down?"

"Rupert!" I hissed.

"Stay where you fucking are. Don't get involved. Guys like them don't have a moral code. I'm turning onto the club's street now. They'll hurt you in a heartbeat. They don't care. Trust me, just stay down."

"I can't just crouch here while he needs help," I insisted.

He roared. "That's exactly what you'll do! Stay the fuck out of this. It's my ass if you get hurt, too."

I sighed. "Where did you say you--?"

"Fuck!"

I held the phone away from my ear at his exclamation.

"Fuck. Fuck. Shit. God damn it!"

I frowned. "What? What is it?'

"An accident. It's blocking the fucking road!"

I winced. "Reroute. How much longer?"

I heard his engine revving before his voice sounded in my ear again.

"Fucking hell, three minutes. I'm three minutes out. I have to take the alleys to get to you."

I sighed. "Better make it two if these guys are really gonna hurt a woman."

"What? No. Bambi, damn it, listen to me!"

But I hung up the phone.

I slipped out of the crevice and stood to my feet. Max's phone was already lighting up again, but I slipped it into my back pocket. I looked around me, trying to figure out what I could grab to use as a weapon before I charged these assholes. I slipped to the front of the dumpster and opened the top. There was nothing but black bags of trash in there. Rotten food that made my nose curl. Leaves that had gotten blown down this way and kicked up into the damn thing.

Then my eyes settled on the glistening object in the corner.

"Bingo."

I jumped and pulled the wine bottle out of the

trash before touching back down onto my feet. Without thinking, I slipped around the corner. Max was grunting as he tried to get up. I heard the pain laced in his voice as the men kept driving their boots into his ribs.

"Get off him!" I roared.

My voice startled the men enough for them to leave Max alone. And before I could think straight, I rushed them. With the bottle over my head and my eyes trained on the men in black, I felt wine dripping down my arm. Over my shirt. Down onto my jeans as I sprinted toward them.

"Dani, no!" Max bellowed.

But it was too late.

The man that had charged Max got a bottle to the back of his neck. And as he sank to his knees, I whipped around and clocked the other man in his jaw. I whirled back around as Max scrambled to his feet. But before I knew it, one of those dumbasses had their arms wrapped around Max, ready to take him back down.

And that shit wasn't flying with me.

"You. Let. Him. Go!"

I punctuated my words with blows to his back. I felt the wine bottle creaking and cracking in my hands. I finally brought it down against the back of the man's head, and it shattered, breaking into pieces as he finally slumped. He took Max to the ground. I saw the man's head bleeding as I drew in shallow breaths through my nose.

"Dani, look out!"

I whipped around, the sharp broken neck of the bottle still clutched in my hand. The other man tackled me to the ground, and I saw something shining in the corner of my eye. He started laughing, taunting me as he straddled my flailing body, holding a knife to my neck.

"You really should learn your place, bitch."

I snarled. "Stay the hell away from us."

I swiped at the man's face with the neck of the bottle, catching him across the cheek. He let out a growl as Max finally rolled the other man off him and charged the guy straddling my body. I heard him grunt as Max pinned him to the brick wall. I scrambled to my feet as the man I loved landed punch after punch. I saw the dude's cheek bleeding. I heard an engine roaring down the alleyway. And once the tires squealed up to my side, it pulled my attention away from the fight.

Long enough to see Rupert come into view.

"Get on his bike!"

Max's voice boomed in my ear as Rupert reached out for me.

"Max, wait. No! Max!"

Rupert forced me onto the back of his bike. "Got her."

Max yelled. "Get her out of here. Now!"

Panic rose up my throat. "Max!"

Rupert sped off, leaving Max with those two brutes. I tried to reach out for him, but I almost fell off the speeding bike in the process. Rupert blazed a trail straight to the road. People honked their horns and cursed at us as we parted the unwilling sea of bodies and engines. I clung to Rupert, trying to crane my neck back to see if I could catch a glimpse of Max.

And just as Rupert got his bike steady, I watched Max sprint away from the alley.

The bike cut a U-turn in the middle of the road. Rupert revved his engine as I watched Max make a mad dash toward his bike. My eyes whipped back to the alleyway, waiting for those men to emerge, to chase us down.

But no one came out.

"Hang on tight, Bambi. We're following him. And don't drop that bottle neck, whatever you do."

I wrapped my arms around him. "Done and done."

The second Max took off on his bike, we followed in pursuit. We raced through town, cutting corners and ducking down alleyways to avoid random stoplights. My heart leapt into my throat as we raced out of there, trying to get ourselves to safety and away from those goons.

"You're a crazy bitch, you know that?"

I grinned at Rupert's words. I wasn't sure why they brought me such pleasure. But they did. I giggled as I drew in a sobering breath, feeling my adrenaline rush slowly coming out of the clouds. My head felt a bit more stable. My hands were no longer shaking. And as I gripped the bloodied neck of that damn wine bottle, I sighed.

Because the fear that had been clawing at my insides finally had a chance to rise up.

The fear and the adrenaline mingled. They met in the middle, forcing me to be aware of my surroundings. It felt like I could hear everything. Smell everything. I felt each breath of wind whipping around my body. I felt more alert than ever before. Something strong took hold of my soul, guiding me through that entire ordeal. Never had I felt so powerful before. So in control of my own destiny.

With every breath I took, I became more aware of myself. More aware of my mind. Of the beating of my heart. Of the way my blood rushed through my ears and how comforting it felt to ride on the back of someone's bike. I loved every part of it.

But I knew I wasn't going to like the scolding Max had in store for me.

Not like you have many options now, anyway.

I'd take whatever he dished out, but in the back of my mind I was confident in my decision. Had I not intervened, there was a chance those men would've taken him down. Possibly even out. And then they would've come after me without him to prevent them from doing so. Even with Rupert's help, Max would've been incapacitated before he got there. It wasn't even as if Max was fully healed from the last encounter.

No, I was confident in the decision I had made to get up and help defend the life of the man I loved. Even if he didn't agree with it. Even if Rupert didn't agree with it. I agreed with it, and that's what mattered. And if Max really wanted me at his side, he'd have to start trusting my intuition. Trusting the moves I decided to make.

Just like I trusted his.

16

MAX

I shook with fury. I felt my nostrils flaring with every breath I took. I paced up and down the driveway. Fuming. Hell, had it been any colder, I probably would've been steaming. Literally. What the fuck was Dani thinking? She could've gotten herself killed! She didn't listen, and it almost backfired.

It didn't backfire, though.

I shoved the voice away. I didn't need a reason. What I needed was for Dani to fucking listen to me. I cracked my neck as I finally heard Rupert's engine off in the distance. I cracked my knuckles as they came careening around the corner. I twisted my back, cracking it into place as they pulled up the driveway.

And the second Dani slipped off the back of his bike, I ripped that bloodied bottle neck from her hand.

"What the ever-blessed hell were you thinking?"

I watched her eyes widen as she leaned against Rupert's bike.

"You were reckless at best. You disobeyed my order, and you almost got yourself killed for it!"

I slammed the bottle neck into Rupert's chest and thumbed over my shoulder. Commanding him to take it into the house and dispose of it.

"You used a weapon that could've left evidence behind for police. You almost killed a man tonight with your reckless actions. You almost got yourself killed, you almost got me killed, and you almost created a scene none of us had the capability to clean up! Do you even get how bad this was, Dani?"

I saw the fear in her eyes. I saw the reflection of my fury in her big, doe eyes, and the only thing I could do was pat myself on the back. Good. If that's what kept her from ever pulling a stunt like this again, then so be it.

Because if I lost Dani due to all of this, I wasn't sure I'd ever forgive myself.

"When I give you an order, I expect you to be like my men. You follow it to the letter, and you don't deviate for any reason. You hear me? If I needed you, I would've called you. Simple as that. But I didn't need you. I had things under control. There's a reason I had you call Rupert. There was a reason, you get that?"

I expected her to start crying or shaking. Or turn away from me and run until she couldn't run any longer. But instead, the fear in her eyes turned to anger. They narrowed into slits and she balled her fists up at her sides.

"Are you done yet?" she asked.

I blinked. "Excuse me?"

She took a step toward me. "You heard me. Are you done yet?"

I slowly peeked over my shoulder and saw Rupert standing on the porch. With my brother. The two of them were sipping beers while watching the show.

Fucking hell. "What could you possibly have to say right now?"

She snickered. "Well, I can start with the fact that I saved your ass."

"You what?"

"You know I did, and yet you're angry about it. If I hadn't intervened with those guys, who knows what would've happened?"

I gritted my teeth. "You would've gotten hurt. That's what would've happened."

"Except it didn't."

"Well, it could have. And that's the fucking point."

"No, the fucking point, Max, is that I didn't listen. And you don't like that. I don't listen to your every word and take it as gospel, and you take issue with that. Which sounds like a personal problem to me. You're not fully healed. At your best? Yes, you would've been fine. But tonight, you weren't. And Rupert wasn't going to get there on time."

"You don't know that."

She nodded. "Yes, I do. I was on the damn phone with him, Max. Watching you get pounded by two dudes who wouldn't stop coming at you."

I glowered. "We're going to talk about this later, you and me."

"No, we're going to talk about it now. You want to know why?"

I heard the guys chuckling behind me and I wanted to slit their throats.

"Fine. I'll tell you anyway. We're going to talk about this now because you warned me this might happen. And now that I'm all in on this, you're the one with cold feet? You're the one telling me to stay out of trouble when I just told you back in that damn club that I was with you, come trouble or high waters? Fuck you, Max. Fuck you for wanting to control me. Because you should know by now that you can't."

She went to brush by me, but that shit wasn't happening. I gripped her arm and spun her around, with my body now facing the guys on the porch. Her eyes glared up at me. She wrenched away from my grasp. But I didn't care. No one talked to me like that.

No one.

"You think I'm a hypocrite?"

Dani snickered. "If that's the only thing you've latched on to, then we might need to go through this one more time."

I pointed in her face. "Woman, I swear to God--"

She smacked my hand away. "Don't you dare chastise me like my parents. Or like my roommate. You're neither. You're supposed to be better than them. Be better than them, Max. Don't be the damn hypocrite you became tonight."

I gripped her shoulders. "I swear to fucking hell, Dani, if you so much as touch me in anger like that again--"

"You'll *what*, Max?"

She shoved my hands off her shoulders and took a step back from me. I searched her eyes, watching them twinkle in the night with fiery rage behind them. I'd never seen that look on her face before. The determination. The anger. The hostility. The brazenness.

It was the sexiest thing I'd ever seen in my fucking life.

"Come here," I growled.

I fisted her arm and drew her into me. My lips crashed down against hers as the hairs on the nape of my neck stood on end. Her hands shoved at my chest and beat against my shoulders. But soon, they slid around my neck, clinging to me as I wrapped my arms around her and picked her up off her feet. My tongue invaded her mouth while I walked her over to the porch.

John and Rupert chuckled at me.

"I think that's our cue," my brother said.

Rupert snickered. "Hungry? I want some wings after tonight."

"Fine. But we're taking my car."

"You can follow me on my bike. I'm getting the hell out of this nastiness about to take place."

My brother chuckled. "Mind if I crash at your place?"

"You know you're always welcome."

It was the last of their conversation I heard before I closed the damn front door on them with Dani's back.

"Oh, Max."

I grunted as I kissed down her neck. I sucked

patches of skin between my teeth and marked her as she whimpered for me. Our clothes came off in a flurry. We left a trail of them from the front door all the way into the kitchen. I gripped her hair, pulling her head back as I raked my teeth down her neck. And as I sat her naked body on the kitchen counter, I forced myself to take a step back, marveling at the beauty of the one woman brave enough to hold her ground with my anger.

17

DANI

When Max stood in front of me, I let my eyes linger on his body. I grinned at the chiseled nature of his muscles. I marveled at the colors swirling around his tattoos. His chest and the tops of his arms were covered in them. He walked over to the fridge, pulled the door open, and reached for something, his eyes studying my naked form.

When he pulled out the strawberry syrup, I giggled. "Where do you think you're putting that?"

He quirked an eyebrow. "Wherever the hell I want."

The pop of the cap made me jump. The fridge fell shut as he walked back over to me. He spread my legs and squeezed the bottle. I gasped as the sticky syrup hit my breasts. It dripped down my stomach and slid between my legs, and I felt Max's eyes following its path.

Once I was covered how he wished, he sat the bottle off to the side.

"Time for dessert," he murmured.

His lips went to my nipple and he sucked it between his teeth. I groaned as my legs spread further, and the syrup trickled against my lower lips. He lapped it up, kissing my body and marking me as his own. Cleaned me of the sticky mess as he sank lower against my body. My core heated. My pussy was wet for him. My entire body pulsed for one thing, and one thing only.

"Max, fuck."

He nipped at my thigh. "Spread those legs for me, gorgeous."

The second his tongue hit my slit, my head fell back. His moans and growls made my skin pucker as he bent over, cleaning up the mess he'd made. I rocked against his face and tugged at his hair. I felt myself climbing that precipice as my juices dripped against his cheeks.

"Yes, Max. Yes. Oh, right there. Oh, right there. Oh, right--no, no, no, no. Come back. Please!"

He chuckled. "You're mine tonight, Dani."

He scooped me off the kitchen counter and carried me into the living room. In a flash, he bent me over the couch, kicking my legs out as my hands planted into the cushions. I felt his cock slapping my ass cheeks. His leaking tip slid up and down my wet slit. My walls fluttered for him. My lips puckered in anticipation. And when he finally dove into my depths, I groaned into the cushion I fisted in my hands.

"Fucking hell, you're so damn tight for me."

His movements were relentless. My tits jumped against the piece of furniture as my body lurched with his movements. His cock grew against my walls. My legs shook before my knees buckled. His hands gripped my hips, holding me up as he continued to fuck me. As he continued to bury himself inside me while the sounds of skin slapping skin filled the space around us.

"Max, oh my God. I can't--it's--I'm so close. Please, don't--oh, no, please."

He pulled out from between my legs. "Not where I want to finish with you, you sexy fucking thing."

I whimpered. "I was so close. Why did you--?"

"Come on. There's more where this came from."

He picked me up, and for the life of me I didn't know how he had the strength. I felt like a limp rag in his arms as he carried me through the damn house. I didn't know where we were going. I didn't know what part of the house we were in. But the second my back fell against a mattress, the familiar smells of his room filled my nose.

He tossed my legs over his shoulder.

"Yes, yes, yes. Please. Please don't stop this time."

I felt his cock at my entrance. "Don't worry. I'm not stopping until we've both had our fill."

He slammed into my body and my back arched. He rested against the backs of my legs, pinning me to the mattress as he fucked me senseless. Groans fell from my lips. My eyes rolled into the back of my head. My toes curled and my hands slapped his forearms as he stroked me perfectly, grinding his pelvis against my throbbing clit. I panted his name. Fireworks burst behind my eyelids as that coil in my gut wound tighter. And tighter.

And tighter.

"Max, don't stop. Max, don't stop. I'll do anything, just don't stop. Please."

He growled. "Anything?"

I nodded quickly. "Anything, if you'll let me come. Anything. I swear. Please. Just--I need it. I need you. Please."

He swiveled his hips as his fingers slipped between my pussy folds.

"Then, come for me, gorgeous."

"Oh, fuck yes!"

The second his thumb slid against my clit, it was game over for me. The world spun around my head while the room tilted, causing me to feel dizzy. My body locked out. My walls trapped his cock. I felt my body pulling him in deeper as groans and grunts fell from his lips. I wrapped my hands around his forearms, feeling his muscles pulsing as his cock emptied itself into me. And as my pussy massaged him for all he had to give, he collapsed against me.

With his dick still sheathed in my warmth, his face fell into the crook of my neck. Our intermingled fluids ran down my ass crack, wetting the bed beneath me. I didn't care, though. Not when I was with Max. As I slid my fingertips up and down his spine, counting the divots I felt, I smiled to myself.

I knew, without a shadow of a doubt, that I loved this man.

And I hoped, one day, he'd come to feel the same about me.

18

MAX

I didn't want to move. Her entire body had molded to me, and I'd never felt more safe in my entire life. Not that I'd admit that to anyone. Ever. But, it didn't stop how I felt. I kissed the crook of her neck as her pussy walls clamped down against me. And as I groaned with pleasure, I heard her giggle.

That soft, sweet, innocent little giggle Dani had.

"You okay down there?" she asked.

"I'm fabulous. You?"

She snickered. "A bit hard to breathe. But other than that, I'm good."

I pushed myself up. "That better?"

Her eyes fell to my chest tattoo. "Much."

I grinned. "Why don't I go get us some water?"

"Will you tell me more about your tattoos when you get back?"

"I'd love to."

She smiled. "Okay. Thank you."

Her voice was so soft. So sweet. Laced with nothing but good intentions. It was torture, peeling myself away from her. Watching her gasp as I pulled my dick out made me want to shove myself back in. Over and over, until she reached her pleasurable heights again. But she was sweaty. She glistened with stickiness I hadn't gotten with my tongue. So I figured some water was in order.

Before we both slipped into the shower together.

"Oh, shit," she said.

I stood to my feet. "What's up?"

"Do you know where my phone is? I have to text Hannah."

"Uh, I can search for it as I'm getting water."

"Will you? Please? I just have to text her so she doesn't freak out on me again. Doesn't really make for a nice rooming situation if your roommate's constantly pissed at you."

"She sounds a bit high strung."

"She is. But that's beside the point. Will you look for it?"

I grinned. "I guess I can."

She smiled. "Thank you."

I found her entire purse by the door and figured it was in there. I also found my phone, which was on the floor by her pants. I scooped up our clothes and everything else before grabbing each of us some water from the fridge. I carried our shit in my arms before dumping it out on my bed, and I quickly tossed Dani her purse.

"Thank you so much. This shouldn't take but a… few… small… there. Text sent."

She showed me the confirmation screen on her phone before tossing it back to the floor. Which made me chuckle.

"Nothing else pressing to do?" I asked.

She grinned. "Not unless you're the pressing thing."

I licked my lips. "I can definitely be that."

"Well, then hand me a bottle of water and let's get this show on the road!"

I laughed as I tossed it to her and she caught it. She leaned against the wall behind my bed, the sheets slipping away from her body and revealing her luxurious curves to me as I climbed back onto the bed. She cracked her water open and took a few long pulls, giving me ample time to study the crevices of her body I hadn't seen just yet.

Like the soft scar in the crook of her waist. And the faded pock marks on her left upper arm. And the slight crookedness of her pinky as she held it out while downing her bottle of water.

I couldn't take my eyes off her.

"So your tattoos."

Her voice pulled me from my trance. "What about them?"

"I really like that sunset."

I grinned. "It's my favorite part of the tattoo."

"Do all of the guys have a sunset like that?"

I shook my head. "Nope. That's unique to me. I

got it after John stepped down and made me president of the club."

"So does he have a sunset? Since he was once president?"

"Nope. The base tattoo you see right here--with the rose and the vines and the mantra?--every guy inducted into the Red Thorns has that. When John was president, he got a separate tattoo. A rose on his left upper arm, with the beginning and end dates of his run in that position wrapped around it. Like a ribbon."

"Why the sunset, then?"

I paused. "I wanted a new day to rise on the Red Thorns. I wanted to completely overhaul the group and get them away from some of the shit they'd gotten themselves into. We'll never be fully safe, but I wanted to make things as safe as possible for them."

She smiled. "The dawning of a new day."

"Exactly."

Her fingers rose and danced along my tattoo. "Will anyone ever have the same kind of tattoo one day? Or will it only ever be you?"

I chuckled. "Only my woman will have this tattoo. One day, at least."

She giggled. "Oh, really now?"

I nodded. "Really, really."

"And where do you expect your woman to get this tattoo? Assuming she obliges."

"Well, seeing as she just told me she'd do anything for an orgasm, I don't think she has a leg to stand on."

Her lips parted in shock. "My parents would freak out if I got a tattoo."

"You're a big girl, Dani. I think you'll be fine."

"No, I just meant--"

"Gorgeous, you hit a thug in the back of the head with an empty wine bottle. I think you can make the decision to get your own tattoo. You know where I think it might look good?"

"Max, I just don't know if--"

I traced my finger along her left breast. "Right there."

She blushed. "You think?"

Then I traced my finger along the valley of her breasts. "Or right there."

"That would hurt, though, right?"

I chuckled, sliding my finger all the way to her outer thigh. "Or even right here."

She slapped my hand away. "Down, boy. Our water isn't gone just yet."

I grinned. "What happens when it's gone?"

"You're bad, you know that?"

"Very. You're just now learning this?"

She shook her head. "Never a dull moment with you, is there?"

I picked up my water bottle. "Not when my father is sending people after me, no."

She paused. "Wait, what?"

I chugged back some of my water before she turned to face me.

"Did you just say your father's the one sending men after you?"

I sighed. "I don't have a way to be sure of it just yet. But my gut tells me that's what's really happening."

"Wait, but why? I don't think I've even heard you mention anything about your parents. And now, your father is the one hunting you down?"

"To be fair, my father hunts a lot of people down. Doesn't make me special."

"I--you--but--what the fuck does that even mean?"

I snickered. "Cussing suits you."

"Seriously, Max. Why do you think your own father is the one sending these people after you?"

I clasped my hands behind my head. "For one, my family situation is complicated. At best. In my father's world, money makes everything go round. And he's never had a soft spot for the likes of me. John? Sure. Because John's more of a pushover than I am. He can manipulate my brother easier than he can me."

"So you really think your father doesn't like you?"

I scoffed. "I know he doesn't."

"Why not? I mean, you're his son."

I shrugged. "Been asking myself that question my entire life. If you figure out the answer, let me know."

She sighed. "I'm so sorry, Max."

"Don't be. I didn't tell you any of that so you could feel sorry for me. You had questions you wanted answered, so I answered them."

"Do you see your father often?"

"When he wants something, sure. When he has no need for me, I don't even get a text message."

"I'm so sor--"

I placed my finger against her lips. "No more apologizing. You have nothing to apologize for. Understood?"

She kissed my finger softly. "Understood."

Fire pooled in my gut. "Good. Now, are you done with your water?"

She held up the empty bottle. "Completely drained it. Why?"

"Because I'm ready for round two."

"Max!"

She squealed as I rolled her over and pinned her beneath me. I crashed my lips against hers and felt our tongues collide, something that would always make my cock stand at attention. I gathered her in my arms and slid off the bed. I hoisted her against me, feeling how sticky she was. And as I walked us into the bathroom, my cock leaked with anticipation of what was to come: the water sliding down her soft curves, the steam swirling around us and blanketing us from the harshness of the world, her sounds flooding my ears as I filled her body with my own. And her sighs of content after she collapsed into my arms and curled against me once we'd both had our fill for the night.

19

DANI

The first thing I felt was a press of his lips against my shoulder. I drew in a deep breath, shifting my sore body as his muscles moved with me. His lips puckered again, this time kissing my upper arm and working down until he kissed every tip of my fingers as I rolled over onto my back.

I groaned. "Not again. I can't take it."

Max chuckled. "Don't worry. I won't put you through the wringer this morning."

"*This* morning?"

I peeked an eye open and watched him grin at me. He lay there at my side, his fingers threading themselves with mine. Max looked positively spent first thing in the morning. His hair was a disheveled mess. His eyes were still half-hooded with sleep. Or lust. Or maybe both. I reached out and traced the small mark I'd left on his shoulder last night. My teeth marks looked so small compared to the rest of him. I let my fingers ramble over the soft red marks I'd left behind.

"Got pretty frisky in the shower there, gorgeous."

I snickered. "Says the man who practically invaded my body."

"Are you complaining?"

I giggled sleepily. "Not one bit."

"Good."

His arms hooked underneath mine and he pulled me against him. He rolled over, my tired body draped over his like a blanket. I rested my head on his chest, listening to his heart beating against my ear. I let my eyes fall closed again as his even breaths lulled me back to sleep. The feeling of his fingers running through my hair sent chills throughout my entire body. I didn't want to leave. I didn't want to get up. I didn't want to go back to campus.

But I knew I'd have to eventually.

After falling in and out of sleep with him until almost noon, I relegated myself to fate. I pulled myself out of bed, fumbled around with my clothes, and let Max take me back. I wasn't sure what day it was, honestly. As I leaned against him, with the motorcycle almost putting me back to sleep, I had no idea what time it was. Or what day of the week.

For all I knew, I'd missed my classes again.

"We're here."

His rumbling voice cut through the haze of my sleepiness and I sighed. I pulled my helmet off and slipped off his bike, my heart already aching to be with him again. I pressed a soft kiss to his cheek. He grinned at me before tossing me a playful wink. And after giving my ass a soft pat, he sent me away to my dorm building.

While he rode off into the sunset.

Sunrise.

Wait, no. The sun was too high in the sky for a sunrise.

Is it almost lunch time?

I yawned as I clutched my purse. I fumbled my way inside and into the elevator. I'd never felt so tired, yet so amazing, in all my life. I couldn't wipe the goofy grin off my face as I made my way to my dorm room. Not even Hannah could ruin this for me. I'd done as she asked, so she didn't have a reason to be upset. I'd messaged her last night to let her know I wasn't going to be back before morning.

So hopefully, things would be better.

"And where the hell were you all night?"

Or maybe not. "I sent you a message."

"Yeah, telling me you weren't coming in last night. What were you up to?"

I dropped my purse. "I was with Max."

She sighed. "Of course you were. Ruining your life, one step at a time."

I climbed into my bed. "I don't need your judgment, Hannah. I get enough of it from my parents. I know what I'm doing. And if you don't trust that, then that's your fault."

"It's not that I don't trust you. I'm just worried. You missed your classes again. That's the second time in two weeks you've missed an entire day of school for him. And for what?"

I slid under the covers. "Well, I don't know what to tell you. I have it under control. So you can stop punishing me for finally getting out there. Like you wanted me to at the beginning of the semester, you jerk."

"Fine. Whatever."

"Yeah, whatever."

And, despite the tension, I didn't have any issues falling right back asleep.

When my eyes opened from my nap, it was almost dark out. The sun was setting, and it jolted me right out of bed. I practically rolled out of bed and crawled to my purse to yank my phone out. Holy shit, it was already past six o'clock in the evening.

How long was I out?

I scrambled to my feet and searched around for my books. I had to do whatever I needed to do to catch up for today. I frantically logged into my school account and found the lectures. My lucky day, apparently. Because both of them were already posted.

One absence in each of my classes. I can't do more than two.

I flipped my calendar opened and started checking things off. I was ahead on my reading, so all I needed to do was refresh my mind with the questions at the back. I was already jotting down notes from my first lecture of the day, so I had that going for me. And thankfully, the material was still pretty easy.

Then my eyes fell to something in my calendar. Something that was circled in red. Written in green. And bolded with a highlighter, just so it was extra obnoxious.

"Oh, no," I murmured.

I had a paper due tomorrow afternoon.

I turned the lecture off and shuffled things around. I pulled up a Word document and found the requirements for the paper. I groaned at the sight of a needed bibliography. Of *course* a bibliography would be involved. I'd be up all night pulling this off. Easily. And since I still had no idea what the hell I was writing for this paper, I still had to research and piece an outline together before I did anything else.

And of course, my phone started vibrating with a call.

"Not now, Satan," I whispered.

The vibrating stopped, but quickly picked back up. Again, and again. Until I couldn't focus enough to do my research anyway. I groaned as I rummaged around for my phone. My hand finally settled on it and I picked it up. Great. Mom was calling. Which meant Dad wasn't too far behind.

Such bad timing.

I put on my chipper voice. "Hi, Mom!"

"Well, there's my little sweetheart. It's been a while since we've heard from you."

Dad chuckled. "Not drowning in those books yet, are you?"

If you only knew. "Well, I'm not going to lie. One of my professors is terrible with deadlines, so I'm scrambling to make some last-minute edits to a paper before I turn it in tomorrow."

Dad sighed. "Ugh, I remember those kinds of professors. Don't worry, they aren't all like that. Just go with the flow as best as you can and take breaks when necessary."

"Exactly, sweetheart," Mom said, "don't overdo it. I know you're proud of your A's, and we are, too--"

"Don't make her compromise her good grades. That's not the point of college."

Mom sighed. "It's also not the point to stress yourself out to the point of not enjoying anything."

I licked my lips. "I can leave you two alone, if you want me to."

Dad chuckled. "Not necessary. We just wanted to call and see how school's treating you."

I lied through my teeth. "Oh, everything's fine. Like I said, just this dumb paper that's been plaguing me, but I'm almost done with it anyway."

Mom snickered. "That's my girl. Make sure to treat yourself tonight before you go to bed. You deserve it."

"Oh! Before you go, get this. One of your mother's friends has a son who just came back from two years travelling abroad."

I nodded mindlessly. "That's nice."

"And he's such a nice boy. Very respectful. Cute, too. Your father wasn't happy with me--"

"Eh, I suppose he could be a worse kid."

Mom laughed. "But I took the liberty of passing on your number."

I blinked. "Wait, what?"

Mom sighed. "I know, I know. I got a bit hasty. But he really is a good kid. And he doesn't live far from your campus! He told me he'd call you sometime soon and ask you to dinner or a movie or something like that. Isn't that nice?"

Dad butted in. "And I approve, too. So no using me to wiggle out of this. It's good for you to get out and live a little. You can't stay cooped up in your dorm room all the time."

My heart thundered in my chest. "You gave out my number?"

The delight in Mom's voice made me confused. "Oh, you're going to adore him. Ask him about his adventures. I'm sure he's got so many stories to tell."

"As well as a future in acupuncture. Don't forget about that."

I paused. "Acupuncture?"

Mom clapped her hands. "Yes! He's very well studied. His name is Kline. He's not quite thirty yet. Just turned twenty-nine. And he's got that nice dark hair I know you like. Please tell me you'll say yes if he calls."

What the fuck? "Mom, I don't know. I'm--I'm pretty busy with school. I don't really want to see someone right now, because I'm just getting into my core classes. It's just a bit much to juggle right now."

Dad snickered. "Oh, come on, you party pooper. Even *I'm* on board with this one, and that's saying something. Just one date. Coffee. You can squeeze in coffee, I'm sure."

I sighed. "I'll think about it. How does that sound?"

Mom clicked her tongue. "Well, it's not a no. I'll take it. For now."

"But princess, if he calls and you get a weird vibe-- or you meet and you don't feel comfortable--just leave. Or hang up. No harm done."

"He's not going to be like that. I promise. You trust me, right?"

Uh… "I mean, you did marry Dad."

He snickered. "Awww, thanks, princess."

"Exactly. Just give it a shot. Or at least consider it. Have a few conversations with him. Get out and spread those wings of yours. Make a few memories. You're in college. And while we're both proud of you, we also don't want you to miss out on all the fun things college has to offer."

"Just--not too much fun. Dad's rules."

Could this call get any worse? "Not too much fun. Got it. You guys, I really have to get back to this paper. I'm so sorry."

"No, no, no! Don't let us hold you up, sweetheart."

"We'll talk soon, princess. Love you."

I smiled. "I love you guys, too."

And as I hung up the phone, only one question ran through my head.

What the fuck just happened with my life?

20

MAX

John cracked open another beer. "All right. Give me the rundown one last time. Because I swear to fuck, if I figure out you're hiding anything else, I'm gonna kill you myself."

Rupert nodded. "I'm with him. I didn't even know your father paid you a visit."

I paused. "I'm pretty sure I mentioned that."

Rupert snickered. "Trust me, I'd remember if you did."

John chugged his drink back. "Give us the rundown one more time. And don't leave anything out."

I sighed. "Well, the two of you know about Dad coming to visit me in the garage. Yes?"

John nodded. "With the goons."

Rupert reached for a slice of pizza. "That practically beat you into the wall. Yep."

I rolled my eyes. "Yeah, so that happened. Then

Dani and I kicked things off a bit. Then that night happened where I took her back to her dorm and I got jumped."

John pointed at me. "You said Benji called you and said he wanted to talk?"

I nodded. "Before I got jumped, yeah."

Rupert cocked his head. "That's a bit weird, don't you think?"

I shrugged. "I didn't think anything of it until Benji came to visit me in the garage himself."

John pointed at me. "This is the part I want to hear again. What happened?"

Rupert chewed his pizza as loud as fucking sin as I tried gathering my thoughts.

"It was the weirdest thing. I asked him where the hell he'd been. Because other than the meeting I called to inform the crew about the jump, he was nowhere to be found. Not answering anyone's calls. Not showing up for shit. It was weird to me, especially since he wanted to talk."

John nodded. "What happened once he got here?"

"I don't know. He was just... weird. Off. Very nonchalant about things. I got onto him about being absent and shit always taking priority in his life over the club, and then he wonders why I don't induct him."

Rupert swallowed. "I thought you didn't want to induct him anyway."

"I don't. But Benji doesn't get why. I went ahead and laid that shit out for him in the hopes that it would completely deter him from trying again."

John paused. "Why does he attend the meetings if he's not part of the crew?"

"To keep his ass out of trouble. Remember the last time we tried to keep him out of the group?"

Rupert's eyes widened. "How the fuck did I forget about that?"

John groaned. "Do we even know how the fuck he blew that car sky high?"

I shrugged. "Doesn't matter. What matters is that even if I'm involving Benji on a 'trial basis,' I know where he is and what he's doing."

John nodded. "Until now."

I pointed. "Exactly. He was much too relaxed in my garage when he was talking with me. And he didn't ride up on his bike, either."

Rupert blinked. "What?"

"Yeah. That was weird to me, too. I chased him off once he started mouthing off at me, and he ran down the road until he was out of sight. He wasn't on his bike when he came to visit."

John snickered. "Well, how the fuck did he get here?"

All of us fell silent, and I knew they were thinking what I was.

"No," Rupert said.

I shrugged. "It's all very fishy. Even for Benji. You have to at least admit that."

John shook his head. "I'm with Rupert on this one. I mean, this is Benji we're talking about. Do you really think he's got something to do with all of this?"

I reached for some pizza. "If anything, that's what

my gut's been telling me this entire time. I'm sure of it. Somehow, Benji has gotten himself involved in some shit. I mean, when he was in the garage with me, he kept talking about how he didn't need the Red Thorns anyway. How he had his own plans. His own time now to make his own moves. I thought he was just mouthing off after I told him the reasons why he'd never be inducted into the crew. But now?"

John and Rupert looked at one another as I took a massive bite of my pizza.

"Now I'm almost certain he's involved somehow."

Rupert chuckled. "Come on. Do you really think Benji is heading all of this up?"

John nodded. "Yeah. Benji's not known for his organization. Or his thirst for revenge."

"See, that's what I can't put together. My guess is that he's gotten in over his head with someone else. Maybe, in the heat of some moment, he entangled himself with someone else to piss someone off that pissed him off. Benji might not like revenge, but he doesn't like feeling like an idiot."

Rupert shrugged. "Then he needs to stop being an idiot."

John chuckled. "Well, outside of all that, that theory sounds more plausible than Benji coming out of the woodwork and being a plotting mastermind."

I sighed. "If I run with the theory and how Benji's mind works, I'm thinking that someone's convinced him that he could do better with someone else rather than with us."

John paused. "You mean, used the fact that we

won't induct him to show him that we don't care about it."

I snapped my fingers. "Bingo."

John sighed. "As much as I hate to admit it, it makes sense."

I shook my head. "Trust me, I don't get any fun out of it, either."

Rupert reached for more pizza. "The kid never could see past the end of his fucking nose."

"That doesn't matter," I said as I grabbed my beer. "What matters is that he knows things about us that he could pass along to the wrong people. People like my father."

Rupert coughed. "Wait a second."

John held up his finger. "Hold on. You think Benji is working with our father?"

I snickered. "Your guess is as good as mine. All I know is that there's been a little too much beating going on in my life, and those two enjoy dropping in on me in my garage at inopportune times. And think about it. The two of them together? Dad with his manipulative ways, and Benji being as gullible as he always is? That's a disaster waiting to happen."

John grimaced. "I don't like the sound of any of this."

Rupert put his food down. "So what do we do about it? If all of this is true, where the fuck do we go from here?"

I paused. "As much as I hate to admit it, I think I have to pay him a visit."

Rupert's eyebrows rose. "Your father? You, go to

him? Without him summoning for you like some warlock?"

I nodded. "I think it's the only way. Lay down my theories. See how he reacts. Even my father isn't infallible when it comes to involuntary twitches of his face."

John cleared his throat. "Well, I'm going with you then."

"No, you're not."

"He's my father, too. I don't want you doing this alone."

"And I don't want you getting hurt any further than you've already gotten hurt."

John rolled his shoulders back. "Max, you're not going to bench me because I'm damaged goods. Got it? I'm going with you. And that's fucking final."

I sighed as I looked over at my brother. He was the strongest man I'd ever known. After he pulled through all of his surgeries, he'd swallowed his pride long enough to step back and let me have a crack at the show. It took a lot of guts for him to step down like that. Usually, presidents tried to make a comeback after injuries like the ones he sustained. But it just wasn't possible. With the permanent damage and never being able to ride a bike again, it took a great toll on his ability to govern.

I still respected him for approaching me the way he did and passing the torch. And I needed to treat him as such.

"Fine. You ready?"

John blinked. "What?"

I stood up. "Let's go. You said you wanted to go with me. No time like the present."

Rupert choked on his beer. "Wait, now? You're going now?"

I nodded. "Yeah. We're going now."

I stared at John and waited for him to stand. Even with his cane, he walked tall with pride. I threw back the rest of my beer, knowing damn good and well I'd need the courage in order to face my father with something like this.

I turned to Rupert. "Keep your wits about you while we're doing this. I want you to call around and see if anyone's heard from Benji lately. I mean, anything. A text. A drive-by. Him yelling at them from across the street. I want to know if he's been spotted by any of us lately."

Rupert nodded. "I'll put out feelers and make some calls."

I drew in a deep breath. "Good. After you're done with that, warn the rest of the crew that Benji can't be trusted any longer. No one is to speak about business with him. No one is to inform him about meetings. Nothing, until we can get this sorted out."

John piped up. "Are you going to warn Dani about Benji, too?"

I reached for my jacket. "I think Dani knew he was untrustworthy before I did, to be honest."

I shrugged it on and took one last look around the backyard before I turned to my brother.

"Ready to go?" I asked.

He held his arm out. "Lead the way."

Rupert stood quickly. "Max?"

I peered over my shoulder. "Yep?"

He sighed. "Just--would you try not to get yourself killed? Okay?"

I sighed. "Yeah. I'll do my best."

21

DANI

I groaned as I rolled over. My arm fell over my eyes as I tried to shield myself from the light. I felt the morning sun against my body as it slowly woke me from the temporary death I called 'sleep.'

Get up. You've got class.

I sighed as my arm fell away from my face. I had plenty of time to get to class. Especially since they weren't until the afternoon, anyway. I wasn't worried about that. But it did tickle my funny bone that I'd woken up in the same position I fell asleep in last night.

"Must've been tired," I murmured.

I pushed myself up in bed and stretched out my arms. Slipping off my leather jacket, I hung it up on the post of my bed and slid to my feet, making my way over to the small coffee maker in the corner. After pouring some of that hot honey in the bottom of my mug, I slid it onto the small platform.

"Come to mama," I whispered.

I pressed the 'brew' button before it started blinking at me. Right. My roommate hated me. Usually, after she used the coffee maker, she'd leave it prepped for me. And vice versa, if I was the first one up. I stumbled around, trying to prepare the small device. I poured a bit of the coffee grounds onto the floor at my feet and cursed underneath my breath. I needed this coffee more than I could stand. Especially if I wanted to get some last-minute studying completed.

And get this paper touched up.

"Thank fuck for groveling," I murmured.

After practically begging my professor, he'd given me an extension on the paper. It wasn't the best thing to do to try and build rapport with my professors, but at least it gave me some breathing room. I didn't want to take advantage of the man's time, either. I wanted to get this paper done, succinct, and perfect well before the end of the extension date.

But, when my eyes found the digital clock on Hannah's desk, they bulged.

"It's already one-thirty!?"

Holy shit. If I didn't hustle, I'd be late for class. For my afternoon classes, of all things! I took a few hot sips of my coffee and drew in a deep breath. I looked down at my outfit and groaned to myself. My clothes were wrinkled. But at least I had them on. All I had to do was wipe my face down, gurgle some mouthwash, and I'd be ready to go.

Get to it. Class is in half an hour.

I scooped up my shower caddy and made a break

for the bathroom. I washed my face and brushed my teeth, deciding to take my coffee with me. I slid back into the dorm room with only twenty minutes to go. I dumped my coffee into a thermos my father had bought me during my freshman year, then gathered my things. I put my laptop in my backpack and picked up my books. I rushed out the door, almost forgetting to close it. I locked it up so Hannah didn't have anything to bitch about, then I ran down the hallway.

With only ten minutes to get to class.

Even though I felt like a badass since running with Max, that didn't mean I wanted to flunk out of all my classes. School was still important to me. Even if something else had also become important. And as I booked it to class, a terrifying scenario crossed my mind. One that had me clinging to my things for dear life.

"All right, class. Today's lecture in on--"

"Yes! I made it!"

I walked through the doorway and every head in the classroom turned to face me. My jaw fell open as my professor looked at me down his nose. Beyond his glasses. Completely unimpressed with my outburst.

"Or maybe not?" I asked softly.

"Are you going to take a seat? Or do you want to give the lecture today?" he asked.

I was so wrapped up in my biggest fear coming to light that I wasn't paying attention. I leapt up the steps two at a time and slammed my shoulder into the door of the school building. I needed a clock. I searched the walls for a clock. I couldn't be late. The universe had to have mercy on me at some point in time.

And in the process of searching for a clock, I walked around the corner, running straight into someone before my things went tumbling from my arms.

Including my coffee.

"Shit, shit, shit, shit. I'm so sorry. That was totally me."

"You're right. It was totally you."

I slowly looked up from my crouched position and watched Benji's face come into view. Every muscle in my body locked up as he grinned down at me. My eyes rolled down his body. I saw the coffee that had splattered all over his pants. His boots. There were even a few speckles on his leather jacket.

A sin that I knew wouldn't go unpunished.

"You don't happen to have any napkins on you, would you, Bambi?" he asked.

I swallowed hard. "Nope. Can't say I do."

He crooked an eyebrow. "What are you still doing down there, Bambi? Care to stand for me?"

I sat on the floor. "I'm good. Thanks."

I gathered my books and my notebooks and shoved them into my backpack. I wanted him to go away. All I wanted was for him to disappear into nothingness. I zipped my backpack up before I reached for my thermos. I outstretched my hand, easing myself forward to get it.

Before I could, Benji kicked it over into a corner. "Oops."

I scrambled for it. "Shit. Come on, seriously?"

Benji snickered. "Why don't you try getting up? Unless Max has you conditioned to be on your knees."

I snatched up my thermos. "Max doesn't have me conditioned for anything, asshole."

He chuckled. "Whoa, ho, ho! Look who's finally sticking up for herself. I give it a four for execution and creativity."

"Do you even know what those words mean?"

"I'm in college, Bambi. Of course I know what those words mean."

I stood, walking back over to my backpack. But, Benji snatched it up. I tried to take it from him. Mostly because I felt time passing us by much too quickly. I needed to be in class. I needed to be in my seat. I didn't need to be out here, fielding Benji's insane bullying tactics.

"Give it to me," I said.

He grinned. "I don't think Max would approve of that."

I lunged for it. "Give me my stuff, Benji."

He held it higher. "Or you'll what?"

I stood on my tiptoes to try and reach my bag. And the second I felt a pressure against my stomach, I went tumbling backwards. I slammed straight into the wall, cracking the back of my head against it. And as Benji's laughter filled my ears, something hard got tossed against my chest.

"Not so tough without your boyfriend, are you?"

I blinked. "He's gonna kill you when he finds out what you're doing."

Benji snickered. "What? You think he doesn't

know? You should know Max better than that right now. He already knows, sweet cheeks."

"That's not true. You're lying. I know how he operates. If he knew what you were doing--"

"He'd what?"

Benji took a step toward me and my vision finally focused. He was close. Much too close for my liking. I felt his breath against my neck. I felt the toes of his boots touching my own. I licked my lips, pressing myself further into the wall. Hoping the damn thing would swallow me whole.

"What the hell does Max see in a chick like you anyway?"

I winced. "What's it to you?"

His finger crept up my arm. "No ass. No tits. No curves. Barely anything to grab on to."

I shrugged off his touch. "Don't you dare touch me again."

His smile was wolfish. "No nothing. Just a plain face and a nose that's always buried in a book. You're so... bland."

"Get the hell away from me."

"Know what I think?"

"I don't give a shit what you think."

He chuckled. "I think your pussy's tight, and that's why he keeps you in his bed."

I tried not to let him ruffle my feathers. "At least I have more going for me than a handful of STDs and an inferiority complex so obvious anyone with half a brain could spot it."

He arched an eyebrow. "What did you just say?"

"I thought you were smart enough to be in college. You don't know what I just said?"

He snarled. "What did you just say to me, you bitch?"

I lifted my chin. "I'm not afraid of you. And no matter what you do to me, that isn't changing."

"You should be, little one. You should be very, very afraid."

"Well, I'm not. You don't make much of a formidable enemy. Plus, you can't touch me. Max is going to beat you to a pulp anyway when he feels the knot on the back of my head. He's going to ask me where I got it, and I'm going to be completely honest with him."

"Oh, I'm really hoping you will be."

I blinked. "What?"

He chuckled. "I like it when you challenge me, little deer. Makes my days more interesting."

I felt his hand gripping my forearm and I shook him off.

"Put your hands on me again and see how loud I scream," I hissed.

He smirked. "Oh, I bet Max's entire block already knows that sound."

I wouldn't let his quips get to me. No matter how frightened I really was of this asshole, I wouldn't give him the pleasure of seeing it. I held my ground, locking eyes with Benji and refusing to look away. This little dickhole needed to be taught a lesson in the consequences of being a bully. He wouldn't get away with it when it came to me. I'd stand up to him. I'd give him a taste of his own medicine so he knew he couldn't intimidate me. He moved closer to me. My back was flush with the wall as I pressed my palms into the cool surface. And when Benji's pelvis fell against my own, I wiggled my hands between us.

Before I planted them on his chest and shoved him away.

He stumbled backward as laughter fell from his lips. I glared at him with wild eyes as he slouched against the wall on the other side of the hallway. He licked his lips and blew me a kiss before running a hand through his hair. And as I watched him walk off, his voice hit my ears again.

"You got lucky this time, Bambi. But I wouldn't count on it for next time."

22

MAX

I stared at my brother John as he shrugged his shoulders. Rolling my eyes, I settled my ankle against my opposite knee and leaned back into the plush leather chair of the fireplace room. A room that had held many murder plans and money laundering issues and other 'business decisions' my father made on a weekly basis. This place was my father's true office. Not the one down the hall with books and a desk that never got used. This room was where my father built his empire. At the back of the house, in the shadows, without a place for anyone to hide and eavesdrop.

Just how my father liked it.

John's good leg jiggled up a storm. I could swear I felt the foundation of the house wobbling with every jerking movement. He kept looking around, as if he were expecting some sort of a surprise. I needed him to calm down, though.

He'd never been good at covering up his emotions.

"John, take a breath."

He sighed. "I can't."

"That was the wrong way. Take the breath in."

He glared at me. "Ha. Ha. Ha."

"Look, it's just a house visit. Nothing to get your panties in a bunch about."

He leaned forward. "Says the guy with two healthy legs good for running away on."

I chuckled. "Told you not to come. But, no. You just *had* to."

"I'm not stringing you out to dry. And I sure as hell--"

I chuckled harder. "Aren't incapable? Says the man complaining about just that?"

I felt laughter mounting as my brother kept glaring at me. And for some reason, the look on his face made this all funnier. I pinched my nose to try and stop it. I felt it building up the back of my spine.

This is not the time to laugh. Get yourself under control.

"Sounds like a party in here."

My father's voice pierced through the moment and the laughter was gone. Toast. Dead, just like the rest of my father's hits. John stood from his chair, wobbling around on his cane. And as I pushed myself out of the plush leather cushions, I watched my father head straight for the drink cart and pour himself four entire fingers of brandy.

Not good.

I peeked over at John as he watched our father down the drink. I mean, the man just tipped it back, opened his throat, and practically let it slide down. I'd only seen my father drink like that once in his entire life. And the end result wasn't good for anyone in his wake.

"You two care for a drink?"

I watched him fill his glass for the second time before he turned to us.

"Nah, I'm good. John?"

He shook his head. "I'm the one driving."

Dad nodded. "Suit yourselves. Though this impromptu house call must be serious if you two are declining free top-shelf liquor."

I didn't like the way Dad was studying me.

"You good, Max?"

I paused. "Why wouldn't I be?"

He narrowed his eyes. "That yellow on your face?"

I shrugged. "Not important."

He turned fully toward me. "Who used you as a punching bag?"

I clicked my tongue. "Was kind of hoping you could tell me that."

In the corner of my eye, I saw my brother go stiff. He straightened out his back and turned his shoulder toward the door. Like he actually thought we'd be able to make a break for it if Dad decided to come after us. It was do or die with our father. Always had been. And if he set his sights on someone, no amount of running would get them any further away than Dad wanted them to be.

I knew John wasn't expecting me to come out of the gate so strongly. But I wasn't here to waste anyone's time. There were consequences, in and of themselves, for people that wasted this man's time. And I was suspicious of my father's motives. Always had been. I wouldn't put it past the old man to be pulling strings in the background for some reason. Working his way away from the Red Thorns. Hell, even trying to dismantle us.

There came a time in every organization my father utilized where it eventually got torn down. People got shifted around. New faces came in and old ones mysteriously disappeared. That was how my father kept his reputation fresh and his hands clean. And the Red Thorns were the longest-running organization that had some serious dirt on the man.

Maybe he was doing this because he was done with our help. Maybe he was ready to take us all out. Maybe he had a new crew he was using. That would explain why we hadn't worked in months. Why most of us were scraping the bottom of our savings accounts just to fucking eat.

Come to think of it, that last client we had was when things started going to shit. When that dumbass client refused to pay.

How convenient.

Maybe someone offered him a great deal of money to end my reign in the Red Thorns. Or maybe someone had offered him something sweeter. Power. Control. Ownership over something in exchange for my life.

I stared at my father for what seemed like decades. And when he smiled, the nape of my neck prickled.

"I don't know what you're trying to imply, son."

I shrugged. "I'm not implying anything. I'm asking you a question. Do you know who's coming after me?"

He chuckled. But he didn't say anything. He just kept looking at me before he chuckled. Then, he'd stop. His eyes would find mine. And he'd chuckle again.

"Come on, John. There are no answers for us here," I said.

I turned my back on Ashton before he spoke again.

"Your little club is just that, Max."

I paused. "What?"

"A little club. That's all it is. Maybe your parading around this town like you own the damn place has rubbed some people the wrong way."

My eyes gravitated over to my brother and I saw fear in his eyes. I kept my back to my father, trying to seem unaffected by his words. I didn't like the tone of them, though. That accusing tone. That gaslighting, manipulative bullshit he always pulled on people.

Not on me, though. "That what you think? Or is that what you've heard?"

I slowly turned around and faced my father again, watching as he threw back the rest of his second drink.

"You know my sources are always accurate."

I snickered. "Sources. Got it."

He shrugged. "You're the one that came to ask. I'm sorry the answer isn't more… fulfilling."

"Yeah. Maybe. But, in any case, in this town, there's only a handful of people with the manpower to send trained thugs after me. Twice."

My father's eyes held mine. "Perhaps you should consider the other threats more carefully, son."

I ran my eyes down my father's body, studying his posture. I took in the way he still held his glass, even though he was done with the drink. His shoulders weren't rolled back, but squared off. Ready for a fight. His hands were always his tell, though. My father had this fidgety way about his pinky whenever he got waist-deep into a lie of his. And holding his glass gave that damn pinky something to do other than fly around in the air like it always did.

The hard line of his jaw and the creases in his brow gave me everything I needed to know, though.

"Tell me, Dad. When were you going to tell us you got a better contract with another crew?"

John's voice piped up from behind. "Let's just go. He's not going to tell you anything."

Dad pointed. "Listen to your brother out in the hallway, Max. He's always had a better sense of what's good for him."

"Calling out our positions to your hidden men now, Dad?"

"John knows when to walk away. You'd do well to learn from him."

"Why? So you can manipulate me like you can him?"

John snarled. "Let's go. Now."

I gritted my teeth. "I'm not walking away, John. And I'm not dropping this, Dad, until we get to the bottom of it. Blood doesn't mean shit. Not if you're the one coming for me."

Dad smiled. "You know what? Good for you, Max. That's the first thing you've *ever* said that I respect. And that I agree with. Blood doesn't mean anything when stakes like this are involved."

My nostrils flared. I knew that man was guilty of this. I knew he was behind it. I just didn't know how to go about figuring that out. But now that I knew where the endgame was, maybe I could walk it back from behind. Start at the punchline, and trace it back to this point.

To where I had been jumped. To where I had been cornered on a fucking night out.

To where Dani got roped into this fucked-up nonsense.

"Max."

John's voice pulled me from my trance. "What?"

His hand fell against my shoulder. "Let's go. There's nothing for us here."

Dad pointed to the door. "He's right. You should go."

I shook my head. "No. He's not right because we should go. He's right because there's nothing for us here. Never has been."

John glowered. "Max. Shut up and come on."

Dad nodded. "Have a nice drive, you two."

John practically tugged me into the hallway before I gave in. I drew in a deep breath as we walked through Dad's mansion, with pictures and artwork and crown molding looming over our heads. I was lost in my thoughts as we walked out to John's car. And I knew he was, too. John wasn't silent too often. But when he was by choice? I knew something important was on his mind.

"Food?" I asked.

John unlocked the car. "How the fuck can you think about food right now?"

I ripped open the door. "I'm hungry. I didn't have much pizza. I could go for something."

"Yeah. Sure. Just tell me where to go."

As we pulled down the massive driveway, I kept an eye on my side mirror. Just in case Dad was having us followed.

23

DANI

I was stuck in that place between being awake, but still being numb to the world. My 8 a.m. class had gotten cancelled due to the professor having a family emergency. So I had an extra two hours to sleep this morning. Which was well needed on my end of things. I'd stayed up much too late last night trying to polish up my paper and get it submitted. I wanted that thing in my professor's inbox by the time he got back from his family emergency. I wanted him to see how serious I was about this class, even if I did have to ask for an extension on the paper.

And I hoped he saw that when he got back.

I cleared my throat as my body came to life and I rolled over. I pulled the covers up to my chin, curled my knees into my stomach, and settled in for a little more sleep. Five more minutes. All my body needed was five more minutes.

But I heard my phone vibrating underneath my pillow.

"No, no, not now."

I heard Hannah yawning as I stuffed my hand beneath the cold cushion.

I tried pressing the side button to snooze my alarm, but it kept vibrating. I peeled an eye open and wiped the crust from my eyelashes as I pulled my phone out. Narrowing my eyes as the morning sun blinded me, I flopped onto my back as my phone continued to jiggle in my hand. The string of numbers flashing on my screen gave me pause. Someone was calling me, but I didn't have their number saved.

Who in the world is calling me?

"Pick it up or shut it up," Hannah groaned.

I rolled my eyes as my phone shot the person to my voice mailbox. But the second I put the phone on my chest, it started vibrating again.

"Dani? Seriously?"

I sighed. "I'm getting it, keep your panties on."

With a voice thick with sleep and an eye still crusted shut, I picked up the phone call.

"Hello?"

The person paused. "Oh, my God."

I furrowed my brow. "What?"

"I woke you up. I am so sorry. Your parents told me you had class at eight and ten thirty. I was hoping to catch you in between them."

I pulled my phone away from my ear just in time to see my alarm flashing on the screen. I shook my head and muted the alarm before bringing the phone back to my face. Great. It was nine forty-five and I was on the phone with some random person.

I sighed. "Who is this?"

"I'm sorry. My apologies. This is Kline."

I peeled my other eye open. "Kline?"

Hannah hissed. "Can you take that outside or something?"

I waved my hand at her. "I don't know a Kline. How did y--?"

Oh. Him.

He chuckled. "I, uh, I got your number from your mother. You know how those things go. Your mom and my mom practically have our lives planned out already. First dates. Our proposal. The wedding. How many kids we'll have."

I rubbed my eye. "Kline. Right. Sorry. Uh, yeah. Mom did tell me about you. You're the acupuncture guy."

He chuckled again. "I've never had anyone call me that before, but yeah, I'm the acupuncture guy."

I pushed myself up from bed and slung my feet over the edge. I had to wake myself up. I had to get a fresh set of clothes on and get my ass to class. I blinked slowly a few times, trying to pull myself out of my hazy trance. I watched Hannah turn her back to me, curling up tight beneath her covers.

But I knew she was still listening.

"Dani?"

I cleared my throat. "Yes. Sorry."

"So what do you say to their plan?"

I snickered. "I'm a bit young for kids."

He snickered. "Well, I was going to take you out to coffee first. You know, do things the right way."

"Like getting my number from my mother before you even know what I look like?"

"Oh, you better believe pictures were exchanged. You're very beautiful, by the way."

I blushed. "Oh. Well, thank you."

He chuckled. "No thanks needed for the truth. So what do you say to our first date?"

"To what?"

"Our first date. Coffee. Would you like to get some with me?"

He's got a nice laugh.

I felt groggy. But, more than that, I felt cornered. On the one hand, this was what I wanted, right? A nice man. A nice husband. A clean-cut house in the suburbs. A pearl white SUV for me to drive our three kids around in. He fit perfectly into my future plans.

But—Max.

Max was everything I didn't know I needed. And I was already too deep into him to start back-peddling now. Maybe in another life, I would've considered saying yes. Maybe, had he come along a bit sooner, I would've gone out to coffee with him. But I loved Max. And there was no turning my back on that. I gave Max my word, and that meant something to me.

"I'm sorry, Kline. My mother can be very pushy at times, and she kind of gets ahead of herself when she sees something she wants. I'm actually seeing someone currently. And I don't think it's fair to him for me to accept a coffee date with a stranger."

He paused. "Oh. I--I didn't know that. My mother didn't--she didn't say anything like that. Do your parents know? Or something? I mean, not that it's any of my business."

I snickered. "No, no. It's fine. It's new. And it's... kind of out of the ordinary for me. But I've told him that I'm not seeing anyone else but him, and that means something to me."

"Of course. I'd never want someone to go back on their word like that."

"I'm glad you understand."

"You sound like a wonderful girl."

I ran my hand through my hair. "Eh, you know. I try where I can."

He chuckled. "I'm sure you do more than try."

I blushed again. "But you know, if you want me to keep your number around, I can hand it out to some of the nice girls on campus. You know, if strange women are your thing."

"No, no. That isn't necessary. To be honest, this is pretty out of the ordinary for me. Usually my parents are very pushy with this kind of thing. But your picture just..."

I slipped off the edge of my bed. "I appreciate the compliment. And I'm sorry you got wrapped up into this."

"Again, you don't have to apologize. He's a lucky man."

I smiled. "Thank you. I'm a lucky girl, too. And I am sorry for the position you've been put in. Believe it or not, my parents don't know every little detail of my life."

"Good for you. Keep a bit for yourself. Because if there's anything we need when growing up with Korean parents, it's a bit of privacy."

I giggled. "You're right about that one."

He chuckled. "You have a good day in classes. And, if things go south with you and your guy, give me a call. I'd still love to take you out to coffee."

I grabbed my mug. "I'll keep that in mind. Thanks."

I hung up the phone and tossed it on top of my bag. I set about making myself some coffee to wake me up before my ten-thirty class. But as the coffee percolated into my mug, I felt a pair of eyes on me.

"Morning, Hannah."

She shuffled around. "Who was that?"

I shrugged. "A guy my mom wants me to go out with."

"Did you say no?"

I slowly looked over at her. "Gee. I don't know, Hannah."

She sighed. "Dani, what if he's a good guy? What if you just passed up your opportunity to--?"

"I mean, he probably is. He sounds like a good guy."

"So why not give him a shot? Just a shot. That's all I'm asking."

"No, Hannah. What you're asking is that I slowly migrate myself away from Max because you don't approve of him."

"Can you blame me for that? I mean, look at the guy. It doesn't take a genius to know he's into some shady shit. You really want yourself getting hurt because of his actions? Because that's how you get yourself killed."

I rolled my eyes. "I need coffee before this conversation."

She sat up. "Or maybe you just need to listen to me for once."

I picked up my mug. "No. For once, what I need to do is listen to my heart. Listen to my gut. Listen to what my own body is telling me. My entire life has revolved around what others want me to do. You, of all people, know that."

"I'm not dictating your future here, Dani. I'm just trying to--"

"Save me? Do me a solid? Get me out of trouble I'm not actually in?"

She threw her hands in the air. "How can you not see the trouble that comes with this guy?"

I sipped my coffee black. "Hannah, I've had enough of this shit. I've chosen Max. That's final. If you don't like it, find another roommate. Or, better yet, I'll put in for a transfer."

She scoffed. "Now look who's getting all worked up over nothing."

"Over nothing?"

I placed my coffee down and glared at her.

"Over nothing, Hannah? You mean to tell me that giving me the cold shoulder for days, blowing up my phone and yelling at me once I get back, constantly chastising me for my decisions, and ultimately jumping down my throat every second you get is nothing? You're really trying to sell that to me?"

She shook her head. "All I'm saying is--"

I held my hand up. "I know exactly what you're saying. You don't like Max. You think he's dangerous. You think I have no business being with him. And I hear you, Hannah. I've registered it. I've logged it away as your opinion. And then, I've made my own decision to stick with him because that's what *I* want."

"You're making a mistake, Dani."

"Maybe I am. But it's a mistake *I've* made. And I have no intention of turning my back on that man until he turns his first. Because that's what he means to me."

She snickered. "If I didn't know any better, I'd say you're in love."

I shrugged. "Maybe I am."

Her face fell. "Are you serious?"

"What?"

"Are you in love with that man?"

"If I am, you'd be the last to know at this point."

She leapt out of bed. "Are you seriously telling me that you're in love with a man who wears leather, rides a bike, smokes like a freight train, and looks like he could kill you with his bare hands? Seriously, Dani!?"

I grinned. "You're cute when you're upset. You know that?"

"Ugh!"

I giggled. "Hannah, I know you don't approve of Max. But listen to me when I say your disapproval isn't going to make me change my mind. I really care about the man. He makes me happy. He takes care of me. I mean, he may not be what you've always pictured in your head or what you want for me. But you of all people don't get to decide who that person is in my life. I do. That's under my control. And I choose him."

"Of course you do."

"So you can either get on board or get off. The choice is yours. But I can tell you what I will do."

I waited until Hannah looked me square in my face before I piped up again.

"I won't live in a dorm room with this kind of tension any longer. It's wreaking havoc on my study habits. It's impeding my sleep."

She frowned. "You sure that's not Max?"

"I've pulled many all-nighters in the past and been fine. But this tension between us? That's what's doing the most damage. Some nights when I'd actually like to come back, I choose not to because I know you're here."

"What?"

"And some days, when I know I should come back and study, I end up not doing that at all and calling Max instead because being around him is better than being here. In this dorm. Or on campus, where I know I'm going to run into you."

"You're just trying to make me feel bad."

"Whatever you believe, that's your call. But this is on you at this point. You want to have a friendship with me? By all means. I'm more than open to it. You're important to me. But you're not important enough to weather this tension and this anger any longer. Either get okay with things, or I'm applying for another roommate at the end of the week."

She balked. "You wouldn't do that in the middle of the semester. That's insane!"

I picked up my coffee. "No, Hannah. What's insane is you thinking you can change my mind by constantly turning your back on me. And trust me, one of those times, you're going to turn back around and I'm going to be walking away. For good."

I sipped my coffee as Hannah searched for her words.

"Dani... I--"

"Whatever it is, I know you mean it. So, just know I mean it, too. I'm done defending myself. I'm done taking this energy that should be thrown into my studies and throwing it at you instead. Max has showed me how to stand on my own. How to be brave. How to dig deep and figure out who I really am and what I really want from my own life. I'm not trading that in for a guy who 'might be nice' because my roommate thinks her anger is going to turn my head, too. Because it won't."

She licked her lips. "I'm sorry, Dani. I didn't real-ize--I mean, I didn't mean--I just..."

I sighed as I continued sipping my coffee. Watching her struggle for the words.

"I'm just sorry, okay?"

I nodded slowly. "Me, too, Hannah. Me, too."

I finished my coffee and started packing my things away. I had ten minutes to throw on something decent before I had to head to class. Yet again, I'd be rushing. And it wasn't Max's fault. I shoved my things into my backpack, shook my mug over my open mouth to get the last drops of coffee, then stripped myself down. I pulled on a pair of black skinny jeans and paired it with a simple red T-shirt before slipping my leather coat up my arms. And after putting on a pair of my flats, I picked up my backpack.

"Don't wait up," I said.

And that was the last thing I said to Hannah before leaving for class.

24

MAX

My gaze dropped to the bubbling foam at the very top of my beer. The pitcher the waitress had brought Rupert and me was fresh. Cold. Crispy to its core. But for the first time in my life, I was too angry to drink it. Too angry to taste it.

All I wanted to do was hear the glass shatter against the wall.

"So you ready to talk?"

Rupert's voice pulled my eyes up and I watched him take a pull from his own glass of beer.

"I'll take that as a no," he murmured.

My eyes fell back to my drink. "He's guilty."

"Wait, what?"

I turned the glass around on the tabletop. "My father's guilty as sin."

"So he's the one doing all this shit to you?"

I nodded. "Looks that way. John still isn't sure, but I am."

"What makes you so sure?"

I snickered. "You know my old man's a piece of work."

"Well, yeah. But what's his motivation? Did he at least give you that? Because what we've brainstormed doesn't really add up."

"My gut tells me he's working with another crew. That's why we haven't had work in months. And it conveniently started when that bullshit client we almost got ourselves killed for up and decided not to pay us a penny."

He paused. "You think that shit has something to do with all of this?"

I nodded. "Yeah. I do."

I finally looked back up at Rupert and saw confusion littered across his face. Yeah, I know. We didn't have all the pieces. But the pieces we did have all pointed toward my father. My father stood to gain the most and lose the most, no matter what angle we looked at this situation from. My father was the only one who knew my stomping grounds well enough to be able to send a professional team directly to where I was. Hell, he was the only one with enough money and enough anger in his heart towards me to hire multiple professional teams in the first place.

I leaned back. "It's him. I know it is."

Rupert shook his head. "Knowing and proving are different."

"We don't have to take this to the police. We aren't putting the man on trial. We're trying to figure out who's trying to get me killed."

"And you're accusing your father of it, Max."

"Are you telling me my father would do anything but kill me? You're really trying to sell that point?"

He shook his head. "No. I'm just trying to play devil's advocate as best as I can."

"Might want to leave that to my father. He's a professional at playing devil's anything."

I finally took a pull from my beer and I didn't stop until the glass was drained. I set it back down onto the table and Rupert filled it up. Then the glass returned promptly back to my lips. Part of me wanted to drown out all of this nonsense. Part of me was ready to wake up from this massive nightmare with two random women in my bed, searching for a third round. But the rest of me knew this wasn't a nightmare. Everything good--and bad--happening right now was real.

And Dani was the only thing I had going for me.

"So let me ask you this."

I nodded. "Sure."

"If you think your father's in play with all of this, should we start doing drive bys on campus? You know, for Bambi's sake?"

I sighed. "I don't know. I honestly--"

I cracked my neck before my eyes fell back to my beer once more.

"I honestly don't know where the hell to go from here."

Rupert sighed. "Oh, boy."

I shook my head. "I just need some time to process all this shit. I need some time to pilfer through what my father said to see if he might've hinted at anything I didn't catch in the heat of the moment."

"What exactly did your father say?"

"He was cryptic. As always. Warned me about slinging accusations around and that he didn't appreciate me coming to his place only to accuse him of what I was."

"What did he say that proved his guilt to you? That's really all I'm concerned about."

I closed my eyes and relived the moment.

"Dad was acting funny. Finicky. I mean, he wasn't shuffling around or anything. But he had a very tight grip on the crystal glass he was holding. I watched that man sling back two massive drinks before he was even remotely ready to speak with us."

Rupert drew in a deep breath. "So something must've happened before you two arrived?"

I opened my eyes. "Or he was that nervous to speak with us in the first place."

"How do you figure?"

"My father has this tell. A tell he's aware of. His pinky likes to twitch and exercise its free will to move whenever he's lying. Or manipulating. I caught it early as a child. It's how I was able to circumvent my father's anger a lot as a kid. But as we grew up, he started finding ways to conceal it."

"How so?"

I shrugged. "Keeping that hand in his pants pocket. Fiddling with a coin, or leaning his hand against the wall."

"Or holding on to a drink."

I nodded. "Exactly. Even though he slung back both of those drinks, not once did he put that glass down. He clung to it so tightly his knuckles were white. And the only time his hand ever relaxed around that glass was when he proclaimed that blood didn't matter in affairs like this."

"Wait, wait, wait. Back up. What did he say?"

"Like I said, things were getting tense. John was in the hallway, calling out for me to come on. That we needed to leave. Dad told me I needed to listen to my older brother and I said, and I quote, 'I'm not walking away, John. And I'm not dropping this, Dad, until we get to the bottom of it. Blood doesn't mean shit. Not if you're the one coming for me.'"

He blinked. "You said that to your father?"

"Yep. And just after his hand relaxed against that crystal glass, he said, and I fucking quote, 'You know what? Good for you, Max. That's the first thing you've *ever* said that I respect. And that I agree with. Blood doesn't mean anything when stakes like this are involved.'"

He paused. "Holy fuck, your father's guilty."

I nodded. "Yep."

"What the hell does he get out of trying to kill you, though? That doesn't make any fucking sense."

"I know. And all I've got there are theories. Maybe he's trying to dismantle the Red Thorns. Maybe he really does have it all-out for me like that. During the meeting, though, Dad mentioned something about us being small time."

"Us, meaning…?"

"The crew. He said we were small-time, and that riding around town like we owned the place had probably pissed some people off."

"And if he's working with another crew, he might be talking about the fact that they're pissed off."

I nodded slowly. "My fear is that we're about to get into a turf war with another gang, only my father's going to be at the helm of it all."

"And we all know how that ended the last time."

I gnawed on the inside of my cheek. "Yeah. We do."

The last time there had been a turf war, John ended up in the hospital for weeks. In a coma for part of his stay. It ended with my own flesh and blood being permanently disfigured with the inability to ever get back on a bike. And that was with Dad on our side. Technically.

The havoc my father could wreak on our club if he was on the opposite side made me shiver.

Rupert poured himself another glass. "Okay, speaking of facts for a second, your father's been content for years using us as anything from errand boys to security detail."

I nodded. "This is true."

"And we've never let him down. At all. We're consistent."

"And affordable."

"Plus, we're low-key. That last client? That's as noisy as shit has ever gotten for us. Because usually, our heads are down. I mean, ever since you stepped up to the plate, our enemies have become at least neutral. Some of them even allies."

"Until now."

He sighed. "You think your father's working with one of our allies?"

I paused. "I think my father is working with someone who wants us out of the way. Whether it's an ally or someone who's neutral--or even someone who's new--I don't know. But none of that matters. The only thing that matters is their current motive."

"Which is to get you out of the picture. Obviously."

"Yep."

I threw back my second beer before Rupert refilled my glass.

"You know what I think?" he asked.

I cleared my throat. "Give it to me."

"I think we need to stop looking at this practically and start looking at it through the lens of your father's eyes. Because if he's really at the head of all this, logic doesn't get us anywhere. Because your father doesn't operate on it."

I pointed at him. "That's the smartest thing you've said since we arrived here."

He blinked. "I don't know if that's a compliment or an insult."

I grinned. "Good luck."

"Hey, Max!"

My head panned towards the voice. "Tiger! Holy shit, where the hell have you been?"

The man with three scars tearing down his face

walked up to our booth and shook my hand. He leaned down for a pat on the back, and I held him a little longer than he was probably expecting.

"Man, it's good to see you on two feet again. I didn't think you'd ever get out of the hospital. How's the leg doing?" I asked.

He bent his knee for me. "After the four surgeries, it's doing fantastic. Sorry I was out of commission so long."

"Man, you know you don't have to apologize for shit like that. Especially after shoving your wife out from in front of a truck like that."

Rupert chuckled. "Yeah. Only you could take a hit from a semi and walk it off after some surgeries."

Tiger chuckled. "So I miss anything? Got any jobs I could hop on? We could really use the money."

I sipped my beer. "I'm working on the job front. We've run into some snags. Some shit that's happened since you've been gone. But any one of these guys will fill you in on what's happening."

He furrowed his brow. "Something I should be worried about?"

"Not to freak you out, but yeah."

I watched Bub slap his hand against Tiger's back before he winked at me.

"Someone around here's chasing our damn president down. Not very nice, if you ask me."

Tiger's eyes narrowed. "Are you fucking kidding me? Who? Who are they? Tell me, and there's no need for anything else."

I chuckled. "You need to take a seat and keep on

resting. And Bub! Try not to freak him out on his first night back. He's got pins in his leg, remember?"

Bub smiled. "Ah, I'm just messin'. You know Max can handle himself."

Tiger studied my face. "Are the bags underneath your eyes yellow? Holy shit, did someone actually land a punch?"

Bub wrapped his arm around Tiger's shoulders. "Come on. Your 'welcome back' drinks are on me. We've got a lot to talk about."

I nodded. "I appreciate that, Bub. Thanks."

He winked. "Anytime, Max."

I watched the two men walk away as I sipped my third drink. Rupert topped it off before he held it in the air, beckoning for another pitcher to be brought to the table. I caught eyes with some of my men. Bushley and Mark. Grandfather and Sully. I waved at them and they came over to talk. Filling me in on their lives, their girls, and their adventures. I sat there and continued to drink, listening to every story they had for me. I loved hearing about their lives. What they got up to when we weren't working.

I liked the fact that my men felt safe enough to live their lives. To go on adventures. To play with their children in the backyard and take vacations.

That was why this situation pissed me off so much. Because looming threats like this made my men fear for their safety. The safety of their families. Soon none of them would be on vacation. Or enjoying their lives. None of them would let their children play outside.

Soon the paranoia would take hold, and that's when mistakes were made.

"Think you should slow down on those drinks?" Rupert asked.

I drained my fifth--no, sixth? No, fifth--drink before I waved my hand at him.

"Hush. Larry here's telling me about his trip to the mountains. You get any fishing done? I know how much you like to sit and fish," I said.

I listened to Larry's fishing trip stories and nodded as Panther talked about his newly-wedded wife. I slung back drinks and laughed with the guys, giving absolutely no fucks about how much I was drinking. This was just as much my night to enjoy as it was theirs. And I needed to enjoy something after that fucked-up meeting with my father.

What I didn't take into account was all of that beer on an angry, empty stomach.

And as Rupert helped me stumble out of the bar, I wondered if he was right.

I wondered if we needed to start doing drive-bys near campus to make sure Dani stayed safe through all this.

25

DANI

I slipped into my car and decided to go hang out with Max for a little while. After my morning classes and that awful conversation with Kline, I needed to see him. Hold him. Kiss him. Hear his voice in my ear. I couldn't sleep. I'd barely eaten all day. I felt guilty for some reason. Even though I knew I hadn't done anything wrong. I just didn't want Max to be upset with me. I didn't want him thinking that I was straying, or whatever. I wanted him and only him. No matter what came our way.

"Text message from Mom. Do you want me to read it?"

My SUV came alive with the Bluetooth automation voice. I peeked down at the dashboard and reached over, pressing the red 'X' button. I didn't need to be speaking with my mother right now. Especially since I knew what she was calling to talk about. I mean, it was eleven o'clock at night! What did she think I was doing right now?

"Incoming call, Mom."

I rolled my eyes. "Really?"

"Incoming call, Mom."

I groaned. "Come on."

"Incoming call, Mom. Do you want me to pick up?"

I sighed. "Yes. Pick up the call."

"Danika?"

"Yeah?"

"Oh! Hi, sweetheart. Is now a good time for a quick chat?"

"Is that what your text was about?"

"It was, yes."

"So since I didn't answer, you decided to call anyway?"

She paused. "Are you busy?"

I sighed. "I've just got a lot on my plate. There's a reason why I didn't answer your text in the first place."

"Well, I promise I'll make this qui--are you in the car or something? You sound a bit echo-y."

"I am in the car. I'm coming back from a new study place I found. I need to catch the library before midnight."

She snickered. "My busy little bee. I won't keep you very long, then. I'm on speaker, right? You're not holding the phone and driving?"

I rolled my eyes. "What is it, Mom?"

"Fine, fine. So testy lately. So Kline's mother called me this morning."

"That doesn't shock me. Kline called me *very* early this morning. Not sure if it's rude or pretentious."

She gasped. "Danika! What in the world? Are you stressed or something?"

"Mom, we're almost at midterms. I'm a bit stressed, yes."

"Well, why don't you try to tone down the attitude a bit. I've never had to worry about that with you. Don't make me start worrying about it now."

Dani, the good little girl. "Mom, I can't really talk about this right now. Can we do this some other time?"

"I said I'd make it quick. I just want to talk about what happened. She told me a very interesting tidbit that I wasn't sure about and wanted to confirm it with you."

I turned on my blinker. "What did she tell you?"

Don't get me wrong, I adored my mother. But I was tired of playing this 'good girl' shtick. I was tired of my mother constantly being in my business. Constantly trying to force me into things. Granted, I hadn't made things easy on her. I practically shoved that poster board of my perfect life in her face every day after high school. All she was doing was trying to help me achieve it.

Keep your cool, Dani. It's as easy as the lie you just fed her.

Holy hell, I was lying to my parents now. That wasn't a thing I ever did. I didn't want to make it a habit, either. I gripped my steering wheel as I heard my mother whispering in the background. To my father, no doubt. I heard a small click sound on my side of things and I knew I was on speakerphone.

Which meant I had to be overly careful about what I said.

Dad could suss out lies from a mile away, after all.

"Mom, look. I'm almost at the library and I need to hop off soon. But I know you're disappointed. I know you were banking on this. I never said I'd agree to go out with him, though. I told you I'd think about it, and I did. I decided not to get coffee with him. That's all that happened."

She sighed. "Is it because you're already seeing someone? Because that's what Kline's mother told me you said to her son. That you were seeing someone."

I bit my tongue. "Oh."

"Are you?"

"Am I what?"

"Seeing someone."

I held my breath, wondering what in the world I needed to do. I mean, I was almost at Max's place. What would happen if I was still on the phone with her and Max saw me outside? The lie I had already told would be blown out of the water. It would be an absolute nightmare. And I didn't have the stomach to lie to her again. Especially with my father secretly listening in.

So, don't lie.

"Dani? You still there?" Mom asked.

I sighed. "Mom, it's nothing serious."

She gasped. "Oh. My. Gosh. You are seeing someone!"

Dad butted in. "What's his name and where did

you meet him? I want to shake his hand before you two go any further."

I rolled my eyes. This incessant helicopter parenting was getting very, very old.

"No one is shaking anyone's hand when I'm still trying to figure things out myself," I said.

Mom squealed. "Have you been on a date with him? What's his name? What does he look like? Have you two had coffee yet? Has it progressed to dinner? Oh, I bet he took you out somewhere nice, didn't he? Tell us everything."

Dad harrumphed. "I still want to shake his hand before he takes you anywhere."

I rolled my eyes. "His name is Max. Everything is fresh and new. We're still just talking. I just didn't find it fair or proper to accept a coffee date with some other guy while I'm talking to another. I don't like that."

"Oh, no no," Mom said hastily, "you made the right decision."

Dad sighed. "Max who? What's his last name?"

I pulled into Max's driveway. "I gotta go, guys. I'll call when I can."

"Wait, at least tell us what you--!"

I hung up the phone call and turned off the car. Then I decided to turn my phone off, too. I noticed there was a truck in Max's driveway. A truck that looked oddly familiar. It wasn't John's. He drove a beat-up hatchback.

Who in the world is at Max's place?

I turned my car off and slipped out. I headed for the front door and didn't even bother knocking. Mostly because the door was already ajar in the first place. I softly pushed it open and stuck my head in, and the smell of booze filled my nostrils.

"Max? You here?" I called out.

"Bambi?"

Rupert's voice came around the corner and it hit me. That's why the truck looked so familiar. It was Rupert's. I walked inside and closed the door behind me, locking it for good measure.

"Rupert? Where's Max?" I called out.

I watched him duck around the corner with a cocky grin on his face.

"Hey, Max! Your girl's here!"

I winced. "Yeah. Thanks."

"Dani!?"

I paused. "Uh oh."

Rupert nodded. "It's been a night."

"Da-ha-ha-haaaaa-niiiiii!"

My eyebrows rose. "Oh, boy."

Rupert chuckled. "Did I mention it's been a night?"

I watched Max stumble around the corner before Rupert held out his arm. He caught Max just as he tripped, saving him from falling flat on his face. I put my hand to my mouth and tried to hold back my giggles. Max's hair was disheveled and his eyes were half-hooded with drunkenness.

That explains the smell of booze.

Max held his arms out. "Dani, dear. You sexy little thing. Come give me a kiss."

He threw himself headfirst down the hallway and it

was all I could do to get underneath him. I caught him just before he tumbled to the floor, with Rupert rushing up behind him. I pressed my hands against his chest. I helped him stand up as he practically pawed me in front of his best friend. He squeezed my ass. Massaged my tits. Licked his lips as he rubbed his pelvis against my own.

I crooked an eyebrow. "Someone's a bit frisky tonight."

Max winked. "I'm always frisky when you're around."

I peeked over at Rupert. "Did the two of you have a little too much fun tonight?"

Rupert frowned. "Actually, not really. Max here had a bad afternoon. Been chronically drunk since dinner time. I'm actually glad you're here."

I paused. "A bad day? What happened?"

Max took my hand. "Bah. Who the fuck cares? You're here, and that's all that matters. Come here."

"I'm com--oh!"

Rupert waved at us. "Have fun, you two!"

Max dragged me down the hallway before we stumbled into his bedroom. I barely got the door closed behind me before he ripped my leather jacket down my arms. I spun around, watching as he fought his own arms to get out of his coat. He spun around like a dog trying to catch its tail, shrugging the leather off. Only for it to fold over onto itself and pinch his skin.

"Ah. Shit. The fuck? What the--who the hell made this? I need a new coat!"

I giggled. "Here. Let me help, Drunkie McDrunkerton."

He stumbled around and could hardly stand up as I helped him out of his things. I tossed his jacket to the floor. I peeled his shirt over his head. I tried not to stare at his tattoos too much as I pulled his belt through its loops. I tossed the leather to the ground before leading him over to his bed. I crouched down, feeling him fist my hair as I helped him out of his boots.

"These jeans are next, beautiful. And when they come off? You're gittin' it good."

I snickered. "Gittin' it, huh? Can't wait, hot stuff."

I slid his socks off before I stood up. I pushed his chest playfully, watching his back fall to the mattress. I stepped away from his body, walking around to the other side of the bed. And as he rolled over to keep me in view, I started taking my own clothes off.

"Hell yeah, gorgeous. Show me that body."

I grinned at him. "That's what I plan on doing if you can stay awake long enough."

The truth of the matter is that I already saw his eyes fluttering closed. As much as he wanted to stay awake, he simply couldn't. I only got my shoes and my jacket off before his soft snoring filled the room. And just to tickle my own funny bone, I took off my bra and tossed it at his face.

Startling him awake before he held it above his eyes.

"Nice," he murmured.

I snickered. "Come on. Let's cuddle for a bit."

"You know I want more than a cuddle, gorgeous."

"I know, I know, you big lug. But cuddling always leads to the best sex, don't you think?"

He chuckled as he barrel-rolled himself to the top of the bed. Watching him trying to get beneath the covers made me snicker and giggle to myself. He looked like a fish out of water. Or a fully grown adult having to learn how to use his arms and legs again. I slapped my hand over my mouth as he finally got beneath the covers. Because the satisfied groan he let out sounded like he had exploded in his pants.

"Feeling good there, Max?"

His eyes fell closed. "Better if you're here."

I smiled softly. "Coming right up."

Still in my jeans and my blouse, I slipped underneath the covers with him. I scooted close, pressing my leg between his. His hand cupped my cheek. His lips found mine. And even though the taste of beer was overwhelming, it didn't stop me from indulging. It didn't stop me from tasting him. It didn't stop me from rolling on top of him, settling between his legs, and letting our tongues fall together.

"Mmmm, Dani."

I giggled. "Hi there."

His hands fell to my ass cheeks, giving them a bit of a squeeze. And as I rested my ear against his chest, his hand started stroking my tendrils. I felt my own eyes slowly drooping. I felt myself melting into his body. He pulled the covers over us and kissed the top of my head, then resumed untangling the curls in my hair with his fingertips.

"It's good to see you, Dani."

I nuzzled against his chest. "It's good to see you, too."

"What made you come over?"

I can't tell him now. He's plastered. "I missed you, is all."

"I missed you, too."

I kissed his chest. "You sure you don't want to talk about what happened today?"

"Nope. Really don't."

"Well, if you ever want to talk about it, I'm here. Okay? Believe it or not, I'm here for more than just sex."

He paused. "Is that how you feel?"

I looked up at him. "What?"

He peered down at me. "Do you feel like you're here just to be my sex doll?"

I snickered. "I suppose I wouldn't quite put it like that."

His voice hardened. "Dani."

"No, Max. I don't feel like that. I feel like you genuinely care about me."

"Good. Because I do."

My heart soared with his words. "I do, too. I'm pretty awesome, you know."

He snickered. "Smooth."

I kissed his chest again. "I care a lot about you, too. I just want to make sure you're okay."

"I'm okay. I promise."

"I don't take promises lightly."

"Neither do I. Promise."

I giggled. "You thirsty or anything?"

He gripped me tight. "Don't you dare get up."

"Okay, okay, okay. I'm not going anywhere."

He sighed. "Good. I'm glad."

Something had him worked up. I wasn't an idiot. He was drunk, uncontrollable, and an absolute pile of mush right now. This wasn't the Max I knew. And while this side of him wasn't a bad thing, I knew that whatever happened had to have been rough if he'd gotten himself this drunk.

"Max?"

He didn't respond, so I peeked up at him.

"Max, there's something I need to tell you."

His soft snores graced my ears again and I sighed.

"I guess it can wait until tomorrow."

But I didn't want to put off telling him about Kline any longer than I had to. I didn't want it to come off as if I had been hiding something from him. Clearly, he had enough on his plate right now. So, clearing the air as soon as possible would be good for the both of us.

Preferably sooner rather than later.

26

MAX

My head pounded against my skull. Wait, that didn't make sense. My brain pounded against my skull. My body felt as if it were sinking into the bowels of hell, never to return, no matter how much I clamored for the surface. I tossed my arm over my eyes. My stomach felt as if it were in the Olympics for gymnastics. It tumbled and twirled and swirled and kicked. I felt like I was going to be sick.

"Shit."

I rolled over as I heaved. I hung my head off the edge of the bed, but nothing came up. Just some spit that dribbled onto the carpeted floor and a bit of bile that fell from my mouth out of nowhere. And with every heave, my stomach shook. It trembled with the need for an apology. I hadn't felt sick like this after drinking in years. Ever since I'd stepped into the role as president of the Red Thorns, I didn't do anything that made me feel out of control.

"You're an idiot."

I murmured the words before I heaved again. Only this time, I felt something cool against the nape of my neck. I reached up to grab at whoever was in the room with me, but my reflexes were off. I felt as if I were moving at the speed of a panther. With excessive reflexes, quick as lightning.

In reality, though, I barely got my hand over my head. Much less in a position to grab at someone.

"Here. Drink."

Dani's voice hit my ears and the night came flooding back all at once. My head felt like it was in a vise grip as I groaned and screwed my eyes shut. I felt something dancing against my lips and I wrapped them around it. A straw. It was a plastic straw that...

"Mmm, my God."

Holy shit, the ice cold water tasted fantastic.

Dani stroked my hair. "Not too quickly. You'll throw it back up. Slow gulps. There we go."

I breathed through my nose and swallowed with my throat. I timed it just right, and my body groaned in disappointment when the cup was empty. I felt the cool washcloth being plucked from my neck and I saw it appear beneath me, wiping up the small stains I made on the carpet beneath my face.

"Can you get to the kitchen? Rupert's cooked breakfast."

Her voice was so soft. So breathless. So... kind. I gravitated toward it as her hands threaded underneath my arms. She helped me up as the room spun around me. I draped myself over her as I stumbled out of bed.

We fell against the wall and I heard her grunt, shooting me into protective mode. I gripped her hips and pulled her against me before the two of us fell back to the bed.

With her body falling right on top of me.

"Max! Max, are you okay? Did I hurt you?"

I chuckled. "You could never hurt me, gorgeous."

She sighed. "Okay. Let's try this again. Rupert! We're really coming this time!"

He chuckled. "Good! Because shit's getting cold!"

"All right, Max. Come on. Up we go, big boy."

I grinned. "You know you like it."

She giggled. "Never said I didn't."

She helped me stumble into the kitchen where the smell of eggs and toast made my mouth water. She sat me down at the table next to John, who stared at me with a look I didn't even want to process right now. And as I watched Dani go back over to the stove, Rupert handed her the spatula.

"Did you turn them already, Rupe?"

"Nope. Didn't need it. Does he need anything?"

"Water, for right now. I'd like to get him to eat, too, if possible."

"You think you made enough food?"

I cleared my throat. "Dani, you said Rupert cooked."

She peered over shoulder. "He did."

John snickered. "He cooked the eggs. Dani threw together everything else."

She waved the spatula around. "So I cooked up some bacon and pancakes. Sue me."

Rupert nodded. "And toast."

John put his hand on my shoulder. "I made the coffee, though. Don't worry."

I nodded. "Good. Rupert's coffee is shit."

Dani giggled as Rupert tossed me a glare, and the entire scene made me smile. Like a goofy little schoolgirl. Dani, standing at the stove throwing down a breakfast that made my stomach growl in hunger. My brother, sitting next to me, looking as spry as ever. My best friend, hanging out with us. A house full of people who cared about one another.

In another life, maybe, I would've actually thought I deserved something like this.

"So! How you feeling, champ?"

Rupert's voice made me wince. "I'm good. Though you can bring your voice down a bit."

Dani giggled. "He's not yelling, Max."

I pointed. "You, too. In fact, everyone whisper. That'll do just fine."

John leaned against my ear. "Like this?"

I pulled away from him. "You spit on me, you fucker."

Dani turned the bacon. "Settle down, you two. The food's almost ready."

Rupert shook his head. "I swear, you two are like kids."

Dani snickered. "Three, you mean."

And the look she gave 'Rupe' made me chuckle until my stomach protested the movement.

I watched as Dani filled the kitchen table with food. With drinks. With ice water and coffee and orange juice. Since when the hell did we have orange juice? Rupert passed out silverware and John got up to get the syrup. The butter. The salt and pepper. We all sat down to a wonderful meal, but even though I needed the food and the water, I couldn't take my eyes off her.

Off Dani.

Off this incredible young woman that had come into my life.

"So, John? What do you think? As the resident breakfast maker, of course," Dani said.

I watched John take a bite of bacon and eggs before practically inhaling a pancake in one breath. All he could do was hold up a thumb and nod his head before he got back to devouring his plate. That was the most praise I'd ever seen him give anyone on their cooking. Because John was incredibly picky about how his food was cooked.

Could this girl get any better?

"Max?"

"Hmm?"

Dani pointed to my water. "Drink. Please. You need to hydrate."

I reached for my glass. "As you wish, gorgeous."

I winked at her and watched her blush as Rupert chuckled.

"To what do we owe this feast?" John finally asked.

Dani shrugged. "I don't know. No reason, really. I got up around seven and decided Max might be hungry once he woke up. I was certainly hungry. And if I was cooking for us, it seemed rude not to cook for everyone else. Though, Rupert, you should have someone check out that snoring issue. You were pulling the curtains in from the other side of the house."

My eyes widened as John practically choked on his food. He barely got it down before he started laughing, and I couldn't help but join in. Dani shrugged and went back to eating her food while Rupert's jaw swung against the table.

"Did you guys hear what she just said to me!?" he exclaimed.

Dani nodded. "They did. But it's true. You should have a doctor look at that. Not good for a man your age."

John roared with laughter and I had tears springing to my eyes.

"I told you!" I managed to say.

John pointed at him. "We fucking told you that you snore like a damn chorus of chainsaws."

Dani cocked her head. "I thought it sounded more like a wood chipper. You know, he's got those little breaks in it. Like this."

She tried to mimic the sound of his snoring and I couldn't take it. I wiped the tears away from my eyes as Rupert sat there, angrily stuffing his face with food. That's how good Dani's food was. No one wanted to stop eating it. They just wanted to experience whatever emotions they felt *while* eating it.

"You guys are asshats."

Dani playfully gasped. "Why, I never in a million years thought I'd hear some old crotchety bastard say such awful things."

"Oh my God!" John bellowed.

I bent over and let my forehead rest against the table. The laughter was killing me. I needed water, but I couldn't drink it. I needed food, but I couldn't eat it. I felt Dani slip her foot beside mine beneath the table and it shot chills up and down my leg. And after we were all finally done laughing, even Rupert was chuckling along with us.

"You've got spunk. I see why Max likes you," he said.

I eyed him carefully. "Down, boy."

Rupert held up his hands. "What? Just stating the obvious."

Dani smiled. "I like you guys anyway. You're nice company. And I like cooking for people, so I'm glad you're enjoying the food."

"It's great," John said with his mouth full.

Before he went back in for a second plate.

I couldn't believe how seamlessly Dani fit in with the two most important people in my life. We did more laughing at the breakfast table than anything else, and it felt fantastic. It was absolutely what I needed, and I felt refreshed after it was all said and done. We cleared out any hope of having leftovers. I drank more water than I could possibly stand. And I even managed to top it all off with a wonderful cup of John's coffee.

"So, Bambi."

"Yes, Rupe?"

Rupert snickered. "Nice nickname. Anyway, what made you stop by last night?"

John put his silverware down. "Yeah, I'd like to know that, too. Just a surprise for Max, or something?"

She shrugged. "Well, there was something I wanted to talk to Max about. But I figured it could wait until he was a little more sober."

Rupert snorted. "Good plan."

I rolled my eyes. "I wasn't that bad."

Dani's face fell flat. "You were heaving over the edge of your bed when you first woke up."

Rupert nodded. "And you were trying to strip me down last night."

John cackled. "He was what!?"

I pursed my lips. "No I wasn't, asshole."

Rupert held his hands up. "Bible. Fucking hand on the Bible, dude. You were trying to strip me down because, and I quote! 'You wanted to make sure things still worked for Dani.'"

Everyone fell apart in laughter as I slumped back into my seat. Fucking hell, I'd never live this shit down. But their laughter didn't deter me from the point I'd caught.

Which was the fact that Dani wanted to talk.

"What's on your mind, gorgeous?"

She was still trying to recover from her laughter.

"I mean, when you're done laughing at my expense."

She held her hand up. "Sorry! I'm sorry. I'm sorry. Hoooo, holy hell. I haven't laughed that much in ages."

John sat back. "You and the rest of the table."

We all fell silent for a moment before Dani cleared her throat.

"I was actually wanting to talk with you about your plans for today. Got anything special going on?"

I shrugged. "Other than drowning myself in water, no. Why?"

She grinned. "I wanted to see if you could take me to get that tattoo."

Rupert and John stared at Dani as my heart stopped in my chest. The tattoo. *The* tattoo. Was she serious? I felt my insides warming. I felt my heart coming back to life as fireworks went off inside my brain.

"Are you serious?" I asked.

And when she smiled brightly, I knew the answer before she said it.

"Dead serious, handsome."

27

DANI

I looked down at the stencil on my outer thigh and I sighed. I wrung my hands together as I sat in the one chair all of the other Red Thorns had gotten their tattoos done in. It was intricate. Even though I was told not to touch it, I wanted to run my fingers across it. The small emblem. The rose, with its thorns. The cute little sunset background. Mine was much smaller than Max's, but they were identical in all of their ways.

And that made me feel special.

"It's not that bad. I promise, gorgeous."

I looked over at Max as he took my sweating hand.

"Sorry," I said softly.

He grinned. "No need. Rupert's hands sweat, too, when he's nervous."

I snickered. "Should I ask as to how you know that?"

"Let's just say Rupert isn't as tough with some things as he is with others."

"Please tell me he hates balloons. Or clowns. Or cotton balls."

"Actually, he's not a fan of needles."

I blinked. "I bet his tattoos were rough, then."

He snickered. "I can attest personally to that, yeah."

My jaw dropped open. "Oh, he's so going to kill you when he finds out I know that."

"And how's he going to find out?"

Max leaned in close and I felt his breath against my lips. I eased myself back into the chair, gazing into his eyes as he smiled at me. I loved it when he smiled. His eyes wrinkled at the edges and his entire face lit up. My heart skipped a beat when he softly pressed his lips against the tip of my nose. Our fingers threaded together. I squeezed his hand tight. And as I drew in a deep breath, I felt a chill work its way up my spine.

"There's something I want to tell you, gorgeous. You know, before you make this commitment."

I blinked. "Is something wrong?"

He shook his head. "No, no. Nothing's wrong. I mean, unless what I have to say is bad news."

"What is it?"

He licked his lips. "Dani, I--"

His eyes caved first. The softness of their gaze warmed my heart. Then his mouth caved. His smile grew wider, and I felt my neck flushing with anticipation. He pulled his chair closer to me, his nose nuzzling softly against my own. And when my eyes fell closed, I felt what he was trying to tell me.

"What is it?" I whispered.

I felt my heart hammering against my chest as I prepared myself for the admission.

"Open your eyes."

They flew open. "Sorry."

He chuckled. "No need to be. I just want to look at you when I say it."

"Yes?"

His smile faded into a grin. "I love you, Dani."

My mouth went dry. "You--you do?"

He chuckled. "Yeah, I do. I've known it for a long time, actually. Ever since the first time I kissed you. But the other night, when you attacked that guy with the wine bottle? I knew without a shadow of a doubt that you were the only woman on the face of this earth for me."

I let out a shuddering breath. "Oh, Max. I love you, too. I love you so, so much."

His hand slipped against my cheek as he turned my lips into his. And when I felt his tongue fall against my own, my heart soared with delight. I cocked my body toward him as I felt his hand sliding down my side. I moaned down the back of his throat, wanting nothing more than to experience the whole of him. My nipples puckered. My thighs clenched together. I wanted to straddle his lap and show him exactly how much I adored him.

But the footsteps coming down the hallway ripped us away from one another.

"All right, I've got the specific colors suggested," the artist said as he came in. "Ready for the outline? We can see how you're feeling after I get done with it."

I wiped at my lip softly. "Um, yeah. That sounds-- that sounds great. Max?"

He nodded. "We'll see how it goes after the outline."

The tattoo artist sat down. "Perfect. Now, the important part is to hold still. If you want to do a test feel on the back of your hand or your arm, we can do that. Otherwise, it might be best if Max here holds your leg down. Not hard. But just so we make sure you don't jump when I touch your skin for the first time."

I nodded. "Max, are you okay with that?"

He turned my leg softly before pressing his hands against it, pinning it to the tattoo chair.

"Ready when you are," he said.

I was scared at first. But when the tattoo needle came down against my skin, I realized why the artist wanted to do that. The initial contact was a jolt to my system. Electricity buzzed throughout my muscles. I felt my thigh contract and Max started massaging me with his hands. The artist took his time, slowly tracing over the outline in a barely-there black line. I watched with wide eyes. I was curious, more than anything. And after the outline was done, he picked the needle up.

"All right. How are you feeling?"

I drew in a deep breath. "Surprisingly okay. What comes next?"

Max took my hand. "The shading. The coloring. This part is a little more intense, so squeeze my hand if you need to."

The tattoo artist started gathering colors. "You think you can hold still for the initial contact?"

I nodded. "Now that I know what it feels like? Yes."

Max kissed my temple. "Good girl."

His words made me melt as the tattoo artist continued his work of art.

There were moments where the pain was a bit much. Where I felt my face flushing and my heart beating harder than it should. I needed two breaks with the shading as it grew closer to my hip bone. But it still wasn't that bad. The anticipation of the new experience was worse than the experience itself. And when the tattoo artist wiped at my finished design, tears sprang to my eyes.

"So what do you think?" Max asked.

My eyes fluttered up to his as the tattoo artist slid something along my irritated skin.

"I think everything I thought I knew about myself was a lie. This is me, Max. I'm yours."

And the smile that lit up his face was one I knew I'd never forget.

28

MAX

I tightened my grip around her waist as I slowly came to. The sun just barely streamed through the windows as my eyes cracked open. The smell of her hair filled my nostrils. The feel of her body permeated my muscles. Dani was in bed with me. Her ass against my pelvis. Her leg threaded between my own. I'd never felt so alive and fulfilled in all my life.

So this is what love feels like.

I pressed a tired kiss against her bare shoulder, cherishing every second I had with her. Dani skipped classes just for me yesterday. And, according to her, she wasn't going today, either. I knew I needed to make her go to classes. I worried that she was giving up too much of her life that she enjoyed just to be with me. I didn't want to be the negative force in her life that led her away from a life that might have been better for her. But, hearing her tell me I was the only thing she wanted while looking up at me with those doe eyes of hers?

It was too much to resist.

My hand slid down her leg until I hit the gauze wrap around her thigh. I traced my fingertips along the smooth surface, knowing exactly the pattern her tattoo took. Her shoulder rose and fell with her even breaths. She slept so soundly next to me, and that swelled my chest with pride. Sleep was the most vulnerable state anyone could be in around anyone else. And Dani trusted me with her body while she was asleep.

I took that trust to heart.

"I'll protect you from anything," I whispered.

I still don't know how it happened. How the fuck she chose me out of the numerous other men out there that I knew were much better for her. But I sure as hell wasn't squandering it. I felt her shift against me and I moved, watching as she rolled over onto her back. Her soft breasts bounced against my body and her hair splayed out over my pillows.

I sighed. "You're perfect, Dani."

How lucky I am that you've chosen me.

I couldn't contain myself. I had to kiss her. I knew it might wake her up, but I couldn't wait a second longer. I pressed my lips softly against hers, feeling her stir beneath me. A soft giggle rose from her lips as her arms threaded around my neck. Her mouth opened up for me. Her sleepy tongue fell against my own. Fucking hell, even her morning kisses tasted like heaven.

Usually, morning kisses tasted like shit.

"Mmmm, hi, handsome."

I chuckled. "Morning, gorgeous."

She yawned. "Oh, sorry. Sorry. The breath, oh."

I smiled. "Your breath is fine."

"Mmm, no. Not even kind of. Ugh. I need some water. Can I brush my teeth first?"

I quickly slid on top of her body. "You're going nowhere."

Her sleepy eyes fell open as she grinned up at me. Her fingertips ran along my shoulders. Rumbled down my arms. Tracing my muscles, like she always enjoyed doing. I'd build them ten times bigger for her, if that's what she wanted. I'd tattoo the whole of my body, if that's what would make her happy. And as my lips fell to the crook of her neck, her body arched against me.

Her moans fueling me onward.

"Oh, Max."

I kissed down the valley of her breasts.

"Shit, Max."

I nibbled at her hip bones as my hand covered the whole of her gauze-wrapped tattoo.

"Max, I need--"

"Mmm, I know exactly what you need."

Her legs parted further. "I just--please? Can I--can I, please?"

My eyes whipped up to hers. "Always, if you ask that nicely."

I buried myself between her legs. I filled my bedroom with her sounds. I found my breakfast between her thighs as I lapped her up and swallowed her down. I couldn't contain my growls. Every time her pussy pulsed for me, I bucked my cock against the sheets of my bed. She overwhelmed me. Every part of her. The sounds. The scents. The way her body moved.

All of it worked together to build this incredible woman I had fallen in love with.

"Max, please! I'm so close. I'm so close. I love you. I love you. I love you. Max!"

"Holy fuck, I love you, too."

I let her use my face however she pleased. And as her juices dripped down my chin, I felt her explode against me. I wrapped my arms around her thighs. I held her close to me, taking great care not to hurt her tattoo. I sucked her clit between my lips and flicked my tongue across it, holding her in place as she bucked like a bronco. I wanted my fill of her. And I certainly wasn't done yet.

It wasn't until those beautiful words fell from her mouth that my head popped up.

"I need you inside me. Please!"

Her words were so desperate. So wanton. So needy. And damn it, if it wasn't fucking perfect. I rushed up her body and crashed our lips together. I fell between her legs as the heat of her pussy called to me. I lined myself up as I hovered over her glorious form, her soft curves rolling and tumbling for my viewing pleasure. I'd never get sick of the view from up here. The way her skin flushed for me. The way her eyes begged for me. The way her body shook in my wake.

"I love you so much," I murmured.

I pushed into her body and our hips fell together. Her entire body wrapped around me, locking me in tight. Her arms went around my neck and her legs wound around my waist. And as I pounded into her, shaking the entire bed against the wall, I felt her quickly pulling me to my end.

"Fuck, Dani."

"Max, yes. Yes. Yes!"

"Shit. Holy fuck, what have you done to me?"

"I love you. I love you so much. I'm so close. Max, please. Please. Please."

I grunted. "Just. Like. That."

I slammed myself against her as my lips fell to hers. I felt her body pulling me in. Massaging me to my end as goosebumps scattered along my body. I unraveled her hands from my neck, rutting against her as I threaded our fingers together. I pinned her hands above her head, opening her up to me. Kissing down her neck. Marking her skin. Sucking in patches and nibbling on them until nothing was left but dark red marks.

"I'm coming," she choked out.

And when her walls clamped me in their vise grip, I met my end with her.

Chanting how much I loved her as it fell effortlessly from my lips.

29

DANI

One, two, three. Breathe!
    One, two, three. Breathe!
Underwater. Turn. Push. Mermaid.
One, two, three. Breathe!

I felt the water gracing my skin as I soared through the pool. I felt the waterproof bandaging from the student's health office on campus protesting my every move. I knew I couldn't be in the water. I knew I shouldn't have been swimming. But damn it, I couldn't help myself.

One, two, three. Breathe!
One, two, three. Breathe!

I needed to blow off steam. I needed to center myself. Because after blowing off classes yesterday and the day before, I was feeling a bit overwhelmed. I didn't want to let my parents down. I didn't want them to throw away all this money on my education. But I also didn't want to waste their time and their hope on something I wasn't even sure I wanted any longer.

One, two, three. Breathe!

One, two, three. Breathe!

I drew in deep breaths. I kept checking in with my waterproof wrapping. Even though plastic wrap was a bad idea, I had layers of it wrapped around my leg over the gauze, with some waterproof stuff on top that the doctor at the student's office gave me. Three layers between it and the water sloshing against my skin. That was enough to protect it, right?

I really hoped so.

One, two, three. Breathe!

One, two, three. Breathe!

I touched my hand against the side of the pool and switched strokes. I threw myself onto my back, kicking and stroking as I stared up at the ceiling. With my hair underneath a rubber cap and my goggles much too tight on my face, I heaved for air. I felt my body finally winding down. After a sleepless night of nothing but studying, catching up, and reading, I needed a way to exert all of this nervous energy. I felt myself turning into something new. Something greater. Something I knew my parents wouldn't approve of.

And finally showing that to them made me sick to my stomach.

Max had turned my life upside down in the best way possible. I'd never felt so in tune with myself. Ever. I felt like I was just getting to know myself. My whole self. And it felt fantastic. The part of me that Max helped me to open up felt more natural than anything

I'd ever done with my life up until this point. I'd never been able to look at something and know so confidently that I wanted it. That I needed it.

Every time I looked at Max, I felt that way.

Your parents are going to kill you for it.

I stumbled with my turn under the water and scraped my toe. I cursed beneath the surface and forced myself back up, gasping for air in the process. I looked down and saw wisps of blood mixing in with the water. I tilted myself onto my back, floating as I brought my foot out of the water. Damn it, I'd really scraped my big toe up good. It stung, too.

I wasn't done swimming, though.

I turned around and started with a breaststroke, moving beneath the water like a graceful frog, as weird as that sounded. And as I worked my heart rate up again, my thoughts fell back to my parents.

I wasn't sure what they'd think. I mean, I knew what they would think once they figured out what was really going on. But my father took my change in major hard enough. He'd shunned me for three days because I didn't want to follow in his medical footsteps. It had been torturous, too. I loved my father. The nickname 'Daddy's girl' was apt for me. I loved him dearly. I wanted him to be happy with me. To be proud of me.

And I knew he wouldn't be if I told him any of this.

He's a criminal, Danika!

My father's voice echoed off the corners of my mind as my hands slapped against the edge of the pool.

He's a biker, for God's sake!

I pushed off the wall, the water rippling over my back.

A man with no prospects. How could you do this to yourself? To us!? As a family!?

I kept kicking beneath the water, leaving my father's voice behind in my wake. I swam beneath the surface, straining my lungs as the wall on the other side came into view. I pulled myself through the crystal liquid, kicking with all my might. My lungs protested. My eyes began to dim. And just when I felt my hand touch the wall, I came up for the biggest, most refreshing breath of air to date.

"Hiya, Bambi."

Through my goggles, I saw him. Benji, with that cocky little grin on his face. I gazed up into his menacing eyes, watching as he crouched down in front of me.

"That a new tattoo I spy on that thigh of yours? Got it wrapped up pretty tight. Why don't you come a little closer so I can get a good look at it?"

I pushed off the edge of the pool, desperate to get away from him. But he reached out quickly and caught my wrist.

"Let me go," I hissed.

His grip tightened. "You made a mistake, little deer. I know exactly what that tattoo is. And it makes you one of them. For *life*. Your timing couldn't have been any worse."

"Let. Me. Go!"

He chuckled. "Your mistake is my gain, I suppose."

I struggled to break free, but he wouldn't release me. I pressed my feet against the edge of the pool, but I felt the bandages around my thigh giving way. I gasped and quickly straightened my legs. If any water got up underneath those wrappings, I could get an infection. So I splashed him with water. Trying to get it in his eyes so he'd let me loose.

But all he did was bark with laughter.

"Cute. I'll give you that."

I snarled. "I swear to fuck, Benji, if you don't let me go, I'll scream."

He looked me dead in my eyes. "Yes. Yes, you will."

I thought he was going to drag me out of the pool. Just hoist me up and have his way with me. I didn't like the twinkle in his eye. I didn't like the feeling of his skin against my own. But, instead of pulling me out, he released my wrist. I quickly pushed off the edge of the pool, treading water a few feet away from the edge. And as he stood to his feet, smirking down his nose at me, he straightened up his jacket.

"Watch yourself, Bambi. This town isn't going to be good for the Red Thorns anymore."

My heart raced. "What are you talking about?"

He slid his hands into his pockets. "You'll see. I promise you, you'll see."

His laughter echoed off the walls as he made his way to the exit. I watched him the entire way, feeling those bandages getting looser around my thigh. He peered over his shoulder at me and winked, then disappeared out the door. And the second I could, I scrambled to the edge of the pool.

Where I hoisted myself out.

I quickly unwrapped the bandages and sighed with relief. No water had gotten in, though my skin looked irritated. I needed to air it out and get some Vaseline on it. So I slipped my goggles off and ripped off my rubber cap.

"Shit," I groaned.

As I stood to my feet, Benji's words tumbled around in my head. What did he mean by all of that? Did this have something to do with Max? Or the crew? Had they done something?

Am I in trouble?

I didn't know what to do, but I knew who to call. I had to talk with Max. I scrambled to my feet and ran into the locker room, desperate to gather my things. I slipped into my clothes, pulled my hair up into a bun and shoved my things into my backpack. Max needed to know what happened. He needed to know that Benji was bad. That Benji wasn't on his side.

And there wasn't a moment to waste.

30

MAX

"Rupert, I'm telling you. You paid last time. You had to settle that tab when I was drunk off my ass. So I'm picking this one up."

He shook his head. "I invited you out. It's my tab."

I yanked the check from him. "Tough shit, asshole."

He grinned. "I'm getting the next one."

"Yeah, you are. And we're taking shots on that one, too."

As I handed my card and my check to the waitress, I heard my phone ringing with a familiar tune. Usually, I had my phone on silent. But, with shit the way it was right now, I had my ringer on constantly. I didn't want to miss a call. Or a text. Or a voicemail. Or any notification from my guys, for that matter. But when I heard the ringtone I'd set specifically for Dani ringing from my pocket, I didn't hesitate to pick it up.

"Hey there, gorgeou--"

"Max! Max. Holy shit, thank God. You have to listen."

I quickly stood. "Where are you and what's wrong?"

Rupert stood with me, concern etched over his face.

"Max, you have to listen to me. I just--hold on. Fuck, I can't--"

"Deep breaths. Are you on campus?"

The waitress came back with my check and I nodded at her, stuffing everything into my pocket.

"I got the tip. Let's get out of here," Rupert whispered.

I pointed at the table. "Dani!"

She gasped. "Sorry, sorry. I just--I uh, I was at the pool, and I was swimming--"

"With your tattoo? Did you have it covered?"

"Damn it with the tattoo, Max! Benji was there!"

I felt my blood boiling. "What the fuck did he do to you?"

I grabbed Rupert and dragged him out of the bar. I felt all eyes on us as we rushed out the front doors. We got out to our bikes and I put her on speaker so Rupert could hear. Just in case I needed an alibi before I killed Benji myself.

"Dani, are you there?" I asked.

She sniffled. "Max, something bad is happening. This isn't like all the other times. He was talking nonsense. Talking crazy."

I growled. "Did he hurt you?"

"Benji. He-he-he--uh… he grabbed my wrist so I couldn't go anywhere. But--but I'm not hurt."

My eyes held Rupert's and I watched my best friend's face turn red.

"Where are you? Start with that question," I said.

"No, Max. Please, listen to--"

I bellowed. "Where are you!?"

Rupert squeezed my shoulder, trying to get me to calm down as Dani sniffled again.

"I'm on campus. In my dorm. He lives in my dorm building, right? Fuck. That's not good. None of this is good."

"What did he say to you? Try to recall, word for word, what he said."

She sniffled. "This wasn't like the other times he's ever cornered me, Max. He seemed… I don't know. More serious somehow. Like this wasn't just his typical bullshit he likes to rattle off. He meant what he was saying when he said something was going to happen. I'm scared, Max. What if he comes to my dorm room?"

"I'll kill him if he does that."

"Don't say that," she whispered.

"I don't say shit I don't mean. Are you alone in your dorm?"

She sighed. "Yeah. Hannah's not here. We're still not on good terms."

I nodded. "Okay. Lock your door. Stay put. I'm coming to get you. We can talk then. Face to face."

I heard a knock in the background and Dani yelped. I

heard her talking in muffled tones before something like a door opened. I whipped my leg around my bike. I pointed to Rupert and pointed to his bike. Then I flashed a small signal. One all of the guys knew by heart. With my pointer finger in the air and my thumb off to the side, I made the motion like I was shooting off a gun into the air.

Signaling for him to round up the guys at my place.

"Sorry. I'm sorry. That was Hannah. She's wondering what's going on. I think I look really flustered," she said.

I cranked up my bike. "You're going to come stay with me for a while. We'll figure out your classes as we can. Understand me? Pack a bag, get your toiletries, and pack up your electronics."

She swallowed hard. "Okay. Max?"

"Yes?"

"Please hurry."

I heard her voice crack. I heard it shaking as she uttered those small little words. I hated how scared my girl sounded. How weak she probably felt. And all because of me. Because I was an idiot. Because I was weak myself.

Because I was a selfish asshole.

"I'm leaving the bar now. I'm less than ten minutes out. Lock your door and don't you leave until I call. Got it?"

She sniffled. "Got it."

"Good. I love you."

She lowered her voice. "Love you, too."

I hung up the phone and looked over at Rupert. Who still hadn't fucking left. I glared at him as I slid my phone into my pocket and kicked up my kickstand.

"The fuck you still doing here?" I asked.

He gave me a grim look. "So, Benji does have a hand in this after all?"

I sucked air through my teeth. "Sounds like it."

"Little rat bastard. I never liked him, you know. Always thought he was a slippery little dude with a bad attitude and an uncanny knack for getting other people in trouble on his account."

I revved my engine. "Yeah, well. Not happening again. You know what to do. See you tonight."

I was pissed. So pissed that my vision started tunneling. My cousin had fucked around with my girl for the last goddamn time. It was time to teach this asshole a lesson in learning his place. And if he didn't want to stay in his damn place, I'd beat him into submission and nail him there for good. I knew Benji saw me as a peacekeeper. Someone willing to bend over and take it up the ass just to make sure no one broke out into a fight.

Well, Benji was about to get a taste of what I called 'peacekeeping tactics.'

"Max, look out!"

I whipped my head up and watched Rupert's eyes grow wide before a sharp pain in the back of my head sent me plummeting to the ground. I felt my bike fall on top of me, pinning me. The engine still churned. The bike was warming as it vibrated against me. But every time I moved to get the bike off me, a searing pain in the back of my head stopped me in my tracks.

"Get the hell off me, you piece of--mmph. Fuck. Oh, no you don't."

I coughed. "Rupert?"

I heard punches landing and boots scuffling against the tarmac.

"Rupert?"

I heard him grunting. I heard bones cracking. I felt something connect with the side of my head and it made me vomit. I felt it rising up the back of my throat. I turned my head off to the side and heaved with the pain coursing down my spine. Fucking hell. I knew enough to know I had a concussion. The one thing I couldn't do was lose consciousness.

Honk your horn.

I felt my hand along my bike. As Rupert cursed and grunted and gurgled, I slid my hand along the hot metal. I continued vomiting onto the pavement, feeling it trickle down my skin. And just as I reached the handlebar, I heard a gruff voice in my ear.

"Surprise, bitch."

A sharp pain raked up my arm and I yanked it back. I fell to the ground, staring up at the sky as I choked on my own vomit. I didn't hear Rupert any longer. I saw the sky fading into darkness from the bright blue it boasted of today. And as the world continued to go dark on me, only one thing crossed my mind.

Dani.

As my world fell silent, the only thing I could think about was Dani.

And whether or not she was all right.

31

DANI

I peeked out the window and listened to the sounds of people walking by. Giggling. Laughing. Having the time of their lives. And what was I doing?

Fearing for my own safety.

Hannah sighed. "You're stressing me out. Will you sit down already?"

I shook my head. "Can't. Something isn't right."

And it was the truth. I had spoken to Max half an hour ago, and he still hadn't arrived. Too much time had passed.

Something's happened to Max.

Hannah slapped her book closed. "Damn it, Dani. Sit down, would you? You're going to give all of us a heart attack."

I sighed. "Something's wrong. I can't sit down when something's wrong."

Her voice lowered. "No shit."

I whipped around. "The hell's that supposed to mean?"

She snickered. "You're dating a criminal, Dani. Of course something isn't right."

"You wouldn't understand. Just go back to studying."

"What? I don't understand because I've never been there, done that with a criminal? Well, let me fix your perception of me for a second. Because I have been. I've done the bad boy thing to piss my parents off. I've done the rebellion thing. It's overdone and overdue. This is exactly what I was worried about when you hooked up with him in the first place."

"Can it, Hannah. I'm trying to listen out."

"And this will keep happening, too. This is his life, Dani. This is how this man gets by. That's how guys like this are. It's not a one-off thing for them. I wanted something better for you. Something nicer. Something easier."

I growled. "I don't want easy."

She sighed. "I don't even know who you are anymore."

I stared at her. "Maybe you didn't know who I was in the first place."

I turned back toward the window. I didn't need to be dealing with her shit right now. I had enough on my plate. Like figuring out what the hell had happened to Max. He should've been here by now. I knew he wasn't far away. But how the hell could I help him?

I don't even know where he is.

"Pack. I have to keep packing."

Hannah snickered. "Yeah. What's with that anyway? You're packing as if you're going away for the summer or something."

"Again, wouldn't understand."

"Try me."

"No, thanks. I've heard enough of your mouth to last a lifetime."

She scoffed. "I don't know what you've done with the Dani I love and cherish, but I'd like her back, please."

I shoved shirts into my bag. "Yeah, well, she's not coming back. Don't like it? Get a new roommate."

I walked over to my closet and ripped it open. If I had more time to pack, then I might as well pack as much as I could. I ripped shirts off the hangers. I pulled open drawers and picked up socks. Panties. Jeans. I shoved it all into my bag until the damn thing wouldn't zip. Then I paused to see if I heard Max. I walked back to the window. I peeked out it again. And when I didn't hear him, I rushed to my bag.

Pouring the contents out over my bed.

"Now, what are you doing?"

I shook my head. "Will you shut the fuck up? No one wants to hear you talk anymore."

Hannah paused. "Wow. I knew this man might change you. But I didn't think he'd make you into a bully, Dani."

I sighed. "When you stop bullying me about my choices in men, I'll stop bullying you about your unwanted opinions on every single part of my life. Okay?"

I looked back at her and her gaze dropped to her book. She flipped it back open and I started rolling my clothes down as small as I could get them. If I had things my way, I'd just move in with Max. Commute to and from school. Save my parents' money on campus housing. But I'd settle for a new roommate.

No, not a new roommate. A new dorm.

I needed a new dorm.

I picked up my phone and sent a text message to Max. Where the hell was he? I needed to know what was going on. I leaned against my bed and started looking up the paperwork information for requesting a dorm room change. I needed something across campus, even if that meant my classes would be a hike. Preferably, the dorm room across the street from campus police.

What's that dorm building's name again?

"And another thing, Dani. What is it with you and this--?"

I groaned. "Hannah, I can't with you right now. Max is in trouble, I need to figure out what the hell's happened, and the last thing I need to be doing is bickering with you. You want to bicker with someone? Call my parents. They'll bicker with you until you're blue in the face. But unless you want to be my friend again, I have no interest in speaking with you. Let alone fighting with you. I'll be doing that enough with my parents once they find out everything that's going on."

She paused. "Trouble? And you want to help this man? Do you even hear yourself?"

I whipped around on her. "I hear myself just fine!"

My voice bellowed over our dorm room and Hannah winced. Physically winced. I felt my fists balling up and my heart rate skyrocketing out of control. I needed her to back off. I needed her to be done with this shit for a little while. I turned around and took in deep breaths, forcing myself to continue packing. Because the more time that passed, the more I was convinced I wasn't ever coming back to this damn room.

"What do you think you're going to do, Dani?"

Hannah's voice was light. Calm. Collected. A far cry from the tinny, prissy voice I'd gotten lately from her. I felt my back tense as my movements paused. I clutched a pair of jeans to my stomach as Hannah stood behind me. Hovering. Interjecting. Poking her nose around where it didn't belong.

"If Max really is in trouble, what in the world do you think you can do for him?" she asked.

I snickered. "You have no idea what I'm capable of."

"Do you have a gun?"

I turned around. "What?"

She shrugged. "He carries a gun, right? Do you have one so you can shoot your way to him?"

"That isn't the--"

"Do you have anyone else you can call? A friend of his?"

"I can call them, yeah."

"Do you have their numbers? Right now? So you can stop blowing up his phone and call them?"

I swallowed hard. "All I have to do is--"

"Do you know where he goes to hide? Where he goes to hang out? Where he might flee to if he's in trouble? Do you two have a rendezvous point? A code word, in case shit goes south?"

I blinked. "What in the world is up with your questions?"

Her face fell. "Like I said, been there, done it. You're not capable of helping him. You don't have the tools to save him from whatever it is you think he's gotten wrapped up in. If you march out those doors, the only thing you are is dead."

"And how do you know that?"

"Judging by how frantic you've been for the past forty minutes? I'd say that's enough for me to go 'I just know, Dani.'"

I blinked. "It's been forty minutes now?"

I whipped back around to my bag and started packing quicker. I rolled up my things and shoved them inside, finally getting all of my clothes in there. She didn't understand. Even if she thought she understood, she didn't. Obviously, she hadn't loved her guy like I did if she wasn't still with him. I loved Max. And he loved me. And together, we were unstoppable.

"If he doesn't pull up in ten minutes, I'm going to look for him myself."

Hannah put her hand on my shoulder. "And what do you think you're going to do? Seriously? Consider that question for a second."

I slapped her hand away and spun around. I was tired of her antics. Tired of her judgment. Tired of her fucking bullshit. I unbuckled my jeans and pushed them down my legs. I pulled up the gauze against my thigh, showing her the tattoo. I trembled with fury. I was so angry I could've put my fist through her shocked face. And when her eyes slowly slid back up to my own, I forced myself to talk evenly.

"There isn't anything you can say that's going to change my mind, Hannah. I love him. I'm with him until the end. Whether you care about it, or not."

She took a step back. "Holy fuck, is that thing real?"

I pulled my pants up. "Yes."

She shook her head. "Jesus. Who are you? Where did this person come from? My God, if your parents knew--"

"They don't, and they won't. Not until I tell them. You got that? They don't need to know. I'm a grown-ass woman living in a grown-ass world with grown-ass issues. I don't need permission, or approval, or a go-ahead from any of you. I'm finally figuring things out for myself. And I just wish you were on board."

"When it's turned you into this, how can I be on board? This isn't you, Dani."

"You have no idea what 'me' is. You've only known me for a little over a year. All you know is the scared little girl I was coming into college. Weren't you the one that wanted to get me out there? Weren't you the one that wanted to get me laid?"

She shook her head. "This isn't on me. This is all you. I meant going to some parties, Dani. Dating a few boys and finding one you might have liked."

"Yeah, well. I found one I loved. That I've given my all to."

She blinked. "You haven't--?"

"Like I'd fucking tell you anyway. Look, Hannah, I can't force this on you. Do I wish you were on my side? Yep. Do I wish we were still friends? Yep."

"We're still friends."

"We're hardly roommates, Hannah! Look at us! I can't stand you! And you can't stand me, either. I'm done trying. I'm done trying to make you see my way with things. If you can't take me as I am like this, then I don't think we can--"

"Don't you dare. Don't you dare say what you're about to say."

I swallowed. "I still love you. I always will. You were my first roommate. My first ever friend on campus. But, I can't keep doing this. I *won't* keep doing this."

I turned my back to her and slid my toiletries into the open spaces in my bag. I couldn't utter the words. I didn't have the strength. But damn it, part of me wanted to. I felt my throat tighten as Hannah sniffled behind me. I didn't want to lose my best friend over this. But I couldn't deal with her incessant criticism, either. Not any longer. It was too much, and I'd had enough.

"That how you really feel?"

Hannah voice was so soft that it almost broke my heart.

Almost.

"Yes. It's how I really feel."

She snickered. "Fine, then. I'll find somewhere else to live."

I zipped up my bag. "Not a problem. I'm already looking at new dorm buildings as we speak. Since I'm apparently the issue, it's my responsibility to move anyway. Happy trails."

"Wait, Dani. Stop. Please. We can talk this out. We can--"

I unlocked the door and ripped it open, slamming it against the wall. I still didn't hear Max's bike off in the distance, but I couldn't wait a second longer. I had a car. A nice one, at that. I could go out looking for him if I had to. And, if all else failed, I'd get a hotel close to campus for the night with the bit of money I had in my account. I knew that would raise suspicions with my parents. I knew it would prompt them to call me. But the idea was there as a last-ditch resort.

"Dani!"

Hannah yelled my voice down the hallway as I stopped outside the elevator. I jammed my hand into the buttons, thankful the door opened up immediately. I pulled my phone out as I stepped inside. I heard Hannah rushing down the hallway toward me.

"Dani, wait. Please!"

I pressed my finger against the 'door close' button, watching as she faded away. The doors closed before I heard her fists slam against it, and the elevator started moving. I sighed with relief. I looked up and watched the levels tick by. Until I was all the way at the bottom.

Then I started for my car.

I checked my phone and grew more anxious. I had

no texts from Max. No phone calls. No voicemails. I stepped outside and felt as if I was being watched, but I wasn't sure if that was my paranoia spiking or not. I hustled to the parking garage, thankful that my car was close. I tossed my things into the back before slipping behind the wheel. And the first thing I did was lock my doors.

Before shooting Max a text.

Me: I don't know what's happening, but I'm heading to your place. If you get this, please meet me there. Or tell John you're okay so he can talk to me. Or Rupert. Or someone. Please.

Tears slid down my cheeks. I didn't even realize I was crying until I felt them dribbling down my neck. I cranked up the engine and backed out of the parking space before a horn started blaring at me. I screamed bloody murder. I looked in my rearview mirror. I saw someone flick me off before they raced off, making their way to the second level of the parking garage. I gripped the steering wheel tightly. And as I sucked down my fear, I eased myself out of the parking space.

Heading straight for the exit of the parking garage.

32

___

MAX

The first thing I felt was the pain at the base of my head. Shit, it felt like someone had impaled me with something. Moving my head hurt. I couldn't even dream of opening my eyes. Were they swollen shut? They didn't feel swollen.

They're heavy.

I went to move my wrists, but couldn't. My eyes snapped open with that truth. My head swam and I felt myself growing nauseous again, so I heaved over to the side. Moving my head was excruciating. I needed a goddamn doctor. But what I needed more than that was to be able to move my arms.

Or my legs, for that matter.

I struggled to get my bearings. When bile wasn't working its way up the back of my throat, my mind swam with so many other questions. Like Rupert. Where the hell was Rupert? Was Dani all right? Who the absolute fuck made this decision to tie me to this chair?

Because it would certainly be their last.

I squinted my eyes as I gazed around the darkened room. There was a light hanging above my head. High above, actually. I tilted my head back, but it was painful to stare into the light. It made my head swim. My eyes felt as if they were screaming. Yep. There was no doubt in my mind that I had a concussion. And every second that passed meant my inevitable death if I didn't get it taken care of.

Where the fuck is Rupert?

I looked around for him. I resisted the urge to call out his name. So far, the only things I knew were this: I was alone in a big room, with ceilings that were vaulted high, and the damn place smelled like rust. And mildew. And there were metal beams holding the ceiling up.

Like a warehouse.

Holy shit, I was tied up in a warehouse somewhere. I had no clue where I was, either. How long had I been knocked out? I needed answers to these questions. My head was on a swivel, no matter how much it hurt. I needed something--anything--to tell me where I was. But, more importantly, I needed to figure out how to get out of these binds around my wrists and ankles.

My eye caught something red and I squinted, cursing the light for shining down onto me instead of at whatever the fuck that was against the wall. I tried scooting my chair, but it didn't budge. And when I say it didn't budge, I mean it didn't move. It didn't tip. It didn't tilt. It didn't do a damn thing.

My eyes fell downward.

I know where I am.

The second those bolted legs came into view, it clicked. The red on the wall. The high beams. The singular light. The metal chair with its legs bolted to the concrete floor. I was in my father's warehouse. A place I'd been many times. I even knew the room I was in. I knew what part of the warehouse and what room he had me tied up in.

And it didn't bode well for me.

My father had his warehouse sectioned off into certain areas. The main room in the middle was for shipping containers and product he moved. Priceless artifacts shipped from one point to another, with him taking a cut off the top. That was, by far, his biggest money maker. So long as he got his fifteen percent and a rental fee for the days someone had to use his warehouse, he asked no questions and didn't poke or prod as to what was being shipped around. This place was always fucking busy.

Which was why it worried me that I heard nothing.

Suddenly, footsteps sounded in the corner. The light grew brighter over my head, forcing my eyes closed. The footsteps grew closer. They shuffled around, and I tried my best to pinpoint the canter of the walk. It sounded familiar. I felt my blood already bubbling as my gut comprehended what my mind was slow to take in.

"How the mighty have fallen."

Benji's voice hit my ear and I wanted to snap his neck.

"Where's Rupert?" I growled.

He dipped down into my view. "Wow. You've seen better days, Maxwell."

I lunged at him. "Don't you dare use my full name, you slimy piece of shit. Where the fuck is Rupert!?"

My roaring voice echoed off the corners of the massive building as Benji stood up. With a crooked grin on his face, he crossed his arms over his chest. I hated how blurry he was. I hated how my mind didn't feel right. Everything was hazy. As if I were walking through fog and reliving memories.

I had to get out of my bonds.

"Are you really going to continue struggling with your brain swelling the way it is?"

I snarled. "Listen here, you slimy snake, I know damn good and well you're working with my father. I know damn good and well you're doing this because I won't let you rush the fucking club. Well, you want to know why I won't let you rush!?"

He snickered. "Because I'm apparently unreliable. Or, so you've told me."

"No. Because you have a future well beyond the club."

He paused. "What?"

I leaned back into the chair. "I pressed college and didn't let you rush because you're smart, Benji. You have a future beyond the club. Beyond the bloodshed. Beyond the firefights and my father's whimsically disgusting ways. I never let you pledge because you're better than that."

"You--you did--you did that for me?"

I nodded. "Yeah. I did, you shithead."

A searing pain cracked me across my face and my head fell to the side. The involuntary roar of pain that escaped my throat before I vomited again reminded me of just how vulnerable I was. I hated that feeling, too. Dread filled my gut. I coughed and sputtered as spit dangled from my lip. Then, I felt someone fist my hair before my eyes found Benji's again.

"You don't get to make that decision for me, El Presidente. It's my life. I do what I want with it. Whether you like that shit or not. Got it?"

He shoved my head, forcing me to heave again. And I made a vow to myself. Then, and there.

Benji dies by my hand.

"You're right," I murmured.

"What was that?"

He dragged my head around for a bit before his gaze found mine.

"Say that one more time, All Powerful One?"

I grimaced. "You're right."

He grinned. "Perfect. Glad you know your place. You're right. I am smarter than all of you. I mean, look at where you're sitting and where I'm, well, standing."

I chuckled. "Cute."

He released my hair. "Yeah, I thought so."

He took a few steps away from me before I licked my lips.

"Tell me where Rupert is."

He shrugged. "And if I don't?"

"You die."

He barked with laughter. "By what hand? Yours? The ones that are bound to that chair?"

"You have no idea what I'm capable of. Don't think that because you're smarter, you're also stronger. Because you're not."

"And yet, here we are."

"Trust me, I'm positive you didn't put me here."

He snarled. "That so?"

I smiled. "That's so, yes. Now, tell me. Where the fuck is Rupert?"

"Probably still face down in the gravel outside the pub. I mean, he put up a pretty good fight. Fruitless, though. A good one nonetheless. But, you know, energy expended for nothing, and all that."

I tugged at my restraints. "If you've hurt him, I swear to God--"

"Oh, we definitely hurt him. That was the goal. But don't worry. What we're going to do to you will make his injuries look like child's play."

I strained at the bonds again. "What the fuck is this all about, anyway? Huh? Because I know you. And even I know this isn't all stemming from the fact that I wouldn't let you become a Red Thorn. You're more even-tempered than that."

He sighed. "You really are an idiot, aren't you?"

I watched as Benji began pacing. He kept sighing. Talking to himself. Almost as if he had gone crazy. I watched him while he moved. My eyes were finally focusing so I could see more of my surroundings. And it confirmed a lot of what I thought. I was in one of the middle rooms. One of my father's sterile rooms. They had no windows. Only one door to get in and out. And everything was covered in plastic wrap. Everything. The red I saw on the wall was actually tape. The ends of the plastic wrap that covered every square inch of the room was bonded together with that red fucking tape my father used.

Oh, this isn't good.

"You know, I've always wondered something."

Benji's voice caught my attention as I tried to work my wrists out of the bonds.

"And what is that, smartypants?"

He snickered. "Cute. I've always wondered why you picked Dani."

I froze. "Don't you dare say her name."

He shrugged. "I mean, she's got no curves. So it can't be her body."

"Don't you talk about her!"

"She's not brave, so it's not her strength."

"You don't know a fucking thing about her."

"She's thrown her life away for you, so it can't be her future. Or any money she might have. Which leaves me with only one option."

I felt my heart rate skyrocketing as I felt the bonds finally loosening around my wrists.

"And what would that be?" I asked.

He grinned. "I guess college virgins really are worth the ride."

I growled. "That's it!"

From the shadows behind Benji emerged two men.

Just as I got one of my hands out of the bonds, they rushed me, forcing my arms back behind the chair. I fought against them, feeling the bolts adhering the chair to the floor slowly giving way. I roared and screamed. I called out for Benji. For my father. I promised death to them all as the two men tied my wrists tighter this time. Almost to a point where I couldn't feel my damn hands.

"Benji, goddamn it! What the fuck are you doing!?"

And as the men dressed in black cracked their knuckles, my cousin smiled. Making my gut seize in something I hadn't felt since I was a child.

Fear.

"Business, Max. That's what this is about. It's always just been business."

DANI

I squealed into the driveway of Max's home. The lights were off. It didn't look like anyone was there. Which didn't bode well for what was coming. I leapt out of my car, grabbing my keys and my phone. I locked everything up and rushed for the front door, banging on it with all of my might.

"Hello!? John, Max! Are you in there!?"

I kept banging and banging, but my efforts were fruitless. The door was locked. The side door was locked. And no matter where I looked, I couldn't find a spare key.

"Fuck!" I exclaimed.

My phone started vibrating and I almost threw it across the lawn. Especially when I saw Hannah's name pop up. I didn't need her shit right now. What I needed was to find Max. I needed to get to him. He needed my help.

Something was very wrong, and the Red Thorns needed my help.

I ignored her phone call and headed back for my car. She called me again and I ignored it again, shooting her to voicemail. But I didn't even get the car cranked up before she called through yet again. I growled to myself. I got the engine running and picked up the phone call through my car's Bluetooth hook-up. I didn't need this. Talking to her was the absolute last thing I wanted to do.

But, if she was going to call me incessantly, I needed to get her to stop.

"Dani?" she breathed.

"What?"

She paused. "I need to tell you something."

"What is it? Make it quick."

My mind was already back to Max. Where was he? Where had he been taken? What the hell was going on? More than an hour had passed since he was due to pick me up on campus. Something was definitely up in all the wrong ways. But all I could do was wait for someone to show up at the house. So, I hunkered down into my seat.

"Spit it out, Hannah. I don't have all night."

She spoke quickly. "I'm sorry but I called your father!"

I blinked. "You did what?"

She sighed. "I called your father, Dani. I was worried. I'm scared for you. I still am. And I know this might make you hate me but I had to do it because you're my best friend. There's only one way this thing with Max is going to end and--"

"Your gut reaction was to call my fucking father about it!? Who the hell do you think you are?"

"I'm your best friend, even if you don't want to accept that right now. You're in trouble, and I know your father can help you."

"Yeah, help me get away from Max, just like you want. Why the fuck can't you just accept things? Why the hell do I always have to be like you? Why can't you just shut your fucking face!?"

She sniffled. "I'm sorry. It's the only thing I could think of."

I stumbled over my words. "What? When? Why-- how--how the hell do you even have his number?"

"He gave it to me at the beginning of our freshman year. Said that if you ever struggled or needed anything and you wouldn't reach out, to call him. He said college was hard, and that you might--"

I leaned up. "I might what?"

She paused. "That you might not be truthful with them once you got out into the real world."

I narrowed my eyes. "What did you do? Tell me exactly what you told him."

"I told him about Max. I told him who he was. *What* he is. And I told him you were in over your head and I didn't know how to help you."

My head spun. I wanted to kill her. For the first time in my life, I understood why people killed other people. My hands gripped the steering wheel. I felt my anger spiraling out of control. How the hell did I get this girl out of my life? How the fuck did I cut her out for good?"

"You listen here, you meddling little bitch--"

"No, for once, you listen to me. I don't want you to hate me over this. That's the last thing I want. But what I want is my friend back. What I want is the real Dani back."

"I am the real Dani!"

"No, you're not! I think you feel that way, but I know this isn't you. I know you."

I growled. "You don't know shit about me."

"I know you feel like you're floundering right now. That you're being pulled in all sorts of directions. But, I promise you, if this is what it takes to keep you safe, then I'm willing to destroy our friendship over it."

I couldn't even catch my breath to respond.

"He's not a good guy, Dani. You don't know him like you think you do. You just like the *idea* of him. Of the danger and the leather and the--"

A loud beep resounded in my car, cutting off Hannah's train of thought. Which was the only thing that saved her from my urge to go back to campus and take a swing at her with a wine bottle in my hand. I didn't recognize the number, and I switched over immediately. I didn't even give my bullshit friend the courtesy of telling her I had another call coming in.

Not like she deserves it.

"Who is this?" I asked.

The man groaned. "Dani. Thank fuck."

Goosebumps prickled my arms. "Rupert. Thank God. Where are you? Are you with Max?"

He groaned. "No."

Something was wrong with his voice. He sounded tired. Or hurt.

"Are you okay?" I asked.

He moaned. "No. The same fuckers who jumped Max at your school came back for him tonight. I tried to stop them, Dani. I did. But they caught us with our guard down."

"Where is he?"

"They took him."

I blinked. "Took him? Took him where. Was he hurt?"

He grunted. "They uh--they, they they--"

"Take a breath, Rupert. You need to talk to me. We need to find him."

He sighed. "They knocked him out cold. Piled him into a dark SUV. I don't know where they went. I'm on my way to John right now. He should be at the house. Max wants me to rally the boys. I need you to call me if you hear from him, okay?"

"Rupert, I'm at the house. No one's here."

He paused. "You're where?"

"Look, it's a lot to explain. Max was supposed to come--"

"I know, I know. He was on his way to get you. You're at the house? You need to get somewhere else. Anywhere else. Somewhere no one would think to find you. Okay?"

"John isn't here! That's what I'm trying to tell you. No one's at the house."

"Fuck," he hissed.

I threw my car in reverse. "I'm going to help you look for Max. Where are some places he might--"

"No, Dani. You do as I'm telling you and you leave this shit to us. This is what we do. We'll find Max. We'll handle this. But, the last thing we need is you getting involved and making things worse."

His words stung, but I moved past it. "He needs me."

"Damn it, Bambi. What Max needs right now is for you to keep yourself safe. I know how much he cares about you. And no matter where he is right now, I know he's worried about you. Don't give him something to worry about once we get him out of this predicament."

I heard him groaning still as I backed into the road.

"I'm telling you, Bambi. I'll find him. We'll get him out. And I'll let you know as soon as it's done. Stay put. Keep whatever door you have locked. Text this number and tell me where you are once you get there. Save it in your phone, too. This is my number. And if you hear from Max, at all, you call me immediately. Got it? Good."

Then, he hung up the phone.

"Dani! Damn it, if you don't pick up this phone back right now--"

I groaned. "Will you shut up, Hannah?"

She paused. "Finally. You're back. Why the hell didn't you tell me you were switching over?"

"Because you're not important right now."

"Wow. Ouch. But, okay. What's going on?"

"Like I'd tell you. I gotta go."

"Dani! Don't hang up. We have to talk. Dan--!"

I cut the call and picked up my phone. I put a temporary block on Hannah's number so I wouldn't be bombarded with her stupid calls or text messages. I'd have to deal with my father later. Because some things were simply more important. I sat in the middle of the darkened road, gripping my steering wheel tightly. I looked into the darkness and felt it staring back at me. Taunting me, as Rupert's words rushed around in my head.

The last thing we need is you getting involved and making things worse.

I stepped on the gas pedal and took off. I didn't know how I was going to find Max, but I sure as hell wasn't sitting around and doing nothing. I wasn't a damsel in distress. I didn't need saving. I didn't need protecting. What I needed was for Max to be alive, to come back safely. I wasn't going to sit around in a driveway or in a dorm room or in a hotel somewhere waiting for my damn phone to ring.

"I'm not the weak girl I used to be," I murmured.

I raced into the darkness. I felt it swallowing me whole as I peeled around the corner. My tattoo called to me. To my soul. To my heart, as it throbbed against my thigh. I was a Red Thorn. Or, close to it. I felt it run through my veins and fill my gut. And if there was one thing I'd learned about the Red Thorns, it was the fact that they fought for what was theirs.

And I sure as hell was going to fight for Max.

MAX

"Max!"

"Dani?"

"Max! Over here!"

I turned around and saw her waving in the distance. A thin figure on the horizon, flagging me down with all her might. I smiled as her voice graced my ear. I whipped my leg over my bike and made the engine roar. I heard her giggling. Even from so far away. And as I grew closer, I saw her hand reaching out for me.

"Get on here, gorgeous."

She laughed. "Take me away, big boy."

She clung to me, and the wind whipped around us. We passed through beautiful wooded areas and tore through a field of wildflowers. Rivers rushed. Fish jumped out of ponds as I wrapped us around the incredible expanse of land in front of us. Her cheek pressed against my back and her hands gripped my shirt. Her legs pressed hard against mine as I picked up the pace.

"Where are we going?" I asked.

She giggled. "You'll see."

I felt her leading me. I felt every turn I had to take just before I took it. The earth spoke to me, guiding me all the way up to a cabin in the woods. There was a lake off in the distance. A beautiful mountain scene right off the front porch. I parked my bike and we slid off, her hand gripping mine as tightly as she could.

"Come on. You're falling behind!"

Then her hand slipped out of my grasp.

"Fuck," I choked out.

Benji's laughter filled my ear instead of hers. And I wanted to gouge his eyes out.

"Hit him again."

A sharp pain worked its way up my abs as my head fell back.

"One more time, just to make sure we drive the point home."

I coughed up blood as a boot connected with my stomach. My head fell forward, my body practically dangling from the chair. I looked down at the floor and it wasn't the lush wildflowers I had been lost in with Dani. It was the cold, hard, concrete floor of my father's warehouse.

With Benji hovering over me like a tyrant.

"You really are something, you know that?"

I spat blood on his boots before he wrenched my head back.

"You really are a son of a bitch. Just like your father."

I growled. "You'll never be who you think you are. From the moment we're born, we have a place in life. And you refuse to accept yours."

He grinned. "Trust me, I learned from the best."

Benji stood back as my head fell off to the side.

"Why don't we try a little more foreplay this time?"

The man dressed in black crammed his steel toe boot into my groin and my eyes rolled back. The pain was unbearable. I could barely see out of my eyes. Blood dripped from places it never should. I couldn't feel my hands. The skin from around my ankles had been ripped away because of how hard I'd struggled against those bonds. And the more maniacal Benji became, the more I feared for my brother. For my boys.

For Dani.

I mean, if my cousin and my own fucking father were willing to come after me like this, what would they do to everyone else? It made me sick to think about. It made my head spin with anger. I gritted my teeth as another punch landed against my jawline. Hoping and praying the man didn't break my fucking jaw in the process. And as my head jerked to the side, I watched blood and spit fly from the tip of my tongue.

"Stop," Benji declared.

"Come on, Max. You're such a slowpoke!"

I chuckled. "I'm going to get you, gorgeous."

She squealed. "No! No tickling! That's not fair!"

"It's completely fair when you're taunting me with your body like this."

We fell to the bed as my hands danced over her body. Over her skin. Along the perfection that was her. I saw her tattoo aching to be kissed. I gripped her waist and let my lips fall against the beautiful colors. My Dani. My beautiful, strong, intelligent Dani. Delicate to the touch, but tough to her core.

"My Bambi," I murmured.

"I wonder how Dani will take her punishment."

Benji's voice ripped me from my happy place and my blood ran cold.

"What the fuck did you say?" I asked.

He chuckled. "You know, she's tougher than she was just a month ago. I'll give her that. But she's still just a weak, scared, confused little deer."

"You won't lay a finger on her. Do you hear me!?"

My head jolted to the side as one of the guys backhanded me across my cheek.

"How easy do you think it will be to make her crack, Max? I mean, really? Because I'm thinking neither of my guys will get a hit in before she starts singing louder than she does in bed with you."

I lunged at him, straining against my bonds. I felt my wrists cracking open and my ankles bleeding. My ass almost got out of the chair as I growled at him. Benji grinned at me.

"Wow, what a show. You're really good at it. But I think we'll just have to look at her funny and she'll break. Like a piece of glass. And then the *real* fun will begin."

"I will slaughter you all. Do you hear me!?"

"It's a nice little hope, isn't it? Thinking you can defend some girl who squeezes your cock nice like that. But really, Max. What are you going to do in your current predicament? I mean, even if you could get out of this place, what kind of condition are you in to go after her?"

I fell back into the chair as sweat dripped down my brow. Every cut and every wound it dripped over only added to my pain. I heard the men snarling. Chuckling. Practically drooling for another slice of me. And as I closed my eyes, I wracked my brain as to how the fuck I was going to get myself out of this situation.

So I could get to Dani.

"She should've never gotten that tattoo, Max. Such a mistake on her part. And yours. If she'd stayed away we wouldn't have had to drag her into this. Why did you drag her into this, anyway?"

I shook my head. "You'll never find her."

He snickered. "What makes you think we already haven't?"

Fucking hell, I wanted to cry. "I'm sure the guys already have her safe somewhere. You'll have to tear through all of them before you get to her."

"Max, you're so stupid."

My eyes flew up to him as he walked toward me.

"We were going to take all of your men out, anyway," he said.

I lunged at him, baring my teeth. He didn't move quickly enough and I sank my mouth against his cheek. I bit down deep and felt his blood in my mouth. The rabid animal finally came loose and I felt the men pulling me back.

"Get him off! Get him off me!"

Benji's shrieks were music to my ears.

"Off, off, get him off, you stupid fuckers!"

The men finally yanked me back and the sound of ripping skin followed me. I watched Benji grab his cheek as blood dripped into his hand. One of the men gripped my cheeks. The other pried my mouth open.

And when I had my chance, I spat the piece of Benji's cheek at him before I grinned.

With that bastard's blood dripping down my chin.

"I'm off," I said with a chuckle.

Benji growled. "That's it. No loose ends. You hear me? They're all dead, including that stupid cock-hugger of yours. By the time I'm done with all of this, every single one of you will be in a casket. But not before I fuck her first. Just to see what the fuck has you so goddamn addicted!"

I chuckled. "Well, you know what they say about family bonds."

He paused. "What's that?"

I snapped the rope around my wrists. "They can be broken in a second."

I stood to my feet as Benji's eyes widened. The straining and the distractions were enough to loosen them. I felt my feet wiggling free as the men came at me. I wrapped my hands around the back of their heads, knocking them together. Benji stumbled back in fear. I reached down and untied my ankles as the men in black struggled to get up from the ground. Their gold fucking rings wouldn't help them this time around.

Not with the fury already balling up my fists.

I leapt away from the chair and made my move. Benji ducked down like the wimpy little pussy he'd always been and I came down with my fist against the nape of his neck. He fell to the ground, his cheek still bleeding. And as the men scrambled from the floor, I kicked him in the stomach.

"Is this what you wanted!? Huh!?"

I kicked him again, feeling his ribs cracking with every connection.

"You tell me where the fuck Dani is now, you piece of shit. Tell me!"

I went to go kick him again, but felt someone grab my jacket. I twisted around, slipping my arms out of it before wrapping it around the man's head. I stepped down onto the back of Benji's head as I tumbled backwards, cutting off the man's ability to breathe. And as my cousin coughed up his own blood, I choked the man out until he lay there lifeless.

"I'm ready for round two, assholes."

The other man in black came at me and I quickly stood up. All the pain in my body faded away with the adrenaline spike as I beat him to a bloody pulp. I got him within fist range and I unloaded. All of my anger. All of my fury. All of my fears. I landed punch after punch to the man's face as it cracked and shattered beneath my knuckles.

"Is. This. What. You. Wanted!?"

I tossed the unconscious man to the ground before I turned back to Benji. He stumbled to his feet, the gaping hole in his cheek making me smile. I made my way for him. He scrambled back toward the wall. Nowhere to go for this scared little animal. Nowhere for him to run.

My nostrils flared. "I told you that you were smart."

"Max, don't. Don't do this. You don't know what's coming."

I fisted his shirt. "But I never told you that you were strong."

"Max, please!"

I mocked him. "Max, please. Wow. Very *cute*, Benji. Now, tell me. Where the fuck is my girl?"

"I-I-I--I don't--"

I slammed him against the wall, watching as his head bounced against the cement.

"Where the fuck is Dani!?"

I punched him across his face before I stood him upright again.

"For every second that passes by, that's another part of your body that doesn't work. Tell me where she is."

He sputtered. "I--she's--"

I kneed him in his gut. "Tell me. Now."

He gasped. "I'm trying. I just--"

I headbutted him, crushing his nose. "Tell me!"

"Your father! She's with your father! He's going after her, damn it. Stop! My damn nose is in my brain, holy fuck!"

I shoved him against the wall one last time. I took a step back, watching as he crumpled to the ground. Someone groaned behind me, but I didn't give a shit as to who it was. What I needed to do was get the hell out of here.

I need a car.

I dipped down to Benji's trembling body, curled up into a ball. I chuckled as I searched his pockets before I finally found them. Keys. They had to be to a vehicle around here somewhere. And as I turned toward the door, I saw one of the guys trying to get up.

"Don't even," I said.

I walked over to him and drew my foot back. I sent it hurling against his face, hearing him gurgle before he passed out again. With the keys in my hand and a goal in mind, I stormed through the door and navigated the dark hallways of the warehouse. Finally pouring out a side exit to go in search of the vehicle.

I needed to get to Dani. I needed to go get her. I needed to get her somewhere safe before I eliminated my father for good. Because if my father got to her first, he would do something worse than kill her. He'd torture her. He'd rape her. Damn it, he might even ship her off somewhere. I knew the kinds of things my father had his hands in. He could make anyone take their own life if he dangled the right thing in front of them. I clicked the alarm button for the car. I saw the lights and heard the horn through the woods that surrounded the warehouse and took off, ignoring the pain in my head as I lunged for the car.

I wasn't going to let anything happen to Dani.

Even if I had to kill my own father myself.

35

DANI

What in the world were you thinking!?

My mother's voice chastised me as I raced down the road. I skidded around corners and sat anxiously at red lights, debating on whether or not to run them. It was dark. The night sky taunted me every time the lights turned green. And once they did, I raced off into the darkness as it rushed by me.

What the hell is wrong with you? Where's your sense?

My father's voice made me wince. I had no idea what in the world he'd say to me once we spoke, but it wouldn't be good. It never was. My father would condemn him. He'd tell me I was no longer allowed to see Max. Hell, he'd probably pull me out of school and refuse to pay for my education if I didn't do as he asked. It wouldn't work, though. My father would eventually get a very stern piece of my mind. Just like Hannah had.

I forbid you to see him. Do you hear me?

"No one can forbid me to do anything," I murmured.

I gripped the steering wheel as the bar came into view. I pressed down onto the gas, shoving my parents' voices out of my head. I didn't want to focus on how my father would berate me. How my mother would probably start crying. How they'd both ask me what in the world I was thinking and what kind of person I had turned into. I forgot about it all. I let it all slip away as my tires skidded into the parking lot. It took all the focus I had to keep control of my SUV as I careened into the handicap spaces.

"Max!" I exclaimed.

I shoved my car door open and turned off the engine. I gripped my keys and made sure I had my phone on me before I leapt out of the car. I had to find him. At the very least, I had to find Rupert. And if he was gathering up the guys, this is where they'd be.

"Max!"

I slammed my car door behind me and my keys dropped from my hand. I grumbled to myself as I picked them up, trying to figure out where I'd go next. This place practically looked deserted. For a biker bar, it was empty of bikes. Hell, it didn't even look like anyone was here.

Was anyone here?

"Rupert? John? Max!?"

I stood up and caught my reflection in the mirror. My worried, sweating, haggard reflection. I shoved my keys into my pocket and drew in a few deep breaths. I wasn't going to find Max in the disheveled condition I was in.

I had to be calm so I could think straight.

Check the bar. Check around back. Head to his house.

I'd break into the damn place if it meant finding something I needed.

Suddenly, a shadow cloaked me. A figure appeared behind me in the reflection of the window and I drew in a deep breath. I let out a scream before the man grabbed me. He pulled me away from my car, causing my feet to stumble over themselves.

"Help!" I roared.

The man clamped his hand over my mouth. "You won't need help where you're going."

My arms flailed. "Let me go."

My words were muffled as I breathed raggedly through my nose.

"Not another sound," he whispered into my ear. "You're coming with me without a fight, or he dies."

I froze. This person was talking about Max. His grip grew tighter and I stopped struggling. I fought the urge to keep screaming. I felt the man's free hand running down my side and I trembled with fear. I felt his hand slip into my pocket and I grimaced at the way his touch felt. He plucked my keys out of my pocket and dangled them in front of me. With a chuckle, they disappeared. And I prayed that he didn't do the same thing with my phone.

"Now, come on. In you go."

He dragged me over to a car before stuffing me into the back seat. I tumbled in headfirst, barely catching myself before I fell to the floorboards. The door slammed behind me as I tried to get my bearings. And the next thing I knew, the car was peeling away from the bar.

I clamored up just enough to watch my pearl white SUV fade away into the night.

I didn't have my purse. Which meant I had no money. I didn't have my keys. Or my driver's license. My only hope was my phone, and there was nowhere to hide in this stupid compact car so I could use it. I sat down onto the seat, facing the man as he drove with black leather gloves on his hands. He was covered from head to toe in black. Even his hair was sleek black. In the darkness, he had on sunglasses. In the soft, cool temperatures of the fall weather, he dressed as if we were in the Arctic. Every inch of him was covered in something.

I have to get out of here.

I looked over at the door handles, but my eyes widened. What the fuck? The insides of the doors didn't have handles. I scooted over to the door, looking around for the lock. I started pressing buttons, but the driver started chuckling.

"Good luck," he said.

I searched around for something. Anything. A weapon. A secret handle. A crowbar. A fucking bobby pin, for crying out loud. Anything to help get me out of this mobile prison. I shoved my shoulder into the door. Then I did it again. And again. Hoping and praying that my sheer force of will would send the thing opening.

The man reached back and fisted my hair.

"Ah!"

He hissed. "Sit still, or you're dead before we get back. Got it?"

I nodded quickly. "Got it."

"Good."

He shoved me down against the seat and I stayed there. I didn't dare look up. I don't know how long I rode in that car, or where the hell he was taking me. But when I heard the creaking of metal against metal, I peeked up.

Only to see us driving through a wrought-iron gate.

The smell of apples was almost overwhelming. The perfectly-groomed trees that lined the manicured lot lined a driveway as it led us up a hill. The mansion at the top made my jaw drop open. There wasn't a mark on the perfectly-poured driveway. The house practically sparkled in the moonlight as it sat there in all its immaculate glory. Everything had a place. Everything had a purpose. Even with the gaudiness of it all, it still felt put-together.

This wasn't the house of a disorganized kidnapper.

My door opening from the outside ripped me from my trance. The man inside reached for my hair again, but I moved backward. I scooted all the way to the other side of the seat, hoping that I might be able to get the other door open. If I could get out of the--

"Ah!"

He grabbed my ankles. "Come here, you little bitch."

I tried to kick my way out, but I was no match for

the man's grip. He pulled me out onto the ground, my back hitting the pavement with a crash. Then he fisted my hair, yanked me up off the ground, and dragged me up the porch. He tossed me into the house as I stumbled over my feet, trying to get my bearings. A massive door closed, making me jump. My eyes darted around as I tried to find my assailant. My kidnapper. The man who meant to do me harm tonight.

My eyes were drawn to the expanse around me.

The black and white marble floors shone by the dim light of the crystal chandelier hanging from the ceiling. The walls were painted a dark color, but the crown molding was a bright, impeccable white. It looked hand-carved. Incredibly ornate. Much too decadent for a machine to have replicated. I slowly turned around. The massive staircase leading up to the second floor was a masterpiece in and of itself. The winding cherry mahogany. The sparkling overlay of the banister. The subtle--

"Come with me."

The man grabbed my hair again. "Shit."

I stumbled after him, trying not to fight too much. Because something told me this man would have no issues killing me at the drop of a hat. He led me through the mansion and out a back door. And when we stepped off his back porch, the scene unfolding in front of me struck me with absolute terror.

There was a crystal clear pool surrounded by concrete. And on the edge of the pool was a lone chair with its back turned towards the water.

And leather ties sitting off to the side.

"No," I said.

I tried to backtrack as the man pushed me toward the chair.

"No, no, no, no. No! I said, no!"

As much as I tried to get away, the man only held me tighter. He picked me up, slinging me over his shoulder and walking me over to the chair. I kicked. I beat him against the back. I did everything I could to get out of his grasp. The freshly-mowed lawn was the last thing I'd smell. The impeccable concrete sculptures that surrounded this dumbass pool would be the last thing I ever saw. How long could I hold my breath? Would it be possible for me to get myself out? Maybe I had something sharp on me. Something that could cut through the--

"And down we go," the man said.

I grunted. "Fuck."

The man sat on top of me as he bound my wrists to the chair. Then he got up and wrestled with my legs as he tied them to the chair as well. The leather cut into my skin. I already felt my hands going numb as my ankles began to swell. I struggled against the bonds, anyway. I couldn't go out like this. There was no way in hell that was happening.

"If you keep struggling, they'll only get tighter."

The smooth voice caught my ear and I whipped my head up. I was ashamed of the frightened tears streaking down my cheeks. The man that had taken me from the parking lot went to stand off to the side with his hands clutched behind his back and his gun shining in the moonlight for my viewing pleasure. My eyes panned over to the man in the dark suit. The only thing with any color on him was his blood red tie.

And his dark green eyes.

He's got Max's eyes.

The man sighed. "Danika Young."

He stood before me with his hands clasped in front of him like some disapproving parent. I couldn't read the expression on his face. But that was mostly because I couldn't look away from his eyes.

It can't be.

He tsked. "I must say, I expected more from my son. Especially when it came to his choice in… women."

I blinked. "Your son?"

He grinned. "Yes. My son. I'm sure you know him. Max?"

Realization slammed into my gut, almost knocking the wind out of me.

Holy shit. The man who had orchestrated my kidnapping was Max's father.

36

MAX

I skidded into a gas station as dirt and dust kicked up behind me. It was the first place I'd seen that was open since I left the warehouse behind. I pushed the car door open and barreled inside, storming through the front doors. The bell above me dinged. People turned to look at me as if I were growing a third head. A couple of the women gasped. A man clutched what looked to be his daughter close to him. They all moved toward the back of the gas station, and it took me a second to remember why.

Because you look like you've got one foot in the grave, asshole.

"Sir?"

I turned my head toward the cashier.

"Phone. Now."

She blinked. "I think you need an ambulance more than a phone."

I strode for her. "Give me a phone. Now. It's an emergency."

Her eyes ran down my face. "Yeah. Obviously."

"And a first aid kit, too. If you have them here."

She pointed. "Down the first aisle."

"I'll tip you forty bucks if you go get it for me and leave your cell unlocked for me to use."

She narrowed her eyes at me as the entire gas station fell silent. I held my breath, staring her down before she shrugged her shoulders. She slipped her phone out of her back pocket and tapped something along the screen. Then she tossed it to me.

"You want one first aid kit? Or four?"

I growled. "As many as you've got over there. And a Mountain Dew."

"You want a sandwich, too?"

"You make 'em?"

She snickered. "No, asshole. I don't. And you got fifteen minutes before I call the cops myself. You're scaring everyone in here."

"Yeah, yeah, yeah."

Focusing on the phone was a chore. Hell, focusing at all was a chore in the first place. Things faded in and out of focus. Some things were blurry, while others hurt to look at. Like how damn bright her fucking phone screen was. I turned the brightness down just so I could type in Dani's number. But it was as if the phone kept moving. For every right number I pressed, I got three wrong. So I had to keep backspacing.

"That'll be sixty bucks for the first aid kits, plus the forty you offered me. So, a hundred bucks and we'll call it even for the night. I'll throw in the drink for free."

I scoffed. "Thanks."

"Hey, I could've pressed the silent alarm button on you."

My head whipped up. "Did you?"

She nodded to her phone. "Why don't you place that call and get out of here, just in case. Okay?"

I growled again. "Yeah. Thanks."

I finally got Dani's number typed in and I called her. It rang and it rang. And it rang some more. I grew frustrated when her voicemail picked up. I hung up and dialed her right back. Surely, she hadn't fallen asleep on me in that damn dorm room of hers.

When she didn't pick up the second time around, I became worried.

"You almost done?" the clerk asked.

I nodded. "One more phone call. It's an emergency."

"By the looks of you? I'd say it is."

I wanted to fly off the handle, but I didn't. I had bigger fish to fry than this woman who kept flexing her muscles at me. It took me ages to type in Rupert's number, but I got it. And when he picked up on the first ring, I almost rejoiced with relief.

"Who the fuck is this?" he growled into the phone.

"Rupert. It's me."

"Max. Holy fuck. Where the hell are you? Are you okay?"

I snickered. "I'm all right. Kind of."

"Kind of? The hell does that mean? Tell me where you are. I'll send someone for you."

I couldn't dwell on the pain. Even though the

weight of my injuries was getting worse, every second I wasted meant Dani's chances of injury grew. I had to find her, and quickly.

"Rupert, listen to me. They're going after Dani."

I heard an engine roar. "I'm close to the school. I'll go and get her. Now, tell me, where are you?"

"I'm going to my father's."

"What? Are you insane? Think rationally for a second. You can't go there by yourself. I think we can *confidently* say he has a hand in this. You need backup. You need to let me help. Wait for me or the boys."

I shook my head. "I can't. I need to go, and now. Go to the school. If she's there, get her the hell out of there. Get her out of town, for all I care. As fast as you can, and don't look back. Then tell John not to come after me. I know he'll try. And I'm telling you, he won't make it out if he does."

He sighed. "Fucking hell, what have we gotten ourselves into?"

"It's messed up, I know. Trust me, I get it. But I trust you to handle this. Don't let me down, Rupert. She means too much to me."

"I won't, boss. Watch your back."

I sighed. "You too."

I hung up the phone and tossed it back to the girl. She caught it with only one hand, and I snatched up the bag. I pulled my wallet out and slapped a hundred dollar bill onto the counter. Then I shoved my wallet into the bag and reached for the drink.

"Anything else I can help you with?" she asked sarcastically.

I paused. "Actually, yeah. There is. If anyone calls you back on that number looking for someone named Max, and their name isn't Rupert or John, tell them to kick fucking rocks."

She grinned. "It'll be my pleasure."

I made my way out of the gas station and I could've sworn I heard everyone collectively sigh with relief. No matter, though. I only had one goal in mind. And that was to get to my father. I knew Rupert would take care of Dani. I knew he'd put her somewhere safe. Now, I had to confront my father. He needed to know that I wouldn't be that easy to wipe off the face of this planet.

And if I got trigger happy enough, I might wipe him off the face of this planet first.

I jumped back into the car that was still running and tossed the first aid kits into the passenger's seat. I didn't bother with the seatbelt as I started ripping the plastic off them. I needed Tylenol. I needed gauze. I needed alcohol wipes to clean my fucking face off as I raced down the road. I cracked the small bottle of pills open in my hand and tossed three of them back. I reached for my drink and drove with my knees as I chugged the caffeine down. Hopefully, that did something for the pain. Because a hospital wasn't in my future until I knew Dani was safe.

Until my father had been dealt with.

"Come on. You can go faster than this."

I ripped open alcohol wipes with my teeth and wiped at my face. I was coated in blood and it hurt to breathe. My nose sat crooked on my face. One of my eyes was completely swollen shut. Too bad none of these first aid kits had a knife or a scalpel in them. Because I could've used my other eye. No matter, though. The alcohol wipes helped to clean off my face. My lips. My neck. My hands. I even tried to wipe some of my shirt off, since it was practically caked in blood.

Not all of it mine, though.

The closer I grew to my father's house, the more I smiled. I couldn't wait to wrap my hands around that man's throat. I couldn't wait to choke the life out of him and see that light dim behind his eyes. Never in my life had I wanted death so badly to fall onto someone. Never in my life had I lusted for blood like this before. I pushed the gas pedal all the way to the floor as some of my pain started to subside. Even the swelling in my eye receded a bit.

A few more pills can't hurt much. I'm a big dude.

I fumbled around for the pills in the passenger's seat. I picked up two more and tossed them back before chugging more of my soda. My vision finally focused for good. I felt my feet planted firmly into reality again. The clouded fog of pain lifted, allowing me to think clearer. See clearer. Carve out a path in front of me quicker.

And as I raced by the signs ushering me into the city limits, I diverted quickly to the left.

"I know a better way than that," I murmured.

I raced along the backroads that I knew cops never policed. There were no stoplights. No cop cars. No stop signs. Nothing. Just winding, open roads that carried me closer to my father's house. Closer to that hill he sat on top of. Closer to that looming house off in the distance. The full moon mocked me as it hung heavily in the sky. The gray clouds slowly covered it up, completely darkening the world below. If there were ever a perfect night for my father to come out and play, it was tonight. A full moon, and yet the world was still dark.

Like his soul.

I'm coming for you, Dad. This is the last playdate you get.

I charged around the corner and skidded onto the main road. My father's wrought iron gates came into view and I made a split second decision. There was no time to punch in the code. And it sure wasn't tactically safe for me to alert my father to the fact that I was here. So I gripped the steering wheel, gritted my teeth, and watched as the speedometer needle in the SUV clocked a buck-ten.

Straight through those fucking gates.

37

DANI

I still couldn't process it. It was like my brain refused to accept the truth right in front of me. This dark, cold, wicked man who had sentenced me to death was Max's father. What a fucking piece of work. This man held me captive like an animal. Tied to a chair, like a pig on a spit over a roasting fire. How in the world did the man I love come from this monstrous man? How was that even possible?

I didn't see any part of Max in him. They didn't look a bit alike. Right down to the fishy little lips on this asshole's face.

Except for those eyes.

The man walked toward me, closing the distance between us. I felt sick to my stomach as the scent of his cologne approached. I wanted to slash him across the face with my nails. I wanted to tell him exactly what I thought of him. His men gave him a wide berth, stepping back the more he stepped forward. From beyond their sunglasses in the dead of night, I saw the fear in their eyes. The whites of their eyes, widening the more he approached me.

They were terrified of him.

And so was I.

"You really aren't what I expected."

He stopped in front of me and he was so close I felt his body heat.

"What did you expect? A model?"

He chuckled. "Nonsense. My son has never been into such trash before. But he usually does take his women a bit more… nonsensical."

"You mean dumb?"

I looked up and saw his grin widening into a plastered-on smile.

"I suppose that's an apt word, yes."

I nodded. "I'll take the compliment, then."

"I wouldn't be so quick to do that. You do have some traits my son seems to gravitate toward."

I flicked my hair away from my face. "Yeah? Like what?"

"For starters, you're a virgin. Or you were, at least. Correct?"

I froze. "Why the hell do you care about that?"

He sighed. "My son enjoys a few of the finer things. Not many of them. But he does have a taste for… soiling the innocent."

"He didn't soil me. If anything, he showed me who I truly am."

"Oh? And are you proud of where this 'new you' is currently sitting?"

I wanted to kick this man right in his balls.

"At any rate, Max has always been selfish. Always thinking of himself before anyone else. I mean, if he had considered you--even for a second--the two of you would've never kicked anything off."

I lunged at him. "I don't give a shit what you think."

He smacked me across the face. "Well, you very well should. Because even though you don't like the reality of your current situation, that doesn't make it any less real."

My head wrenched to the side and I moaned in pain. Holy shit, that hurt. I groaned as I moved my jaw around. I felt something warm trickling against my skin. I whipped my head around and looked up, watching as this disgusting man pulled a handkerchief out of his pocket. Wiping his knuckles. Removing my blood from his hands before he slid a golden ring off his finger.

And began polishing it in front of me.

The rings. Didn't Max say something about rings?

"I must confess, it would've been interesting getting to know you."

I snickered. "Enjoy that one-way road by yourself."

He slipped his ring back on. "But desperate times call for desperate measures. And Max never did enjoy learning lessons as a child. He was my most stubborn one. Then again, all younger children are. Or so I've been told."

He tossed his handkerchief onto my lap and I

parted my legs, watching it fall to the concrete at my feet.

"So, I suppose we should get right to it, yes?" he asked.

I shrugged. "You're the one obviously stalling for time."

His eye twitched. "Is that so, little bird?"

"If anything, I'm a little deer. But who's keeping track?"

"My, my. You really do have a mouth on you."

He cocked his hand back and I flinched. My fear took hold and I cowered away from the man. I didn't want to give in to my fear. I didn't want to show him how absolutely frightened I was.

But I also didn't want to be hit again.

"A good beating always solved things with my oldest son. John. I believe you've already met him."

The man put his hand down and my heart broke for the two brothers.

"He was always so... nosy. I really had to do a number on him to get him to find his place. Max didn't take to that, though. He never liked staying in his lane."

I nodded. "Sounds like the Max I love."

He sighed. "Ah, young love. It's always so romanticized. Tell me, Miss Young. Is this romantic to you?"

He held out his arms as my eyes scaled his body.

"I don't know. I guess, in the right context, this could be considered foreplay."

I heard one of the bodyguards let out a small bout of laughter. And as quick as lightning, Max's father had his gun out. He pointed it at one of the men in back and pulled the trigger, causing me to scream out. My eyes widened. I watched the shadowed man drop to his knees. I heard him gurgling. And as my eyes widened, I watched him fall face-first into the grass as dark liquid tainted the ground beneath him.

"Anyway, where were we?"

I drew in ragged breaths, trying my best not to panic. But I couldn't pull my eyes away from the man on the ground.

"Holy shit, you killed him," I said breathlessly.

"Focus, little bird. We don't have much time."

My eyes whipped up to his. "You killed him!"

"And you're not giving any consideration as to why I brought you here tonight?"

I'm so sick and tired of being compared to hunted animals.

"I take it you're going to tell me. So get it over with," I said.

His frown grew on his face as he walked toward me. I leaned away from him, but it didn't get me out of the way of his touch. His finger traced along my jawline, where his knuckles had connected with my face. He brushed something away and I winced. Then he cupped my cheek.

Making me jerk away from his touch.

"Don't you dare," I growled.

He patted my cheek softly, causing me to wince.

"I have recently discovered that you are quite special to my son. Which is interesting, since it's been so long for him. I haven't had any access to any real leverage against my son. Max keeps himself locked up tight. Like a vault. Again, not like my eldest. Not like John. John was easy to manipulate."

I shook my head. "You're a monster."

He nodded. "I suppose most would consider me as such. But that's not the point. The point is, now I have you."

He turned around and faced me with a wolfish grin on his face.

"I now have access to leverage in Max's life. Through you. And I've waited years for it. That boy has defied me for far too long. He's disobeyed me for far too many years, has hated me his entire life. He never did learn to fear me the way his brother did. To respect me, the way John does. All he ever wanted was to be what I'm not."

I hissed. "Because he's better than you. And he always will be."

The man chuckled. "No. Because he's a fool. Because he doesn't have what it takes to *be* something more. Because he's willing to let other people over-shadow him while he plays in the kiddie pool with his little Red Thorns. Destroying what I created. Dismantling what I willingly handed over to his brother."

I blinked. "You created the Red Thorns?"

He put his hand over his heart. "Oh, that wounds me. I see Max doesn't talk much about it."

I shrugged. "I didn't even know what you looked like until just now. I still don't know your name."

"Such rudeness. Allow me. My name is Ashton Ryddle. At one point in time, I was the president and owner of the Red Thorns. I created them after leaving a crew I was part of. Want to know why I left?"

"Because you're a monster and they wanted no part of your existence?"

He snickered. "So judgmental. But no. I left because I wanted no part in their drug smuggling operations. Not quite my taste in crime."

"A murderer with morals. How quaint."

"Do you know what they did to me, little bird?"

"Deer."

He took a step toward me. "They chained me to the ground, like an animal. They beat me. Kicked me. Gagged me, so I could barely breathe. They took hot irons from a fireplace and burned their tattoos clear off my back. Leaving nothing but roped, thick, disgusting scars I walk around with every fucking day of my life."

I bit my tongue as I heard the man's anger growing in his voice.

"I paid a high price to leave that club. To leave them behind. To this day, I'm the only person to walk away from them. And in my anger, I focused. I established the Red Thorns and ushered them into greatness. I did so well with them that it opened up other doors for me in the business world. Other doors I would've much rather walked through. So it only made sense to pass the crew onto my eldest."

I grimaced. "You mean, the one you can control."

"Of course. It's my club, after all. At their peak, those men made five figures a month with contract work and running weapons. Dealing in shipping artifacts from continent to continent. They were living the high life. Until John decided to get himself wrapped up in a turf war."

I blinked. "Is that why he walks with a cane?"

He waved his hand in the air. "Ah, some shooting. Some accidents. A coma, I think. He really should've known his limits better. Left him unable to ride his stupid bike, so of course he handed my precious club over to Max."

"The one who doesn't listen."

Anger filled his face. "He defies me at every turn. Barges into my home like he owns this place. Demands money and clients and payment as if he actually had any power. Well, he wouldn't have any of that power without me. Without my efforts. Without my sacrifice!"

I tugged at the bonds on my wrists. "If you knew Max at all, you'd know none of that is true. He cares about those men. About that club. He does what's best for them, even if it means sacrificing himself."

His eyes met mine. "Is that what you really think?"

"That's what I know."

He walked over and crouched down in front of me.

"Do you love him, little bird?"

I blinked. "What?"

He gripped my chin. "You heard me. Do you love him?"

I swallowed. "No."

He smiled. "Liar."

I stayed quiet as panic gripped my soul. I saw evil in this man's eyes. They weren't Max's eyes at all. The only thing they shared was color. And that sure as hell didn't make them alike. His hand slid against my cheek. I gritted my teeth to keep the pain at bay as I felt it swelling. His fingertips played with the tendrils of my hair as he twisted one around his index finger. I tried to shake him off, but his finger didn't move. I tried to lean back, but he only came closer. Until his abs sat against my knees and his disgusting breath pulsed against my face.

"In my line of work, little bird, I've become gifted at spotting a liar. At watching for the tells. A fluttering at the throat as the pulse quickens."

His finger slid out of my hair and pressed against the pulse point on my neck.

"Or maybe a brief reflex. A twitch of the finger. A quirk of the lip. A widening of the pupil for the briefest moment."

His finger ran up my neck. Along my jawline. Until he traced my lower lip. I leaned away from him as far as I could get. I felt my chair teetering along the edge of the pool as the two front legs came up. I felt his free hand grip the leg of the chair. He tilted me back quickly and I yelped. He dangled me there, my hair touching the top of the water as I wiggled and strained for dear life.

Then he brought my chair back down onto all fours as he snarled, "You love him, little bird. I know you do. Don't you dare convince yourself that you can lie to me and get away with it. Many people have made that mistake in the past, and it's gotten them killed. And it will be your undoing."

My eyebrows rose. "My lie? Or my love?"

His eye twitched. "Both."

I felt my fear morphing. It spiraled in my gut and fogged up my brain. I kept tugging at my restraints, only feeling them grow tighter as my hands started to tingle. I couldn't wiggle my toes any longer. I felt trapped, like the small animal I had become to these people. And as my tears betrayed my solid façade, I fought to stay in control, to blink them back, to keep a strong outer force against this terrible man as his hand came up to my face.

He wiped away a tear that escaped the side of my eye.

"Don't cry," he whispered. "This will all be over soon."

My lower lip quivered. He stood up and turned his back to me, his hand in the air. With a snap of his fingers, the bodyguards moved. They moved to the body still lying on the grass. The smell of blood and sweat filled the air around me. I closed my eyes, not wanting to see them drag that poor man off. I listened to his body sliding across the grass as more tears leaked down my face. I was in hell. This was what hell felt like.

And I wondered if anyone knew I was even here.

When the shuffling around stopped, I slowly opened my eyes. It took a second for them to adjust through my tears. But when they did, I found myself alone. His father wasn't there any longer. I saw none of the bodyguards. It was just me, this stupid chair, these damn leather bonds, and the very dark puddle in the grass.

That had drag marks leading back to the mansion.

What are they going to do with him?

I started tugging again. As furiously as I could. I didn't know what else to do, and I prayed that one of the knots would come undone with enough manipulation. I craned my neck back to see if I could figure out how the knot was tied. But the more I shifted around, the closer the back legs of my chair got to the edge of the pool. They came so dangerously close that I felt the chair wobble, causing me to cry out.

And as I leaned forward, trying with all my might to keep myself from falling into that damn pool, I smelled something in the air. A stench I couldn't place. One that wrinkled my nose, curled my toes, and brought my eyes to the sky.

Smoke.

I saw smoke rising into the air. Thick, black, heavy smoke coming from a chimney at the side of the mansion. The smell was rancid. It made my stomach turn over onto itself as I sat there, begging myself to wake up from this nightmare. And as my watery gaze fell back onto the pool of blood in the grass, I put two and two together.

Causing me to vomit between my legs.

38

MAX

The gates blew open as I soared through at over a hundred miles an hour. I grunted as the tires rumbled over the spikes that shot up from the concrete. I heard guns firing. I heard the dents in the outside of the SUV getting deeper and deeper. But this was one of my father's SUVs, so I knew it was decked out with the best of the best.

Things like flat-proof tires. Bulletproof windows. Double metal coats to catch hollow-pointed bullets.

I'm coming for you, Dad.

The gunfire kept up until I heard a bullet penetrate the car. I ducked down, trying not to let up on the gas pedal as I careened into one of the apple trees. The entire front of the car dented. I swerved out of the way, scraping the entire length of the car on the passenger's side. Guns kept firing. I heard my tires screaming for mercy as the bullets penetrated to the core of the tire.

Forcing me to race away on the rims.

"Come on. Come on, you piece of shit."

I heard the apple tree crash behind me. The gunfire stopped and men started yelling. I skidded to the stairs of the porch as the rims of the car started sparking. I hoped the damn thing burst into flames and took the entire mansion down with it. With my father trapped inside. I slammed the door open and raced up the porch, listening as men sprinted up the driveway.

They wouldn't catch me, though.

Not until I had my father dead in my hands.

I barreled through the front door, jamming my shoulder into it. I growled out in pain as I looked around with my one good eye. I stormed through the house, searching every room. Checking every corner as my boots sounded loudly against the marble floors.

"Ashton!"

I bellowed throughout the house with my hands cupped along my mouth.

"Ashton! Where the fuck are you!?"

I knew damn good and well my father had already prepared for my arrival. That fucker was always one step ahead of the game. I had something up my sleeve, though. Something I knew he hadn't taken into account.

I knew his weakness.

"Ashton!"

I followed my gut and checked outside before heading upstairs. I wanted to make sure he wasn't up to something out there by that fucking pool of his. I sniffed the air deeply, wrinkling my nose at the scent.

My good eye was already strained from taking in my father's eyesore of a home. Even in the dead of night, I saw my father out there, standing in front of the pool with his hands clasped behind his back.

"I've been expecting you!"

I charged him with my fists balled up. I heard men trampling through the house as they spilled out behind me. They cocked their guns, aiming them at my back. And as my father held up his hand, I reached for his throat.

"I'll die taking you with me," I growled.

He grinned. "What was that?"

I went to clamp down against his throat and he moved off to the side. And when I saw what was behind him, I froze. My jaw dropped open. My heart stilled in my chest. But, it was my father's hand patting me on the back that brought air into my lungs.

What the fuck is Dani doing here?

"You really do enjoy your women with spunk, don't you?"

My father's whisper had nothing on the voice screaming inside my head. I had so much anger built up within me I didn't know what to do with myself. Dani was bound to that chair. With leather. Leather bonds that had seen so many other dead bodies before her. She had a bruise on her cheek and I felt the beast within me snap. The tears streaking her cheeks made me a walking time bomb. I'd never experienced rage like this before. I felt damn near delusional as I kept my eyes locked on her.

"Let her go. She has nothing to do with any of this."

Dad sighed. "Well, I suppose that tattoo on her thigh suggests otherwise."

I slowly looked over at him. "If you tell me--"

He held up his hand. "Young, barely-aged women aren't my thing. I didn't touch her. Mostly."

I lunged at him. "You're the one that hit her."

His men lifted their guns again and I heard Dani whimper. A soft, surreal, panicked sound that stopped me dead in my tracks. Making my father grin.

"Benji told me she's one of you now. You know, your cousin? Which means she's fair game. Just like you are."

I gnashed my teeth. "Why are you doing this?"

My father raised his hand in the air and snapped his fingers. And quicker than I could blink, five of his men surrounded me. I felt the heat of their guns pointed at me. I saw Dani struggling out of the corner of my eye. Trying to get loose from those binds around her wrists and ankles. I knew it was no use, though. The knots my father taught his men to tie grew tighter the more someone struggled.

And if Dani didn't stop, she'd risk losing her appendages.

If he didn't kill us first.

"Max, please. I'm sorry."

The sob in her voice broke my heart. I wanted to go to her. I wanted to save her. But I didn't dare move. I knew the second I did, my father's men would unload on both of us. Pump us full of lead before--

I sniffed the air again. "Who did you incinerate this time?"

Dad shrugged. "Poor Dani. I'm pretty sure it scarred the girl."

"You killed a man in front of her? Are you insane!?"

I took another step toward him and the guys moved in closer. I heard a couple more of them cock their guns as my father's grin grew into a wide, empty smile. A smile that haunted my nightmares. A smile that followed me around as a child, just trying to endure my father's spontaneous wrath.

"It's kind of cute, really. Her trying to save you," he said.

I blinked. "What?"

He nodded. "It's true. Isn't it, little bird?"

"Don't you dare talk to her."

"You might want to answer me if you want him to live, *little bird*."

I heard Dani swallow. "I thought you were at the bar. You never showed up on campus, and I got so worried, and I just--"

Dad interrupted her. "It's cute. But stupid. I have to say, I expected more from a college student."

I snarled. "What do you want?"

He leveled his eyes with me. "Your time is done here, Max. You're finished. Progress requires compromise. And sacrifice. Neither of which you've been good with. And in order for me to expand my business, I need to get my hands into deeper pockets. I need to change up the game. And a certain pesky *thorn* in my side will stand in my way if he finds out what is required to get into said pockets."

I stood my ground. I tried to take even breaths. I knew exactly what my father was saying, though. He'd made new business deals outside of the crew. And it sounded like he was dealing with even more unsavory characters than we were used to. In any other situation, I would've told my father to kick rocks. I would've shot him, taken Dani with me, and gone back to my men just to tell them we were on our own. I had dreams of turning my father's mansion into a place where we all congregated. Where we all lived, if we wanted. A place no one could take from us. A place where we dominated in private, held meetings away from our loved ones, and enjoyed the expansive surroundings before us when we needed time to rest.

I couldn't do any of that with my father about to kill Dani, though.

None of it meant anything if I didn't have her with me.

"You knew I wouldn't let you go through with it. That's why you've done all of this. To get me out of the way."

Dad nodded. "Maybe you're not as stupid as I figured. Nevertheless, I thought I would eliminate the obstacle before it had a chance to fuck up my operations. Just as you would do if you were in my shoes."

I scoffed. "I wouldn't kill my own goddamn son in order to do it."

He growled. "You are no son of mine."

"Good. Because I have a hard time calling you 'Dad' anyway."

"You could've had everything, Max. Everything! You could've ruled at my side. Had all of the wealth and the riches and the women you could've ever wanted. And yet, you chose a life of scraping the bottom of the barrel. Scrounging around for money just to eat at night. You chose a woman like her instead of women who deserve to be with a Ryddle man. You chose a woman that comes from nothing instead of woman of substance."

"You won't speak about her like that a second time around. I can assure you that."

He held out his arms. "You could've chosen all of this! A life of ease and no worry. But you chose back-roads and mediocrity. You chose *them* over your own flesh and blood."

"They're more flesh and blood to me than you'll ever be. You're a disgrace to this family."

He got in my face. "I built this family!"

"You killed our mother and you smiled about it! Because she dared to talk back! Because she dared to stand up and try to course correct you. Because she saw you turning into this monster and wanted to save you. You killed that woman for loving you. And you'll never be my father because of it!"

My father's nostrils flared. I felt my knees weakening as my anger eroded at the rest of the strength I had left. I balled up my fists, ignoring the guns pointed at me. And with every sniffle that came from Dani, the need to rescue her grew inside me. My head swirled with pain. I swallowed down every single bit of bile that crept up the back of my throat. My adrenaline spiked again, dimming the pain. Dimming it just enough for me to focus back on my father.

Whose smile grew even wider.

"Then maybe you should learn from her mistakes," he said.

I shook my head. "I'm going to kill you. I'm going to slaughter you. And then, I'm going to hang you from the highest building in this fucking town as a reminder to what happens when you fuck with the people I love."

Dad wiped at his face. "Really, Max. You should learn a few manners while you're at it."

I held my head high. "You're worthless. You're worth nothing to anyone if they don't fear you. You're nothing but a middleman. And a middleman can always be easily cut out. John? He's a starter. He knows what he wants and he goes after it. That turf war? The one that fucked him up? He started it because he knew we had nothing without a space to call our own. We struck before they saw us coming and it's the only reason we survived. Even when you abandoned us."

He chuckled. "And what are you, Maxwell?"

I got in his face. "I'm a finisher, Dad. I might not always start shit. But I sure as hell end it."

"Which is why you've made my decision very easy."

"Yeah? And what decision is that?"

All of my muscles tensed. I saw something flicker behind my father's eyes and I knew I had to prepare myself. My eyes tunneled. The only thing I saw was the face I wanted to pound into the pavement. I wanted to curb-stomp my father's head until his brains were splattered against the perfect grass of his lawn. I wanted nothing more than to see the evil light in his eyes fade into nothingness before throwing him into that fucking kiln he had in his basement.

"Well? You gonna fill your son in on what you've got planned?"

Dad grinned. "I think you know what comes next."

And as my father turned his back, I heard the darkened men scrambling around me.

"Max, no!"

39

DANI

I watched the fight unfold before me. I saw the five men jump Max as his father started making his way for me. The violence was unlike anything I'd ever witnessed. I screamed for Max. I screamed until my voice went hoarse. Could no one hear us? Did no one understand the insanity unfolding right now? I watched Max spring up from the throng of men. They went flying to the ground, and I couldn't peel my eyes away. He roared like a wild beast. He picked them up with his bare hands and slammed them against the ground. Every move he made was to hurt. To maim. To block.

To kill.

Every time his fist connected, blood splattered. Every time his boots connected, men groaned. Every time he tossed them over his shoulders, bones cracked. Broke. Shattered, for my ears to cringe upon. The animal within him raged, and I watched with fearful awe as he tore through those men like paper fucking sacks.

My blood ran cold as Max unleashed a roar that left me uncontrollably trembling.

"Max! Behind you!"

His eyes found mine before he whipped around. But the guy behind him was already slamming the butt of the gun into his chest. They both went down, and my blood ran cold as I craned my neck to try and see them. Men were piled on top of one another, creating a wall I couldn't see over. And as my heart fluttered in my chest, I drew in another deep breath.

"I wouldn't, if I were you."

His father stepped in front of me, blocking my view. The sounds of my yells were swallowed as my eyes cased up his body. He hovered over me with his hands clasped behind his back. He smiled down at me with a twinkle in his eye that made me want to slap him the way he'd slapped me. My stomach felt sick. I felt like I was going to throw up again. But when that man grabbed my chin, it shocked me back to reality.

And anger filled my chest once more.

I waited with baited breath for him to stay something. As he held my head up, gazing into my eyes, I wondered what other horrors he'd done to people. I'd never forget those evil eyes so long as I lived. They'd haunt me. Forever. They'd define the word 'Satan' for me. Forever.

I thought about all the people who were in the wrong place at the wrong time with this man. People who said the wrong thing. Or said 'hello' to the wrong person. Who made a bad deal in exchange for their soul. Just like Satan himself did. I thought about Max's mother. What she must've gone through before she was so disgustingly killed by this man.

My heart ached for the nightmare that was Max's childhood.

My eyes watered as Max groaned out in pain. The sound of bones crunching and punches landing only backdropped the voice screaming in my head. A voice that kept telling me Hannah was right. A voice that kept telling me I should've listened to her. A voice that kept telling me I had made such a bad decision in falling in love with Max.

My heart still didn't believe it, though.

My heart refused to believe that Max was a bad decision.

His father tilted my head to one side, then the other. And as he studied me closely, my mind fell back to my roommate. The girl who I had once considered my best friend. As much as my heart was angry at me for admitting it, she was right. Just not about Max. I knew Max would never hurt me. I knew he'd never bring me harm. But, I should've taken him--and her-- more seriously when they warned me how dangerous this life could be. I should've listened when they told me about the horrors that might follow him around. About the trouble he might get himself into because of choices he made when he was younger. I mean, I didn't actually believe Max when he told me I might have to die for him. That my love might mean the difference between living and ceasing to exist.

Nor did I figure it would happen so soon.

I don't want to die.

I didn't want to die. I wasn't ready to die. Nor was I ready to watch him die. This entire situation was so convoluted and so full of bullshit. And yet, I wondered how it could've ever been avoided. My mind turned to mush. His father cupped my cheek. And as he pressed into my bruise, I moaned in pain.

"Look at me, little bird."

Reluctantly, I lifted my eyes to his. "What?"

He grinned. "Good girl. You're a very good girl, aren't you?"

"What. The fuck. Do you want?"

He smiled at me. "You don't deserve this, little bird. You deserve so much more. But business is business. And I'm a man of my word."

"Wonderful. Yay for those morals again."

He sighed. "And, unfortunately, we're all making the necessary sacrifices tonight."

He released my chin and bent his lips down to my temple. I tried pulling away from him, but he fisted my hair. He kept my head in place as his lips planted themselves against the shell of my ear. I heard him breathing. I felt him breathing. And as I heard Max growl out in pain again, my jaw quivered.

"And among those sacrifices is you."

My eyes darted around. He couldn't possibly be thinking about what I thought he was. I didn't do anything! I hadn't done anything wrong against this man! He stood up and backed away from me. He moved out of the way and I saw a man jump onto

Max's back. The man took him down, pinning him to the ground while another man kept kicking Max repeatedly in the ribs. I wanted to cry out for him. I wanted to scream at him to get up. That he could do this. That we could do this, together.

But fear blocked off my ability to speak.

"Ready?"

His father stepped back in front of me and I started shaking my head.

"No, no. No. You don't have to do this. Please."

He placed his foot between my legs on the chair. "I really wish I didn't have to."

"Wait. Please. I just--"

He snickered. "Ah, who am I kidding? This is the best part."

"Maaaaaaax!"

His knee flexed and it was as if everything happened in slow motion. The way Ashton's body moved. The way my hair flew about my face. The way I caught a glimpse of Max getting to his feet before the sky came into view. I heard his father chuckling. I heard gunshots ring out. And as the back of my chair hit the water, I let out a deep sigh.

Let's see how well I can hold my breath.

I drew in a deep breath through my nose as water surged around my body. I took in one last glimpse of the sparkling night sky before the water closed in around me. Everything went silent. My lungs inflated with air that would soon run out. My bound appendages prevented me from swimming to safety. Nothing was heard but the sloshing of water. The crashing of waves at the ocean. Hannah's insistent voice ringing out in my head.

Where did this person come from?

This isn't you, Dani.

We're still friends.

He's nothing but trouble. All men like him are.

You're going to get yourself hurt, or worse.

I gazed up through the wavy waters at the sky above. How beautiful it looked as it moved and rejoiced for me. I wasn't sure what the sky was so happy about. But I wanted a slice of it. A slice of that happiness to cover up the fear that clenched my gut. I felt my lungs starting to prickle. I expanded my diaphragm, giving the air somewhere to go. But I knew it wouldn't be long before my body would take over.

And drown itself.

I thought about my parents. About my father, and how he was feeling right now. Probably disappointed in me. Ready to give me the ass-chewing of my life. I thought about my mother. How confused and distraught she must be. Guilt filled my eyes as my tears intermingled with the crystal waters. The anguish this would put them through would do them in. My father, for sure. I blinked, and the nightmare was still going on. My lungs were beginning to burn, my stomach beginning to jump.

I'm sorry, Mom.

I wanted to apologize to them. For hiding it. For lying to them. For not letting them into my life. I wanted to apologize to them for not trusting in their wants and wishes for me. I had convinced myself that they didn't want me to be happy. When the truth of the matter was they wanted nothing but my happiness. And my safety. And my security. I never gave them the chance to be happy for me, even if they didn't understand my choices.

I just assumed they wouldn't understand.

I'm sorry, Dad.

I never gave Hannah a chance either. As the back of my chair hit the bottom of the pool, my lungs felt as if they were on fire. Panic gripped my chest. I felt my stomach jumping again, and I tried with all my might to get it to settle. I wanted to apologize to Hannah. For not listening to her. For not talking to her. For not opening up and letting her in on what I was thinking. What I was feeling. What I really wanted out of my life. I had made assumptions about everyone, just like they had about me. And because I thought I was in the right, I assumed they were all in the wrong.

I guess you were all right, and I'm sorry.

My eyes blinked again. I didn't want to miss a moment of this. I didn't want to miss a moment of the sky undulating before me. I didn't want to miss a moment of recompense as I apologized for my sins. Grief filled my body, overtaking the burning sensation that made me want to accept my fate. I wondered what had happened to Max. Had they killed him already? Were they about to incinerate his body like the other man tonight? I wanted to know. I needed to know. But I felt the leather tightening even further around my wrists. Around my ankles.

Giving me no hope of escaping by myself.

I'm sorry, Max.

I wanted to be stronger for him. I wanted to be better for him. I wanted to be the woman of his dreams. But instead, I ended up being the wounded, hunted animal that became his demise. I blinked again. I felt the water brushing my tears away. I wanted my father. I wanted my Daddy. I wanted him to reach down into the water and pull me back to the surface. I wanted someone to jump in. Anyone. I wanted someone to come save me.

Please, Max. I'm begging you.

I blinked again, and the sky was blocked out by a shadowed figure. A dark, lanky figure, with two green specks near the top. Max's father. Ashton. He was staring at me from the edge of the pool. Blocking out my dying view of the sky. Forcing me to relive the hell that had unfolded tonight. His wavy form waved at me. I watched his hand move side to side. As if to say 'goodbye' himself.

Then he stepped away.

My lungs jumped. My throat moaned. My stomach pulled in and my toes flexed. I screwed my eyes shut and willed myself to hang on just a few seconds longer. Just a few more seconds until someone could get to me. I puffed out my chest and girded my abs. I forced my mind to fall blank so my panic wouldn't override my body's natural need to survive. I felt my head spinning. I felt my arms going numb. My thighs tingled and my calves ached and I hadn't been able to feel my feet for a while now.

Just a little bit longer.

Images popped into my mind. Images of my father, smiling down at me. My mother, hugging me with my college acceptance letter in her hand. The three of us sitting around a table talking about my future. Discussing my options. Laying out the pros and cons. I saw Hannah. An image from my first day on campus. I saw her standing in our empty dorm room with her immaculate decorations and her sparkling jewelry and her makeup sprawled out over her working desk.

I saw Max. Standing on the other side of the road. Sucking down a cigarette as the soft light illuminated his face.

I love you, Max.

Then, I succumbed to my destiny. Accepting my fate, accepting the moment, and allowing my body to relax.

I'm sorry. I'm just not strong enough.

40

MAX

"Maaaaaaaax!"

I whipped my head up and saw my father looking off into the distance. With his hands balled up at his sides, I watched him turn around. And when my eyes gravitated beyond him, something struck me I'd never felt before.

Hopelessness.

"DANI!"

A man crammed his shoulder into my side and took me down. The sound of her hitting the water started the clock ticking down in my head. A minute. I had a minute to get to her. Sixty seconds. And these five assholes wouldn't even let me breathe. No matter what punches I threw, no matter what bones I crunched, they kept coming. Kept doling shit out.

And my father watched it all with a smile on his face.

I threw my elbow back as time counted down in

my head. If Dani was the amazing swimmer I thought she was, I had maybe a minute and a half. The compromise of seventy-five seconds started ticking down in my head.

Seventy-four. Seventy-three. Seventy-two.

If I wanted to save Dani, I had to barrel through these men. I'd have to tear through my father. But it took me damn near ten minutes just to get them unloaded of all their weapons. Guns without magazines littered the ground. Knives I'd smashed into the concrete, rendering them useless, took so much fucking energy out of my bones. But with the splashing of water as the pool buried her beneath its crystal cave, a third round of anger fueled my strength.

Causing me to charge through the men.

Sixty-five. Sixty-four. Sixty-three.

I started for my father before someone wrapped their arm clear around my neck. I coughed and sputtered, and I heard my father's laughter fall heavily against my ears. I brought my hands up to the guy's forearm and dug my jagged nails in. I raked down, feeling his skin give way. Feeling it gather beneath my fingers. He howled in pain as I bit down, ripping a chunk of muscle clear away from his bone.

Like I had done with Benji's cheek.

Fifty-nine. Fifty-eight. Fifty-seven.

"All right. You guys want pain? You've got it."

I cracked my knuckles and spun around. The only thing I knew was hurt. The only thing I smelled was death. Blood spattered against me as I sank my knuckles into the first face I found. Ribs broke against my toes as my boots went flying into their stomachs. Arms flew about. Legs caved in on one another. I rushed back into the mass of men trying to take me down. Determined to be the only one standing by the end of it. I counted down the numbers in my head. I felt Dani's life slipping through my fingers. And as one of the men charged me with a knife I hadn't found, I reached for his forearm.

I spun around, tucking his arm underneath my armpit.

And I broke that son of a bitch's wrist as the knife fell from his hand.

"Fuck!" he roared.

Forty-three. Forty-two. Forty-one.

I was running out of time. I still had four men coming at me as well as my father to contend with. I fought without mercy. I crushed everything in my path. My sole purpose was pain. My final destination was death. Even if I had to drown my father with my own hands, so long as it got me in that pool with Dani, I didn't give a shit about it. I throttled my hand into some man's windpipe. His head wrenched back as I threw my elbow behind me. Another man grunted in pain as someone else came at me, and I wrapped my arm around his neck.

Before snapping it.

Thirty-two. Thirty-one. Thirty.

"She's running out of time, you know!"

My father's taunting voice rattled around in my head. I wouldn't be surprised if I looked up to see him jerking off to all this fucking chaos. That man would get the worst of me. That much was for certain. And as my eyes whipped up, I saw yet another man coming at me, his fists at the ready. I stuck both of my hands out and curled my fingers against my palm, except for my thumbs. And when the man was within arm's reach, I sank my thumbs into his eyes until blood seeped down his face.

Twenty-seven. Twenty-six. Twenty-five.

Every time I put a man on the ground, I thought about her. About how scared she must feel. About the pain she must be in. I pushed through my own to get to her. Because I had to. There was no other choice. I promised her I would protect her. I promised her I'd take care of her. I loved her. I was head over heels in love with Dani. She was my everything, and I was nothing without her.

Twenty-one. Twenty. Nineteen.

The rational part of me chastised me the entire time. With every drop of blood I drew, I knew I wouldn't have been in this situation had I kept a lid on things. I disconnected myself from my emotions for a reason. I didn't care about shit for a reason. I never let people into my life for a reason. But Dani had been relentless. Always running into me, as if she thought she was being cute. As if I didn't know she was actively seeking me out. I knew it from the second time I'd ever laid eyes on her. She looked for any reason to be around me. Any reason to look out for me. She kept her head on a swivel for me. And it was that determination that wore me down.

It was that perseverance that made me weak to her.

Fourteen. Thirteen. Twelve.

I hated myself for caring too much. For breaking my rules. For falling in love and making her a target. It was my fault she was in this position. It was my fault that she had gotten into the crosshairs of my father. I wouldn't let her die for me, though. I wouldn't let her go down for this. If anyone deserved to die, it was me. If anyone needed to die, it should be me.

Not her.

Not the only shred of beauty that had ever come into my world.

Ten. Nine. Eight.

Time was running out. It was now or never. With a guttural roar, I picked my foot up and bashed it into the face of the only other man coming for me. I watched his teeth splatter against the grass. I heard him moaning in pain as his body jumped and writhed. I hated my father for using her like this. For using her as bait against me. I knew she'd be a risk. I knew she'd be a weakness. And I'd pursued it anyway. Selfishness drove me to her.

But love would bring us back together.

Seven. Six. Five.

"Not so fast."

I charged my father, ready to knock him into the pool. Until he pulled a gun out of the holster on his hip. I panted for air. Heaved for it, really. And as the men on the ground that were still alive groaned out in misery, my eyes fell to his gun.

Four. Three. Two.

Time seemed to stand still. My father approached

me, moving away from the edge of the pool. I couldn't take my eyes away from him. I felt him press the barrel of the gun against my chest. My heart hammered against my sternum. His smile faded, and something akin to sorrow replaced it.

Which was impossible. Because my father didn't understand what it was like to feel sorry for anything.

"You can do whatever you want with me. Just let me get her first," I said.

Dad cocked his head. "You really do love her, don't you?"

I refused to answer him and I heard that telltale tick.

"It would do you well to answer me," he said.

I swallowed hard. "Yes. I do."

He snickered. "And here I thought my son was just a one-pump-and-done kind of man."

My nose twitched. "Let me get her out of that pool, and you can have me. Whatever you want to do, I'll let you do it. Just let me get her."

He sighed. "You know I can't do that, son."

"I'm not your son."

"DNA would say differently."

"Experience wouldn't."

His finger twitched against the trigger. "You know, I really am sorry about all this."

I scoffed. "Yeah. I'm sure you are."

My eyes flickered over his shoulder. Down into the pool. Where I saw Dani's immobile form sitting against the bottom of the pool. I didn't see any bubbles. The water was starting to still. And as the clouds moved away from the moon, the glow of the night illuminated my father's disgusting face.

One.

"Dad, please."

He blinked. "Did I just hear my son beg?"

I drew in a ragged breath. "Please. Let me get her. She's already been down there a minute and a half. I've got less than a minute to get her up here and--"

He shoved the barrel further into my chest. "And if I did you this favor, how do you think that would make me look?"

Two. Three. Four. I have to get to her within the next minute. I just have to.

"No one has to know," I said.

He snickered. "Someone always knows, son. You'd do well to learn that lesson now, so no one else has to die."

Ten. Eleven Twelve.

"She doesn't! Have! To die!"

Dad moved the gun to my forehead. "*I'm* sorry it came to this, Maxwell."

Fifteen. Sixteen. Seventeen.

"Over my dead body," I growled.

Eighteen. Nineteen. Twenty.

Thank you for reading RED ROSE. Don't miss RED QUEEN, the final book in Max and Danika's love story, and be sure to join my SMS list below to don't miss any of my future books!

Get an SMS alert when Rebel releases a new book:

Text REBEL to 77948

If you want to support me, consider leaving a review on Amazon. I'd love it!

ABOUT THE AUTHOR

Rebel Hart is an author of Dark Romance novels. Check out all the books in her #1 bestselling series Diamond In The Rough.

NEVER MISS A NEW RELEASE:
Follow Rebel on Amazon
Follow Rebel on Bookbub

Text **REBEL** to 77948 to don't miss any of her books (US only) or sign up at www.RebelHart.net to get an email alert when her next book is out.

authorrebelhart@gmail.com

CONNECT WITH REBEL HART:

ALSO BY REBEL HART

For a full list of my books go to:

www.RebelHart.net

www.ingramcontent.com/pod-product-compliance
Lightning Source LLC
Chambersburg PA
CBHW051631180726
48284CB00006B/1685